Something felt wrong. Deadly wror

A chill shot down her spine, freezing Stormy in her tracks as she tried to process the scene.

Several people, some dressed in business attire, were sprawled across the floor, their noses to the commercial gray carpeting. A small child pressed tightly against a pale woman, his head buried beneath her trembling arm. On the far side of the room, behind thick granite counters, a group of tellers fidgeted anxiously, their hands held high over their heads.

A lone man was still on his feet, pacing and clearly on edge. A nylon stocking distorted his features, dark, baggy pants hung from his gaunt frame, and his long-sleeved shirt had seen better days. A large vanilla-colored cloth bag hung over his right shoulder, its weight pulling him to one side. He nervously waved a pistol in his left hand, aiming between the tellers and those on the floor.

"Don't move a muscle if ya know what's good for ya," he yelled to those on the floor, trying to force a growl into his voice while the gun shook in his hand. "And don't try to be a hero. Heroes end up dead."

Stormy Winters Mystery Novels

The Austin Fires

Shadowed In The Springs

Shadowed
in the Springs

A Stormy Winters
Mystery

S A Slack

A big "thank you" goes out to my mother, Stormy, my sister, Kelly, my daughter, Kristy, and my nephew, C.J

One

Stormy pulled her coat tightly about her as she stepped from the hotel's front doors onto the snow-covered sidewalk beyond. Some thoughtful soul had re-shoveled the walk, making it easier for her to navigate over the icy patches. The weather had turned a bitter cold, and as she headed in the direction of the bank, the wind toyed with her coat as if undecided on whether to let her keep it together or not. She reached into her pockets to pull out gloves and her fingers closed around a furry object lodged deep in the pocket.

"Good," she said to herself, removing the gray earmuffs. "I'm so glad I brought these along." She arranged her dark-blonde hair around the muffs with her fingers to make sure it was in place before donning her gloves. The wind had picked up, blowing robustly off the snow. "Brr, it's freezing out here!"

The sky overhead darkened as heavily laden clouds made their way across the tops of the nearby snow-covered mountains, masking the sun that had only hours before shone brightly down upon the city below. Obviously the old saying held true here: if you don't like the weather, wait a few minutes and it'll change.

Stormy paused for a moment and gazed up at the top of the mountains, her eyes coming to rest on the crest of the famed Pikes Peak. She marveled at the mountain's jagged slopes, now layered with more of the powdered-sugar snow than had been there when she and Lance arrived yesterday afternoon. She never tired of the thrill she felt when looking at these beautiful mountains. She loved visiting Colorado Springs.

I hope it'll be a clear day when Lance and I take the COG railway up to the top of the Peak, she thought. She'd been looking forward to the spectacular view of the city and the valley beyond which her niece, Ann, had talked so much about.

Just then, a car hurrying along the street, caused a spray of icy slush onto the sidewalk in front of Stormy. Her attention was drawn to the roadway. She usually enjoyed the invigorating feeling of the fresh, crisp air that filled her lungs on a winter's day when visiting these colder states, but not today. The nauseating scent of automobile exhaust rebounding off the snow embankment filled her nostrils, making her gag and forcing her to cover her nose with a gloved hand.

Using her walking stick to balance herself, Stormy cautiously continued, avoiding other piles of wet slush that flowed over the curb, deposited there by busy snowplows clearing the city streets. She always felt safer when she brought her stick along, in more ways than one. If it hadn't been for the hip operation, she wouldn't have had to carry it at all. But that was life, and she was now used to the feel of the sturdy black metal wrapped securely in brown leather near its' top section. Actually, she would not be opposed to using it as a weapon in self-defense or to help someone else, if the need arose.

Stormy approached the bank, when a loud commotion interrupted her thoughts. Looking up, she noticed a dark sedan shoot out from an alleyway on the other side of the solid brick building and recklessly fish-tail out onto the street. Correcting its path, the driver turned in her direction and picked up speed, tires slipping on the icy pavement.

As the vehicle sped past her, Stormy got a quick glimpse of the dark-suited figure hunched over the car's steering wheel before her eyes were drawn to the back seat. An auburn-haired woman leaned into the window, an anguished expression upon face. A masculine hand was grasping the woman's shoulder, and Stormy thought she spotted a crooked nose protruding from his rather sharp facial features.

"What an idiot! I'd be worried, too, if someone drove that way in a car I was riding in!"

Stormy continued to watch as the car disappeared around the next corner. With a shake of her head, she turned and continued toward the bank as several other cars passed by, carefully making their way down the street at much more reasonable speeds.

Reaching the bank doors, Stormy pushed one open and stepped in out of the cold. Engulfed in the warm air circulating throughout the foyer, she paused to remove her gloves and earmuffs and tucked them back into her pockets. She continued forward, unbuttoning her coat.

As she entered the main lobby, Stormy slowed.

Something felt wrong. Deadly wrong!

A chill shot down her spine, freezing Stormy in her tracks as she tried to process the scene.

Several people, some dressed in business attire, were sprawled across the floor, their noses to the commercial gray carpeting. A small child pressed tightly against a pale woman, his head buried beneath her trembling arm. On the far side of the room, behind thick granite counters, a group of tellers fidgeted anxiously, their hands held high over their heads.

A lone man was still on his feet, pacing and clearly on edge. A nylon stocking distorted his features, dark, baggy pants hung from his gaunt frame, and his long-sleeved shirt had seen better days. A large vanilla-colored cloth bag hung over his right shoulder, its weight pulling him to one side. He nervously waved a pistol in his left hand, aiming between the tellers and those on the floor.

"Don't move a muscle if ya know what's good for ya," he yelled to those on the floor, trying to force a growl into his voice while the gun shook in his hand. "And don't try to be a hero. Heroes end up dead."

Realizing the danger she found herself in, Stormy looked for a way out. She knew it was important that this man not see her.

He's so nervous, who knows what he might do, she thought, standing perfectly still so as not to catch his eye.

Slowly turning her head to the right, Stormy found herself standing beside a tall cardboard sign: an advertisement about the bank's mortgage rates, printed in bold letters. Praying not to attract the gunman's attention, she inched her way over until she was concealed behind it. Relief flooded over her at the same time she realized that she'd been holding her breath. As she quietly exhaled, she became aware of a small tear in the cardboard at about eye level. She moved forward to watch the scenario unfold, forcing her mind to focus on a course of action. In doing so, the toe of her shoe hit up against the cardboard, tipping it forward. Quick reflexes saved it from falling to the floor as she grabbed at the framework and pulled it back into place. Her heart skipped a few beats as she stood still.

"Hey, who moved?" the gunman yelled, turning the gun toward the sign and scanning the area. "Show yourself."

"Now listen, just settle down. No one's going to stop you," a calm, but commanding voice announced. It appeared to come from somewhere behind the gunman, but Stormy couldn't make out who was speaking.

Spinning back around, the gunman faced the voice, a surprised look crossing his face.

"No!" the gunman commanded, "Uh, stay put."

Forcing her nerves to quiet, Stormy took hold of her emotions and discovered a second hole from which she had a much better view of the entire room. Her eyes were immediately drawn to the source of the voice: a tall, brown-haired man in a grey suit, sporting glasses and a thin, dark mustache. He stood in an office doorway to the left of the tellers' counter. Taking a step forward, the man held his hands out in front of him, palms facing forward.

"Just go," the grey-suited man ordered, gesturing toward the door. "Leave, we won't try to stop you."

Stormy, aware that she'd once again been holding her breath, slowly released it as she turned to glance at the door behind her, wondering if she could reach it.

"I said nobody moves! That includes you, mister! Not another inch." The pitch of the gunman's voice rose as he raised the weapon a few inches higher.

"Whoa, now just a minute, buddy," the grey-suited man said, inching his way a bit closer.

"I said stop!" The gunman's hand shook uncontrollably, his face clouding with anger. He glanced over at the row of tellers behind the counter and his gaze flickered from one teller to the next, then back to the grey-suited man. His expression changed to one of extreme fear, no longer sure that he had the situation under control.

The grey-suited man took a step forward, still holding his hands out in front of him. "Now don't do anything stupid. Just go." As he moved, his glasses slid part way down his sweaty nose, and he unconsciously reached up to push them back into place.

What happened next seemed to Stormy as if it were a scene right out of a Hollywood movie, played out in slow motion. The gun in the thin man's hand exploded with a thunderous roar. The bullet struck the grey-suited man, knocking him backward. His body hit the floor with a resounding thud. Smoke poured from the revolver as the gunman stood frozen in place.

Then the scene sped up and returned to real time. Several loud cries went up from those on the floor and tellers dove under their counters, hoping to escape any shots that might be fired in their direction.

The shock crossed the room to hit Stormy, washing over her like a giant title wave. After a moment, she shook herself loose of its effects and quickly racked her brain for something she could do. A thought entered her mind, and a plan began to form.

"If I time it right, it just might work," she whispered to herself.

"Now look what you made me do," the gunman cried. "You all saw it! It was his fault!" Panicking, he turned and bounded toward the outside doors, gun in one hand, bag of money weighing heavily from his other.

He covered the space much more quickly than Stormy had hoped. When he was almost even with the cardboard sign, she abruptly took a step out from behind it, thrusting her walking stick across his path in an attempt to trip him. But he was too quick. Before she could raise the stick high enough to do any damage, he ran full speed into her, knocking her off her feet. Her stick and purse flew into parts unknown.

Left with a daze of colors dancing through her head and an image of bright orange socks and dirty tennis shoes, Stormy heard the bank door slam shut behind the fleeing gunman.

Two

Stormy lay sprawled on the floor, her vision clearing, as the room burst out in an array of noisy confusion. People started shouting, a woman burst into tears while a man tried to comfort her, and the small child asked his mother if the game was over now and could he get up.

"It's okay folks, he's gone," a blonde-haired woman in a beige sweater and matching pants, with a name tag pinned to her blouse, called out in an attempt to take control of the situation. She had stepped out of a doorway from behind the sign where Stormy had taken shelter and hurried across the room to where the injured man lay. "My name is Ms. Grey. I'm the Bank's Assistant Manager and I've contacted the police. They, along with an ambulance, are on their way. Just stay put until they arrive. They'll have some questions for you."

Stormy sat up and took inventory of her body, wincing at the sore spots the fall had brought on. A younger woman approached her.

"Are you alright?" she asked, helping Stormy to her feet and retrieving her stick and purse for her.

"Yes, I think so, thank you," Stormy replied. "Nothing seems to be broken, but I'll have a few bruises by tonight, I'm sure. How is the man that got shot?" She looked over in his direction. Some of the tellers were near him, blocking any view of the wounded man.

"I don't know," the young woman replied, her mouth a worried frown. "I hope the ambulance gets here soon. What a blessing it is that more of us weren't shot."

"Yes," Stormy agreed. "It could have been quite a blood bath in here before it was over, God forbid. Excuse me, I think I'll go and see how he's doing. Thanks again."

Approaching the group of women, Stormy found that Ms. Grey was on the floor holding a cloth against the unconscious man's shoulder trying to stay the flow of blood until medical help could arrive. On closer inspection, she realized that the cloth was really a white, wool scarf, now stained bright red.

"Is there anything I can do to help?" Stormy inquired. "It looks like he's lost a lot of blood. Who is he?"

"This is Mr. West, the bank's manager," Ms. Grey replied. "And yes, you can help by keeping the customers calm while we wait for the police. I don't know why Charlie, the bank's guard, had to get sick today of all days."

"That's unfortunate," Stormy said. "I'll see what I can do."

She began by checking with the various customers, inquiring how they were doing. Several told her why they'd come to the bank that day.

Stormy chatted with a young gentleman in a business suit that told her he had stepped into the bank for a quick withdrawal before heading home to his wife and children. It was his son's birthday, and they were planning to take him out to Chuckey's for pizza and games.

"Now this had to happen, and I'll be late," he told Stormy. Withdrawing a cell phone from an inner suit coat pocket, he punched a few buttons, then held it up to his ear, "I need to call my wife and let her know I'm okay. She'll worry about me as soon as she hears about this robbery when it airs on the news. Excuse me." He took a step away and spoke into the phone. "Hi, honey, I thought I'd better give you a call and let you know what's going on."

She turned to see how the rest were fairing and found that most were animatedly discussing the events of the robbery. Tellers were handing out bottles of water to each of the customers, along with some little mints from a nearby employee's desk, as they answered the customers' questions and checked to see if they needed any assistance. They assured the customers that after the police investigation, it might be possible to help them finish the transactions they came in for.

Eventually, sirens could be heard in the distance and police cars came roaring up to the front of the bank, an ambulance close behind.

Police officers quickly filed into the bank, followed by a staunch-looking detective and his tall partner. Behind them trailed a couple of paramedics, one holding a large medic's bag, the other rolling a stretcher. The women standing over the injured bank manager waved them over. A third paramedic holding another medic kit set about checking with each customer and bank employee to see if anyone else required medical treatment.

The two detectives fanned out across the room, iPads in hand, and began the task of talking with each person in turn, getting their statements down about the gunman, robbery, and shooting. Bank personnel offered them the use of a few of their offices to conduct more private interviews, which the detectives gladly accepted.

When it came time for Stormy's turn, the staunch-looking detective called her into a small, but pleasantly decorated office for questioning. He introduced himself as Detective Jarvis, waited for Stormy to be seated, and then pressed his stylus to the touch screen of his electronic device on the desktop before looking back up, full of questions.

"I really can't tell you much, Detective," she began in answer to his questions. "I'd just come through the bank's doors and was unbuttoning my coat. When I looked up, I saw a man waving a gun around and telling everyone to stay down."

"At any time did you get a look at his face?" the detective pressed.

"Not really," she said, looking him in the eye. "He had a stocking pulled over his head. But he was a skinny fellow wearing dark brown pants and a black-colored, long-sleeved shirt. I found it odd, though, that he wore no gloves on his hands, considering the cold weather outside. Not to mention that he was committing a crime."

"And what color were his hands, Mrs. Winters?"

"They were a little on the dark side," she paused to consider for a monument, focusing on the dark-green fern pushed to one corner of the desk. "Not really black, but they had sort of an olive-colored complexion to them."

"Okay, that may help in identifying him." The detective punched a few lines with the stylus onto his iPad, then turned his attention back to Stormy. "Now, Ms. Winters, about the man that was shot, the bank's manager. I hear he tried to be a hero and provoked the gunman into shooting him."

"It's Mrs., and he was certainly being a bit foolish in continuing to walk toward the gunman when he had plainly been told to stay where he was," Stormy surmised. She looked out the office's framed, glass door in time to observe two paramedics lifting Mr. West onto the gurney in preparation for a ride to the hospital. "Poor man, he was only trying to get the gunman to leave. I'm sure he must have thought that he would do just that: back off and leave. It seemed to me that the gunman had what he'd come for with the heavy sack he was carrying."

Then, as often happened, Stormy's mind started working a mile a minute, the thoughts flying quickly by. *Why would the man just stick around like that? It was almost as if he were waiting for an accomplice to finish filling up another bag or something. But I didn't see anyone else leave with him, or could he have been waiting for an accomplice in a car to pick him up? Hmmm.* Just then the detective started talking again, breaking into her thoughts.

"Seems like it, doesn't it? Anything else you can think of?" The detective continued typing more notes into his pad.

Leaning forward, Stormy tried to peer at the screen. The detective immediately snapped closed its leather cover and drummed a rhythm on the top of it with the stylus.

"No, I don't think so," she said, adjusting in her seat. "Wait. I did notice something as I fell to the floor as he ran past."

"Ah, and what was that?" Pulling the iPad closer to him, he flipped open to the screen, poised to take further notes.

"I got a quick glance at his socks and shoes," she said, leaning forward in her chair.

"His socks and shoes, Ma'am?" The detective raised one eyebrow, awaiting her answer.

"The socks were a bright orange, and the shoes were a dirty pair of off-white sneakers with several scuff marks running along their sides. It struck me as an odd combination."

"Why? A lot of people wear loud-colored socks these days. And dirty shoes are nothing new."

Stormy watched as the detective shifted in his chair, obviously shoving his feet further underneath the desk between them, a momentary look of discomfort crossing his face.

"That's not it," she explained, pretending she hadn't noticed. "It was the fact that a price sticker was still on one of the socks he was wearing, attesting to the fact that they were recently purchased."

"I guess he wasn't sure yet if he wanted to keep them or take them back," the detective quipped as he made a further notation and then snapped his leather case closed once more. Eyebrows furrowed, he reached inside his shirt pocket and handed her a business card. "Give me a call if you think of anything else. Thank you, Mrs. Winters, you're free to leave."

"Thank you, detective. I'll let you know."

Gathering up her purse and walking stick, and pulling her coat around her once more, Stormy exited the office and headed toward the bank doors. Upon reaching them, she turned to look back in the detective's direction in time to see him step from the office to call his next witness. As he did so, the stylus slipped from his hand and fell to the carpeting. In bending over to retrieve the instrument, his pant legs hiked up, showing off a pair of bright purple socks stuffed into black loafers.

"No wonder." Stormy chuckled to herself, before turning back to the doors.

A polite police officer stationed there held a door open for her. She thanked him and stepped out into the cold as she secured the buttons of her coat. Replacing the muffs over her ears, she retrieved the gloves out of her pockets and slipped them onto her hands.

Stepping onto the sidewalk, she turned toward her hotel. As she did so, a tall young man with short brown hair, sporting a closely cropped goatee on his rugged chin, hailed her. He'd been chatting with another man beside a News vehicle.

"May I have a moment of your time, Ma'am?" he asked, heading her way. The other man followed along with some equipment in tow.

The young man seemed kind and genuine. He wore a warm-looking down jacket, and she could just make out where it said "News 1 Radio" on the breast pocket. The material creased back on itself where it stated the frequency, making it unreadable.

Stormy was still a bit shook up over the events she'd just witnessed, and she hesitated for a moment.

The man didn't wait for an answer.

"I'm Chris Jacobs with News One Radio." he said, extending a hand. "Sorry if we're catching you off guard. I'm on in a few minutes and was hoping you could tell us what you saw in there?"

"Well, I can't tell you much, Mr. Jacobs," she explained, wrapping an arm around her for added warmth while balancing herself on the icy walk with her stick in the other. "I really walked in on the end of it all."

"Please, call me Chris," he smiled.

"And you are?" "Okay, Chris, I'm Stormy Winters," she replied.

"Alright, Stormy Winters, here's what I need: just let me know what things looked like when you walked in and give me a brief description of the suspects when I prompt you. Would that be alright?"

Chris ducked out of the way, as the other young man swung out some sort of antenna from the van.

"Um, okay, but there was only one suspect that I witnessed inside," Stormy replied.

"Great, it'll be just like a conversation, but with this mic in our faces," he chuckled, holding up the black instrument in his hand. "The news van is heated if you'd like to sit in there while we do this." The other young man handed him a microphone.

"No, I'll be just fine here on the sidewalk," she replied. "As long as it doesn't take too long, that is. My husband is waiting for me back at the hotel and he may start to worry if I'm gone much longer."

"It shouldn't take too long," Chris said, adjusting his glove, "but let me know if you change your mind. It's a lot warmer inside the truck than it is out here."

A few minutes later, the young man called out from the direction of the van and then made a fist symbol.

"Okay, Stormy. We're on in a few seconds." Chris straightened up, almost as if he were going on camera.

The crew stood dead quiet as they prepared to go live, with Stormy waiting beside Chris. He seemed to be listening intently to something unseen.

Stormy found the experience both interesting, and a bit nerve racking. She hadn't been on the radio before.

Chris took a sudden deep breath. "That's right, Ted. We are here in front of the First Bank, the site of a robbery that took place under an hour ago. I have here with me, Stormy Winters, a witness to the crime. Stormy, can you tell us what you walked in on?"

"Well Chris, I was fiddling with the buttons on my coat when I entered the bank doors" she began, speaking into the microphone, suddenly shoved into her face. "When I looked up, I noticed that the patrons were face-down on the floor and the tellers held their arms high over their heads. Then I noticed the gunman. He looked pretty nervous but was trying to act as tough as he could."

"And can you give us a general description of the suspect?"

"He had a very thin-looking build. He wore a stocking mask, had on dark clothing, and was holding some type of revolver. I noticed by the way he was acting that he was trying hard to cover up his nervousness."

"What led up to him shooting the bank's manager?"

"Well, he surprised the gunman by coming up from behind him. He told Mr. West . . .." Stormy said.

"Mr. Peter West is the bank manager here and it is uncertain of how serious his wounds are at this time," Chris interrupted, speaking into the mic, then placing it back near Stormy. "Please go on, Ms. Winters."

"Yes, Chris, that's what I understand. The gunman told Mr. West to stay put, not to come any closer, but took one too many steps in the gunman's direction, and the gun went off."

"And that's when the gunman knocked you down and left the bank?"

"Yes, and I really didn't see much more than that." She'd thought to mention the colorful socks and dirty shoes but had decided against it.

"I noticed the medical crew checking you out. I trust you're okay, Stormy?"

"Oh, I'm just a bit sore, Chris. As you mentioned, the man knocked me down as he ran for the front doors. I'll be okay."

"Good to hear that. Thanks for joining us, Stormy. You heard it here." The reporter held the microphone back in front of him as Stormy took a few steps out of his way. "The initial description of the suspect—a thin man, armed and dangerous, wearing dark clothes with a stocking mask pulled over his face. Police are asking for your help. If anyone has any information about this suspect, they ask you to please call the Colorado Springs Police Department. Your name will be held in strict confidence. We'll check in again with the official police statement later on. Reporting live from in front of the First Bank in downtown Colorado Springs, for News One Radio, this is Chris Jacobs."

"Perfect." Chris beamed with enthusiasm after he'd clicked a button on the bottom of the microphone. "That's exactly what we needed. Thanks, Stormy. I hope you didn't mind me calling you by your first name. Here, let me give you my card if anything else comes up. Is there anyone coming to get you?"

"No, my hotel is just down the block, and the walk will do me some good," she replied, taking his card and shoving it into a coat pocket. "And Stormy is fine."

"Sure you don't need a ride?" Chris insisted, handing the microphone to his assistant.

"Yes, I'll be fine."

"Okay," Chris replied. "If you need anything at all while you're here in the Springs, or remember anything more about the robbery, just give me a call."

"Thanks, Chris, I might just do that," Stormy smiled, and using her walking stick, she carefully headed down the sidewalk.

As she walked, she thought about Chris. He seemed like a nice young man. She wondered if Ann was seeing anyone at this time. *Oh Stormy, stop that!* She chuckled to herself. *You don't need to be meddling in Ann's affairs.*

Stormy carefully made her way back to the hotel as the sun began to drop lower in the sky. The evening air held an even chillier wind, and she was glad to step through the doors into the hotel's lobby.

* * *

"There you are," Lance said, as she stepped into their room. "I was starting to wonder what was taking you so long to withdraw that money. I thought maybe you had gotten robbed along the way." His eyes twinkled, a smile playing on his face.

"Well," she began, "that's not far from the truth."

Exhausted, she flopped down on the room's sofa, setting her purse and stick beside her.

"What do you mean?" Lance asked, sitting down beside her.

"When I arrived at the bank," she related, unbuttoning her coat, "and had just barely stepped through the doors into the lobby, I realized that something just didn't feel right. I'd hardly had time to look around the room when I noticed that there were several people lying on the carpeting. Then I spotted a man waving a gun around."

Stormy continued her narrative, including the shooting of the bank's manager, ending with her being knocked to the floor by the fleeing gunman.

"Oh, Storm, are you alright?" Lance studied her, great concern showing in his eyes.

"Nothing that a good, hot bath won't help to cure," she said, rubbing her shoulder. "Though I'll probably have some pretty good-sized bruises by tomorrow morning."

"I'll put some of that warming rub on for you after your bath," Lance offered, helping her remove her coat. "That should help." "Thanks, honey."

"What happened after he knocked you down?" Lance asked, lightly rubbing her shoulder.

"He ran out the bank's doors. I guess he must have had a car nearby or some other plan of escape," she responded. "They were still looking for him, the last I heard."

"He's probably long gone by now," he said. "Hopefully, they'll find him soon and lock him up."

"The police detective at the scene gave me this card in case I could think of anything else." Stormy fished out the card from the depths of her purse and handed it to him.

"What do you mean 'anything else'?" Lance said, taking it from her and looking it over. "What else could you possibly tell him?"

"Not much really. I guess it was because I mentioned the robber having worn bright orange socks and dirty tennis shoes," she replied. "The others had already given him the same description of the assailant: scrawny and thin with a stocking cap over his face. Apparently, they hadn't seen the socks, and the sales sticker attached to one of them. Or else they just didn't think to mention it to the detectives." Stormy shrugged, "Maybe due to the fact that their faces were pressed into the carpeting."

"Bright orange socks, huh? That's interesting."

"Oh," Stormy grinned, "you might hear me on this evening's news report. A nice young reporter from News One Radio interviewed me outside the bank as I was leaving. He, too, gave me his card." Grabbing her coat, she retrieved the newsman's card from a pocket and handed it over.

"I'm married to a celebrity, am I?" Lance teased, looking at this new card before putting his arms around her. "I already knew that. I'll have to see if I can find the interview on the news later. If not, I'll search for it on their website."

He gently kissed her and gave her a hug.

"Ouch!" Stormy said, as she pulled back from his arms and rubbed at her side.

"Sorry, you'd better go get that bath," Lance suggested, helping her up from the sofa. "I'll get it started for you while you grab your things.

Afterwards, I think you'd better lay down for a while."

Three

Tanks rumbled across desolate fields and planes buzzed overhead like hungry mosquitoes in search of life's precious red liquid. Shrill whistles echoed against nearby hills as bombs fell from the sky, causing great explosions that carved gaping holes deep into the earth. Commanders shouted directions to their men, as screams of "Medic!" rang throughout the battlefield. Soldiers lay dying where they had fallen.

Stormy awoke with a start, confusion clouding her mind.

"What's going on?" she mumbled, as a bomb exploded somewhere close by.

Wiping the sleep from her eyes with a finger, she quickly sat up and looked around the room, listening intently. After a few moments, she realized that the sounds of war issued forth from the other side of the room's door. Shoving her feet into her favorite slippers and donning a robe, she hurried to the door, flung it open, and stepped through.

Her alert eyes quickly scanned the area for the approaching army, then came to rest on the form of her husband, who was hunched over his computer. A smile came to her lips as she paused for a moment, admiring his strong physique, the slight graying at his temples marking the wisdom of his years.

"It sounds like a war's going on in here." She padded across the thick, beige carpet of their hotel suite, stopping beside his chair.

"Sorry." Lance reached over, turning the volume down on his laptop, eyes glued to the screen. "Close though. It's World War II, to be precise."

"I thought you were going to lie down for a while after you checked your e-mail," Stormy said, peering down at the screen in time to see another explosion rip through a line of olive-green trucks, flinging them in all directions.

"Well, I was," he responded sheepishly, looking up at her, "but I wanted to see if this new game I downloaded before we left Phoenix was any good. I haven't had the chance to check it out yet. I guess I lost track of the time."

"That sounds like a familiar scenario." A sigh escaped Stormy's lips as she turned and headed back across the room. She sat down on the room's plaid couch and propped her feet up on the matching ottoman.

"Well . . ." Lance's attention was pulled back to the screen as a German tank came into view and began firing upon his armored supply column. He furrowed his brows, the fingers of one hand flying across the laptop's keys, the other hand furiously clicking the mouse, fighting to save his troops from the approaching forces.

Stormy rested against the sofa's high back and smiled to herself. It would be another few minutes before her husband would resurface from his game and they could talk about their plans for the rest of the day. She guessed she could relax a bit more.

Though of retirement age, most people thought that Stormy was a good ten to fifteen years younger than her age. Smooth skin and lovely blue-gray eyes, framed by dark-blonde hair, curled and teased neatly into place, may have attributed to this misconception: one that pleased her to no end. Her make-up was always fresh-looking and lightly applied; she refused to pile it on like some of the women her age, saying that they looked like "ladies plying their trade." Her clothes usually consisted of tailored shirts and pants—blues and browns being her favorite colors—accented by a pair of opened-toed sandals. She claimed that a shoe that totally enclosed her foot was just 'too hot and uncomfortable' for everyday use. She'd had to make an exception, however, being here in the colder weather of Colorado. Her niece, Samantha, would be especially pleased to hear this, having tried to convince her to reconsider her footwear ever since Stormy had broken an exposed toe on a dining room chair a few years back.

Lance, on the other hand, was every bit retired military, right down to the games he chose to play on his computer, or when picking sides for Army vs. Navy in one of his favorite sports, football. One only had to look at Lance to notice the fine military bearing about him from his many years of service in the U. S. Army. Just two years older than his wife, he looked more his age than she did, with his short graying hair, nicely groomed salt and pepper mustache, and the wisdom of the years reflecting forth from soft brown eyes. His nicely tanned skin was the result of many hours spent beneath the hot Arizona sun caring for his prized rose garden.

Stormy thought of how, when the overseas call had come to their home in Phoenix, asking if they would like to attend the Army/Air Force football game with their niece, Ann, they'd quickly agreed.

Stormy's brother, Jared, along with his wife, Diane, were working at the US Embassy in Paris and couldn't get the leave they were hoping to attend the game with their youngest daughter at the prestigious Air Force Academy in Colorado Springs. Though disappointed, they offered their tickets to Stormy and Lance, knowing how much Lance loved football.

Stormy felt close to all of her nieces and nephews, but somehow felt even closer to Ann. Maybe it was because they always seemed to be laughing at something when they spent time together. And what was that saying? 'Laughter is the best medicine!'

Another thing that bonded them was that Stormy could see the same yearning for adventure in Ann that she felt in herself. In fact, a few years ago, when she found out that Ann had been accepted at the Air Force Academy, she was thrilled for her. Almost from the time that Ann could talk, she'd expressed a desire to do two things: travel the world, and follow in her father's and uncle's footsteps, standing up for their great country. Finally, she would be able to do both!

"Okay, I'll save right here," Lance said. He made a few more clicks with his mouse, then closed the laptop. He stood up and crossed the room to sit beside Stormy. "How are you feeling after your rest? Ready for the big game?"

"A little sore, but I wouldn't miss it for the world." Stormy leaned over and kissed Lance. Lance took her gently in his arms and returned the kiss.

"I'd like to pursue this further, but we don't want to miss the opening." Lance sighed, giving Stormy another hug before pulling her to her feet. "Why don't we continue this when we get back later this evening?"

"Sounds like fun to me." Stormy laughed. "I'd better get back into my clothes and check my makeup. I'll be done in a few minutes."

Once ready, the twosome headed down to the hotel's parking lot. Lance unlocked the passenger's side door and held it open for Stormy.

"Thank you." Stormy climbed into the car, settled into the leather seat, and fastened her seat belt.

"Anything for you, my dear," he said, executing a small bow. Smoothing out his salt and pepper mustache, a twinkle in his eyes, he closed her door.

He placed her walking stick onto the rear seat before going around and climbing into the driver's seat. The engine roared to life, and they backed out of the space and exited the parking garage.

Heading along the I-25, they traveled north toward the Air Force Academy. Lance steered the Hyundai carefully along the crowded highway, the traffic coming to a crawl several times as they made their way along the blacktop. The game was a big annual event in the area, and many would be attending it.

Making their way along the rows of seats in the stadium, the two of them pushed through the many groups chatting excitedly with one another. Stormy and Lance found they had excellent seats from which to view the game.

"You chose well when you bought these tickets," Lance exclaimed to Ann as she joined them. Her reddish-brown, shoulder length hair was swept up and pinned to the back of her head and her green eyes shone with excitement. Her light-colored jeans, with matching jacket, accentuated her trim, athletic build.

"That comes from getting your order in early," Ann answered, grinning as she took her seat beside him. "Dad was always a stickler for being early or doing everything early as we grew up. I guess it rubbed off on me." She smiled.

The opening ceremonies began as the Air Force band struck up a melody of patriotic songs and blue-clad cadets marched out onto the field, placing themselves at intervals around the area. A loud roar filled the skies overhead as several jets came into view, streaking across the sky over the stadium.

As Stormy and the others craned their heads upward, she was the first of the trio to spot several individuals jumping from a slower flying plane. As they fell, parachutes shot out above each one, dragging them momentarily upward. Each skillfully guided their chutes to land in the center of the football field as the band continued to play on. An honor guard, made up of more cadets, with airmen carrying rifles over their shoulders flanking them on either side, marched out onto the field as a final parachutist descended from the sky. A large American flag, attached to his shoulder, flapped in the wind.

The band began to play the Star-Spangled Banner and Stormy and Lance stood up with the rest of the crowd. Stormy placed her hand over her heart while Lance stood to attention and saluted. It had only been in recent years that retired military in civilian clothes were given permission to salute. Stormy knew this meant a lot to Lance.

The cadets, stationed out on the field, ran to catch hold of the large flag before it could touch the ground as the parachutist descended to make a perfect landing. Tears filled the corners of Stormy's eyes and spilled down her cheek as her love for this country filled her heart. She noticed that Lance had moist eyes as well when she glanced in his direction. Beyond him stood Ann at attention, saluting in fine form.

The guard presented the colors in fine form, not an airman out of step. Stormy and Lance loved the opportunity to be here on a military base.

Stormy's thoughts turned to the fact that it'd been a few years since Lance had retired from his career in the service, so he didn't get this kind of opportunity to attend military events as often as he'd used to. However, today he'd worn his "Retired Army" cap with a gold leaf emblazoned on it to the game. He'd been given a salute by the guard on duty at the entrance gate to the base after he'd seen Lance's military ID. It'd made Lance feel good and Stormy swell with pride for all the service and sacrifice Lance had made for his country over the many years he'd served. Both their fathers had served in the military and in overseas wars, so serving was a long-standing family tradition.

Everyone's attention was drawn to the sky once more as several F-16s flew overhead, lines of white contrail trailing in streaks behind them. A mighty cheer rose up from the crowd as if a famous baseball player had hit a triple play at the World Series, one of Stormy's favorite sports. Then people took their seats and the game began.

"Well, this should be a good night for the Army to show the Air Force how to play real football," Lance said to his niece, a gleam forming in his eye.

"No, Uncle. I think you've got it backwards," Ann retorted, obviously enjoying the banter between them. "It's the Air Force that will show the Army what's what."

"Oh, boy, I can see we're in for an interesting evening," Stormy said, laughing. "Maybe we should call a truce and get a few hot dogs and sodas."

The crowd roared and cheered as the two teams came head-to-head and began to play ball. Stormy found the game exciting as the teams continued to one-up each other on the field, the score going back and forth. A final play at game's end put the score at 20 to 27, in favor of the Air Force.

"Woohoo!" Ann yelled with the rest of the crowd. A wide grin on her face, she turned to her uncle. "You were saying?"

Lance made his famous puppy dog eyes. "I guess the Army just had one of those off days," he suggested, then smiled. "Just wait until next time. They'll beat those flyboys!"

"We'll see," Ann laughed. She and her uncle posed for photos with Stormy's phone, then it was Stormy's turn.

Stormy and Ann made their way behind Lance, heading out of the bleachers.

"We're hoping to be at the restaurant in about 30 minutes," Lance told his niece. "Will you and your friends be able to get through this crowd in time?"

"We'll sure try," Ann said, smiling at him. "If not, save us a seat. I'll give my parents a quick call on my phone and round up the others. I think you'll like them." Turning around, she dashed off into the sea of bodies.

"If they're as good as Ann, I'm sure we will." "True," Lance agreed.

Stormy followed close behind, walking stick in one hand, as she held tightly to the program of the night's ceremony. She would hold onto the paper and send it off to Ann's parents with copies of the pictures they'd taken. They'd be excited to receive them.

Lance and Stormy dodged several cars backing out in preparation to exit the stadium's parking area. Security personnel, bundled in heavy blue coats and hats, and holding lighted batons, helped to direct the flow of traffic.

As Lance entered the highway it began to snow, coming down slowly at first, then in handfuls, as if the stars were falling from the heavens. It reminded Stormy of a ride she'd been on with her children at Disneyland when they were younger.

"Those are pretty big flakes," Stormy observed. "Good thing they decided to wait until the game was over."

"I put in a word with the man upstairs." Lance pointed toward the sky, his other hand gripping the steering wheel as he slowly followed the car in front of them.

"You've got a pretty good connection I'd say." Stormy laughed as she patted Lance's shoulder.

Four

Lance parked outside of P. F. Chang's, jumped out, and held the car door open for Stormy. Taking her arm, he led the way to the restaurant's doors. They stopped momentarily to admire the two huge stone war horses that were placed outside the restaurant's front entrance. Stormy loved the Oriental culture and their ways. The two years they'd spent in Japan held some very dear memories for both she and Lance. They had made some wonderful friends while Lance had been stationed there, and they still stayed in contact with many of them.

The snow came down in large, heavy flakes, covering the cars in the parking lot with a white blanket that made it hard to tell their individual colors. Even though it was cold outside, Stormy loved this time of year in the Springs. It was like being in a white wonderland full of promise and excitement!

Upon entering the large restaurant, the first thing Stormy noticed was the unusual light fixtures on the ceiling. To her, they looked like huge Japanese drums. With her vivid imagination, she could just imagine entertainers dressed in kimonos up on the ceiling playing them for the diners to enjoy while eating their dinner. She laughed at herself for thinking such a thing, rolling her eyes and slightly shaking her head.

The hostess showed them to their seats at a table near one of the windows, where they had a good view of the falling snow outside. Ann and her friends had arrived just ahead of them and were already perusing the menus. Stormy noticed that each place setting included a set of chopsticks next to the silverware.

"Here's my Aunt and Uncle now," Ann said, lowering her menu to greet them. "Sit over here by me." She patted the seat next to her, looking expectantly at her aunt.

"I'd love to," Stormy replied, sitting down next to her niece. "Have you been here long?"

"No, just a few minutes. But long enough to become quite ravenous with all these wonderful smells in the air." Ann laughed, glancing over at the plates of food on a table nearby.

"Yes, it does smell great and I'm starving, too," Lance agreed, taking the chair beside Stormy. "Who do we have here?" He smiled across the table at the three young people sitting with them.

"These are my friends from the Academy," Ann began, making introductions all around. "This is Mark, Jeff, and Darlene. This is my Aunt Stormy and Uncle Lance from Phoenix; the ones I was telling you about."

"Hi," Stormy greeted them. "It's nice to finally meet some of Ann's friends."

"Yes, it is," Lance said, reaching across the table to shake each of their hands in turn. "How are you?"

"Fine, sir," each one of them answered.

The server approached their table and took their orders. Stormy and Lance decided to order separate dishes and share them between themselves. They did this quite often when they went out to eat. Stormy chose beef and broccoli, while Lance decided on chicken with cashew-peanut sauce. Ann ordered chicken and vegetables, with her friends each choosing their own favorites from the menu.

As they waited for their orders to be prepared, they discussed the day's events and what lay ahead of them.

"Wasn't it you I heard on the radio this evening, Mrs. Winters?" Jeff asked. "Your voice sounds familiar, and I thought I heard Chris Jacobs announce your name."

"Yes, you probably did, Jeff," Stormy replied, taking a sip of her ice-water.

"So, you were there when that man robbed the bank today?" he further inquired, his expression one of concern. "I heard a man was shot. I'm glad to see you're okay."

"You were in a robbery, Aunt Stormy?" Ann asked, obviously upset at the news. "Where, when? Why didn't you mention it to me? Were you hurt?"

"Well, I've not had the time to tell you before now." Stormy finished spreading out her napkin on her lap before looking up at Ann. "And I didn't want to worry you."

"Well, you'd better tell me all about it now," her niece demanded. Ann turned to her friends and said, "Leave it to my Aunt Stormy to be in the middle of the action!"

"After breakfast, I realized that I'd forgotten to withdraw the money I'd meant to before leaving on our trip," she explained. "A bank was just down the block, so I decided to dash over and get some cash out of our account, just in case we needed it for anything. The sidewalk was icy, so it took me a little longer to navigate than I'd first thought it would."

The waiter approached carrying a large serving tray, interrupting the conversation. With a flick of his hand, he unfolded a stand and set the tray on it. Removing a tureen and ladle, he placed it in the center of their table. Its beautiful markings drew everyone's attention as steam poured forth from the opening in its top, the wonderful aroma filling the group with anticipation. The waiter set a bowl in front of each person and encouraged them to try the hot soup, promising to return with their main courses.

After he'd left, they all took turns filling their bowls with the hot Egg Drop soup.

"Do they use real eggs in this soup?" Jeff asked, examining the contents of the bowl in front of him.

"Yes, they do," Stormy answered. "They usually crack the eggs into a bowl and slightly beat them, then drop them into the hot soup when it is almost finished cooking. This is one of my favorite Oriental soups and I make it occasionally at home for Lance and I." She lifted a spoonful to her mouth and sipped the hot liquid. "Delicious," she declared.

They all agreed that it was just what was needed for such a cold day.

"Didn't you notice anything wrong when you got to the bank?" Darlene asked, steering them back to the previous conversation. "No waiting car outside with its motor running or anything like that?"

"Not that I saw, Darlene. There wasn't anyone around outside at all," Stormy answered, then paused. "Well, that's not exactly true, come to think of it. Some nut came shooting out of a side street or alleyway and skidded all over the road, then raced past me down the street."

"They should know better in conditions like these," Ann exclaimed, shaking her head. "They could've lost control and run you down."

"Yes, they could have," Lance put in, giving Stormy's arm a squeeze. "Good thing for us they didn't."

Stormy smiled at him before continuing.

"I'd just walked through the front doors of the bank and was trying to unbutton my coat when I realized something was wrong," she related. "I looked around the lobby and spotted several people down on the floor before noticing a man across the room waving a gun at them."

"What did you think when you saw the gun?" Darlene asked, putting her spoon down on the napkin next to her empty soup dish.

"I didn't know what to think," Stormy replied. "Just that I had to hide. I ducked behind a nearby sign and watched from there. A man from the bank, they said he was the bank manager, tried to talk the robber into leaving but ended up getting shot by him. It took me by such surprise that I was too slow to react as the robber turned and ran in my direction. I'd thought maybe I could trip him with my walking stick, but he was on me before I knew it, knocking me to the ground as he fled past and out the doors."

"Wow! Good thing he didn't get nervous and shoot you, too," Mark said. "People under stress can react before they know what they're doing."

"Mark's a medical intern," Ann explained, her face a mask of emotions. "And I agree with him. You were very blessed, indeed."

"Yes, she was," Lance said, squeezing Stormy's hand before looking over at Mark. "A medic, huh? I had some medical training when I was in the military, but that was some years ago."

"It's always good to know a few things, just in case," Mark said, taking a sip from the teacup in front of him.

"Let's hope they catch the man before he hurts anyone else, or even kills someone," Darlene said, shaking her head. "How's the bank manager doing? Was he badly hurt?"

"He was shot in the shoulder and was still bleeding by the time the paramedics showed up. They think, however, he'll be okay after a stay in the hospital. I was thinking of going by to see him at the hospital tomorrow, if they'll let me."

"That's very thoughtful of you, Aunt Stormy," Ann said, before turning in her chair. "I wonder what's taking the food so long?"

As if on cue, the waiter appeared with a tray filled full of piping hot dishes, and the hungry group dug into their delicious meals.

"They sure know how to prepare cashew sauce here," Lance commented. He skillfully used his chopsticks to pick up a nut and place it in his mouth. He and Stormy loved using chopsticks every opportunity they got since living in Japan, where they'd become quite proficient at using them.

As the group was finishing off the last few bites of their dinners, the waiter brought two dessert plates filled with a wonderful chocolate cake with rich raspberry sauce poured over the top of it. It was one of the desserts the restaurant was famous for.

"This looks great," Mark and Darlene said in unison, reaching for one of the small plates in front of them.

"It sure does," Lance agreed, surveying the chocolate delight with great anticipation. "Help yourselves everyone."

When everyone claimed to be much too full to eat another bite, Lance helped himself to the last piece of cake, using his fork to scrape up the delicious red sauce.

"You'll need to be careful, or you'll end up looking like the Great Wall," Stormy teased him.

The group broke out in laughter as Lance feigned a hurt look.

Stormy kissed his cheek as she swabbed her hands with one of the wet towels that the waiter had placed on the table. She and Lance had been sportingly teasing each other their whole married life.

"Hey, have you found that cache you were looking for yet, Jeff?" Ann asked him, pushing her dessert plate away from her.

"Uh, no, not yet," Jeff said. Stormy sensed he'd had his mind on something else. "I haven't had the time to look, with studies . . . and all."

"What kind of cash are you referring to?" Stormy asked.

"It's actually called geocaching. Haven't you ever heard of them before?" Ann asked her aunt.

"I guess not," Stormy laughed. "Tell me about them."

"Geocaching is really a lot of fun," Mark began. "It's a form of treasure hunting using a navigation system, like a GPS, or Global Positioning System. It began in May of 2000 in Portland, Oregon when a man named Dave Ulmer hid a large bucket near his home, placed a logbook and some other miscellaneous items in it, and let people know about its coordinates via the Internet."

"It caught on as others found out about it and went exploring for his cache," Jeff continued, getting warmed up to the subject. "Then others began copying what he had done by placing caches of their own in various parts of the country and then throughout the world."

"What types of things do they put into these caches?" Stormy asked, wiping a spot of chocolate off her mouth with the corner of her napkin.

"First of all, each one usually contains a logbook, as Mark said the first one did," Ann took over the explanation. "When you find a cache, you will be able to see who else has visited it and where they've come from. And maybe a few other details about themselves and what they may have taken and left in its place. It is important that if you remove an item from someone's cache that you play fair and put one back in from something you have."

"I once found a DVD in one cache containing the most amusing amateur comedy routine. My friends and I got quite a laugh out of it," Jeff chimed in. "I replaced it with a mystery book I'd taken from another cache I'd previously found. After watching the DVD, we placed it in the next cache we came upon so others could enjoy it."

"One time, when I was in the UK, I found a cache containing a plastic bag which held a few rotten apples. I quickly removed and disposed of it. Food is never a good idea to place in a cache as it usually spoils before anyone finds it." Darlene made a face. "I heard of one case where a bear sniffed out a cache that contained some food items that someone had placed inside it and completely destroyed not only the cache, but its entire contents."

"Sounds like these caches have caught on all over the world," Lance put in, warming to the subject.

"Yes, they're in over one hundred countries so far, and growing by the day." Ann drained the water from the glass in front of her, then set it back down on the table.

A waitress came by and asked if anyone would like their glasses refilled. Only Jeff took her up on it.

"We'll have to check out some of these caches while we're here, Lance," Stormy said; the thought of a mystery intrigued her.

"Yes, my thoughts exactly. It sounds like great fun," Lance remarked "And it will be fun trying out our own GPS system this way."

"I can start you out with a few of the coordinates to ones around here, if you'd like," Mark offered, pulling a wallet from his back pocket.

"Sure, that would be great." Stormy took out the small notebook she carried in her purse, along with a black pen, and jotted down the information he provided them.

"It sounds like we'll have to stay an extra day or so," Lance chimed in, looking over at Stormy, a twinkle filling his eyes. "What do you think?"

"I think we'll have to." Stormy smiled.

The group conversed a little longer about the various caches they'd discovered and the things they'd found in them. The discussion switched to the new assignments the Air Force might give to the cadets when they graduated next spring. Excitement filled the air as each one described the places they hoped to be sent to and what their responsibilities might be.

Stormy and Lance responded with lots of good wishes to each of them for the wonderful opportunities that lay ahead, mirroring their enthusiasm.

"We had a great time celebrating with all of you and now we'd better be getting back to our hotel," Stormy said, glancing at her wristwatch. "It's getting late."

"Yes, I guess we'd better go so Stormy doesn't miss out on her beauty sleep," Lance teased, his eyes dancing with mischief. "Of course, I don't see how she could get any lovelier than she already is." Stormy laughed as the others agreed with Lance.

"See you tomorrow morning for church," Ann told her Aunt and Uncle. "I'll meet you at the church building about 7:45 am and we can sit together. Don't be late. The services start at 8 sharp."

"We'll see if Stormy can have her face put together by then," Lance said arising from the table, a twinkle showing in his eyes.

Stormy stood up, firmly punched Lance on the arm, and picked up her purse. He grabbed his arm and feigned pain by letting out a low moan.

The group broke out in laughter as they headed for the restaurant's door.

* * * *

"That was a fun evening," Stormy remarked as she waved a last good-bye to her niece. "I think Ann's friends are nice, and I'm glad to see her so happy."

"Yes, me, too," Lance agreed. "She's had some rough times in the past and she might not have made it through so well without your help." Turning on his signal, and checking his side mirror, he changed lanes. "She's smart and has a good head on her shoulders, and I think she has a lot more confidence now than she used to."

"I was glad she could come and stay with us for a while. I think it was good for her to get away when she did." Stormy replied, her thoughts drifting back to that time.

"Would you like to drive down Academy Blvd. and see if there's been any new development since the last time we were here? I think we might make better time on the surface streets anyway," Lance commented as he scanned the road ahead.

"It would be fun to check. It's been a while since we've been here," Stormy said, coming back to the present.

They turned out onto the Blvd. and headed south.

"This place continues to grow and grow, no matter how the economy is." Lance remarked, steering around a slow-moving car in front of him.

"I'm glad to see that," Stormy mumbled as she stared in the passenger's side mirror.

"What are you looking at, Storm?" Lance asked, noticing that she'd been staring into the mirror more than looking along the boulevard.

"That car behind us: it seems to have been following us for quite some time now. I know it may sound crazy, but I think I've seen it somewhere before. It looks familiar."

Lance looked intently in his rear-view mirror, trying to get a better look at the car following behind, while keeping an eye on the road ahead. He couldn't make it out clearly in the dark of the night, but it appeared to be a late model sports car of some type, maybe dark blue or black in color.

"There's one way to find out," Lance told her. He turned onto a nearby residential street and headed down it.

The dark sports car turned and followed them, all the while keeping its distance.

"See what I mean?" Stormy continued to watch the car in her mirror as Lance drove through the neighborhood.

"Maybe they live around here and it's just a coincidence."

"It might be, but I have an uneasy feeling about it." Stormy continued to watch the dark car behind.

"Let's pull over to the curb and see what they do," Lance suggested. He steered the SUV to a halt in front of a two-story red brick house and turned it off.

The black sports car sped by, the occupants not visible in the dark of the night. It continued down the road and turned onto another residential street.

"It looks like they were just going the same way as we were, and we happened to turn into their neighborhood," Lance assured her, pulling away from the curb.

"Maybe," Stormy said, though she couldn't shake the feeling that there was more to it than that.

Five

Stormy awoke to a fresh white blanket of snow covering the landscape outside their window. Lance must have pulled back the curtains. *It's funny I didn't hear him,* she thought.

Lance emerged from the bathroom, drying his hair with one of the hotel's soft towels. The wonderful smell of his English Leather aftershave reached across the room, filling Stormy's nose. Lance knew it was one of her favorites and had put it on especially for her.

"Good morning, sleepy head. You must have stayed up quite late reading that mystery book of yours," Lance greeted her. "Better get a move-on if we want to eat breakfast before we leave."

"I was just dozing until the bathroom was free," she replied, throwing back the covers. "As for the book, I did stay up a little later than I'd planned, but I had to finish it and see how it ended. It had a pretty good twist in the plot, but then she's always such a good writer. I'll be ready as quickly as I can. I'm starved." Stormy arose from the bed and crossed the room to the closet, pulling it open. Selecting a long, turquoise-colored skirt with matching vest and a long-sleeved ivory blouse, plus some undergarments from the dresser, she headed for the bathroom.

Twenty minutes later, she was fully clothed with makeup applied, pulling on the caramel-colored knee-high boots she was so fond of.

"Are you ready to go yet?" Lance asked impatiently, pulling on his charcoal-colored suit coat, before running a comb through his hair.

"Yep, let's go eat." Stormy smiled as she headed for the door.

They made their way to a table set for two in the hotel's breakfast room off the lobby. The buffet offered many delicious items for guests to choose from.

Stormy helped herself to scrambled eggs and a few pieces of bacon. At the last minute, she grabbed a large blueberry muffin and a small glass of juice before making her way to the table she shared with Lance.

"I see the muffin won out after all," Lance chucked, looking over at her plate.

"Yes," she began, sheepishly, "I tried to ignore it, but couldn't resist taking just one. As you know, blueberry muffins have always been one of my favorite kinds, and it looks almost as good as the jelly-filled sweet roll you're devouring there."

Lance's laugh rang out across the room as he picked up his glass of grapefruit juice and drank down the last of it.

"It's great to find such good citrus juices this time of year," he remarked, setting down the glass. "They must have shipped it in from Arizona."

"Couldn't be from Florida," Stormy stated.

"Of course not," Lance smiled. They had a few orange trees growing in their backyard in Phoenix and enjoyed fresh juice most mornings throughout the growing season.

After they'd finished eating, Stormy returned to their room to retrieve her purse and coat and run a toothbrush quickly over her teeth. She joined Lance, who was waiting for her by the hotel's front entrance.

"Okay, I'm ready," she informed him. "Let's get going."

"Are you sure you have everything?"

"Yes," Stormy said, her blue-gray eyes flashing at him. She passed by him and stepped through the door he held open.

"Race you to the car," she yelled back over her shoulder as she hurried away, balancing herself with her walking stick.

*   *   *   *

Lance pulled into a parking space at the church building. They found Ann waiting for them outside the front doors. They'd made good time, assuring them a nice seat inside for the services.

"I'm always surprised that I need my sunglasses in this kind of weather," Stormy conveyed to her niece as she removed the glasses and placed them inside her purse. "The sun's glare off of the snow is enough to blind me."

"That's one thing that a lot of people don't realize when they're in snowy climates," Ann replied. "The sun's glare off the white snow can, and will, have a very blinding effect on the eyes. So, it's very important to protect one's eyes from its effects when you're out in it."

"I have enough trouble in sunny climates without snow, so I'll be extra careful here in Colorado," Stormy remarked, shrugging out of her coat.

"We'd best be getting to our seats before they start the service," Lance interrupted, stepping between the women.

"Lead the way," she said, turning toward the doors.

The carpeted hallways were filled with friendly faces and excited children walking alongside their families.

Ann led her aunt and uncle through the chapel doors to a row of light blue, soft-padded benches. Stormy glanced up at a woman sitting at an organ near the front of the chapel, off to one side of the pulpit, softly playing hymns as the congregation's members found their seats.

Soon the chapel doors were closed and a friendly looking, middle-aged man in suit and tie stood before them and addressed the group, welcoming everyone to the services.

*   *   *   *

A few hours later, Stormy walked beside Lance, hand in hand as they exited the church.

"It was nice having you both here with me today," Ann exclaimed. She rendered them a warm smile as she buttoned her coat.

"We loved attending with you," Stormy replied, donning her sunglasses once more.

"Yes, thank you for inviting us along," Lance put in, guiding Stormy around an icy patch on the sidewalk. "I really enjoyed the lively discussion in Sunday School."

"Yes, that was interesting. We all need a bit more faith in our lives," Ann replied, before changing the subject. "I brought along some sandwiches and some other things if you would like to join some of us across the street at one of the member's houses for lunch," Ann offered.

"Sounds like a winner," Lance put in, rubbing his hand over his stomach.

"Anything to do with food will get Lance's vote," Stormy said, smiling.

The snow and chill in the air invigorated Stormy and she breathed in deeply, filling her lungs. How she loved the feel of the crisp atmosphere.

The members' home was simple, but beautifully decorated and had a warm, inviting feeling about it as the group stepped inside out of the cold.

"Welcome to my home," said the small Asian woman in greeting. "If you will please remove your shoes and place them on the rack by the door, we will go into the kitchen. My daughter will take your coats and hang them up for you."

"I would like you to meet Linda." Ann introduced the woman. "This is my Aunt Stormy and Uncle Lance. Linda and her husband, Ban, have taken us cadets under their wings. This has been our home away from home."

"It is so nice to meet you and thank you for taking such good care of our niece," Stormy said, shaking the woman's hand. Lance followed suit, adding a slight bow.

"My, what a nice walking stick you have there," their hostess commented, as Stormy leaned her stick against a nearby wall before sitting down at the large wooden table. "And I especially like the Kokopelli design on."

"It's a Southwestern Native American symbol of one of their deities," Stormy explained, "in both the Hopi and Zuni cultures. They associate it with childbirth, animal reproduction, and agriculture. I have always loved its design."

"Stormy likes to collect charms from different areas that we travel to as well," Lance said, taking the seat next to his wife.

"Oh, that's a wonderful idea," a younger, brown-haired woman, seated across the table, chimed in. "Hi, I'm Jill. Will you be looking for one here in the Springs?"

"Yes, I hope to take the time to look while we're here."

"Be sure and take a look out at the Garden of the Gods," Linda suggested. "The gift shop is full of unusual and intriguing items."

"Okay. I will, thank you," Stormy replied. "That sounds like a lot of fun." She looked over at Lance, and from his expression, she knew they'd be checking it out.

Stormy found the meal delicious and the company quite delightful. By the time they'd finished and were ready to leave, Lance and Stormy felt as if they had a whole new group of friends to add to their lives.

"Please feel welcome to come and visit us any time you're in town," Linda warmly told them as they headed out the door. "Our door will always be open to you both."

"We'd love to, thank you," Stormy replied turning to follow Lance down the walk.

"Would you like to see the Air Force Academy Chapel on the base?" Ann said, looking at her wristwatch. "We still have time to make it there and get a good look around before it closes."

"Sounds good to me," Lance said. "We've heard a few things about it and were hoping to see it."

"Yes," Stormy agreed, as they headed across the street to the church's parking lot and their cars.

"Then let's go," Ann remarked, tying the belt of her coat about her waist.

"Why don't you come in our car so you can show us the way," Stormy suggested, gesturing to their vehicle.

"I was hoping I could, as my friends have other engagements to attend to."

"Hop right in, young lady and we'll be off," Lance told her, holding open the back seat's door for her.

"Thanks, Uncle Lance," she said, waving to her friends before climbing in.

*   *   *   *

Once through the South entrance gate to the base, Ann directed them past the stadium where they had attended her graduation the evening before. She instructed her uncle to turn left and continue past the Visiting Quarters and Officers Club. As they neared the mountains, Stormy spotted a large eagle soaring in the sky above.

"Oh look, guys! There's an eagle above those pine trees over there." She pointed it out for them, raising the front windshield visor to give Ann a better view of the magnificent bird. "I think it's a Golden Eagle. Isn't it good luck to see one?"

"That's what I've heard," Ann replied. "I've seen them several times up here as I've gone from building to building between classes, and to PT. I enjoy seeing them as I'm running in the morning. My heart thrills at their beauty each time."

"I just love the way the sun shines off their wings as they turn in flight." Stormy watched the bird as it made lazy circles in the sky above. "It's a good thing that they're protected."

"Let's stop here at the Environmental Overlook," Ann called out, pointing toward the next entrance.

"We'll walk from here to the Chapel. There's a trail around that hill that leads to it but be careful as it may be a bit icy this time of year."

Lance parked the car in an empty space facing out toward the valley, then sat there for a minute or two, drinking in the view.

"Magnificent," Lance exclaimed. He looked out across the base and out toward the city of Colorado Springs. Snow glistened off the covered branches of many of the nearby trees as the foothills flowed into the buildings of the city below them.

"I could sit here for hours absorbing this scene," Stormy said. "It's peaceful, not to mention breathtaking." The eagle flew over them once again. Stormy watched as it swooped toward the ground and then shot back up, a field mouse clutched in its claws. "Even though mice are not my favorite creature, I feel sorry for it."

The three of them exited the car, locked it, and headed for the Air Force Museum and Visitor's Center building across the pavement.

"Welcome to the visitors center, folks," a grey-haired woman greeted them. "Where are y'all from?"

"We're here from Phoenix, Arizona visiting our niece," Lance replied, gesturing to Ann.

"We're glad to have you visit us here today. Please sign our guest book, then have a look at these displays. If you feel like it, follow the signs to the start of the trail that way." She pointed out the doors and to the left of where they stood. "It's a pleasant walk but watch out for the patches of ice."

"You really should see these before we continue," Ann exclaimed.

They walked from exhibit to exhibit, enthralled by each one as they made their way around the room. Afterwards, they left the building and headed for the trail. The asphalt path winded its way in and out of the evergreens. Several joggers in Air Force blue sweats jogged past them. Stormy admired how physically fit they were.

They encountered a few more cadets sitting on benches, enjoying sandwiches while engaged in conversation.

The group had just entered an area where they were all alone, walking carefully over the icy asphalt, when a jogger in long blue sweats, heavy jacket and gloves, sporting a dark ski mask pulled tightly over his face, ran toward them from around a bend in the trail. He bolted by at top speed, plowing into Stormy and knocking her into Ann, who'd been walking beside her. The two of them slipped on the ice beneath their feet and went flying to the ground.

"Hey," Lance cried out as the jogger disappeared around the next bend, never once stopping to look back.

Lance hurried forward to reach the women, who were already attempting to sit up.

"Are you two okay?"

"That idiot should be put on report," Ann said, looking in the direction their assailant had disappeared. "He should know better than that, and what's more, he should have stayed and checked to see if we were alright." She looked down at the scrapes on the palms of her hand. She'd been wearing a pair of gloves earlier but had removed them when they were in the Visitor's Center.

Stormy was examining her left knee just above her boot as Lance helped Ann up, then bent over his wife. There was a small tear near the knee area of her skirt, a ring of blood around its edges.

"Oh, I hope I can fix the tear and get this blood out. This is one of my favorite outfits," she murmured. "I guess I should have changed into my jeans for this outing." She pulled up her skirt to check her knee. The skin was pulled back and bleeding. Pulling a tissue from her skirt pocket, she dabbed at the blood. "Ouch, that smarts."

"Let me get you to that bench over there and we'll have a better look at it." Lance helped her up and she put her weight on his arm. She hobbled over and took a seat on the cold metal.

"And me without my walking stick. I shouldn't have forgotten and left it in the car. I don't know what's worse," she exclaimed, "my banged-up knee or the cold coming through this skirt. Whoa, that's cold!" She raised up enough to tuck her coat under her and sit back down as Lance examined her knee.

"It doesn't look too bad, but we'd better clean it up so we can tell better." He withdrew his handkerchief and held it against the cut. After a couple minutes of pressure, Lance removed the cloth and took a look. The flow of blood had stopped.

"I have a few Band-Aids in my purse. I'll put one on for now, but I'd better clean it off as soon as I can." Stormy dug in her purse and withdrew a large one.

"Here, let me help you, dear." Lance took the strip from her, opened it, and gently applied it to the wounded area. Then he pulled Stormy's skirt back over her legs.

"The Chapel's just around the next bend and down the path. They'll have a restroom there where we can clean up," Ann volunteered, pulling her gloves on. "Do you think you can walk, Aunt Stormy, or should I go get some help?"

"I'll be okay," Stormy replied. She gingerly stood up from the bench with Lance supporting her arm.

"Let's take it easy and go slowly. And keep your eyes out in case some other nut happens to run by without watching where he's going," Lance huffed. Putting his arm around Stormy's waist, and with her holding onto his shoulder, they proceeded around the next corner.

Stormy wasn't so sure it was an accident. It seemed to her that the man had veered toward her at the last minute and deliberately ran her down. What he was thinking, and why he did this were beyond her.

I'd better not tell Lance my suspicions or he'll just worry more, she thought.

As they rounded the next bend, they stopped for a moment to take in the splendid view of the base's chapel, known worldwide for its unique design. Its' large A-framed structure had seventeen spires coming down to the ground from the center seam with another seventeen reaching up toward the sky. Between each spire was thick, colored glass.

"It was created in the nineteen sixties from steel, aluminum, and glass. The seventeen points you see represent fighter jets soaring through the sky." Ann stood looking up at the top of the chapel, shielding her eyes from the sun with her hand. "It was originally designed to have nineteen spires but proved too costly, so they lowered it to seventeen."

"It's impressive, but we'd better get you two inside and to those restrooms to get cleaned up."

Lance continued to help Stormy along the path the rest of the way, with Ann close behind. Once they cleaned up, they both felt better. Stormy's leg was a little sore, so Lance suggested that he go back to bring the car around and take her back to the hotel, but she insisted they continue with the tour. She didn't want to miss out on seeing one inch of this place.

"Okay, but if your knee starts hurting any more than it already does, we're going to take you back to the hotel. Deal?"

"Yes, I'll let you know, Lance," she agreed as they headed through the doorway.

"There's my commander coming out of the Chapel," Ann exclaimed, looking down the walk. "You two look around while I go report the incident to him. I'll join up with you in a few minutes."

"Okay," Stormy said. She tried her weight on the injured knee, and, though a little sore, she thought it would be fine to continue on.

Stormy and Lance marveled at the beauty of the building. The chapel consisted of two floors and a basement below. The building was divided into four main chapels: a Protestant one, a Catholic one, a Jewish one, and a Buddhist one, plus an all-faith one used by Muslim cadets, and those of other faiths.

They enjoyed the stained-glass windows and other beautiful works as they toured through each section. They read that the principal architect was a man named Walter A. Netsch, Jr. who hailed from Chicago, Illinois. The chapel and surrounding areas cost over three and one-half million dollars to build, and much of the costs of the interior sections were donated by various groups and individuals.

Ann joined her aunt and uncle as they were sitting on a pew at the rear of the last of the chapels.

She explained that she and many of the other cadets often met there for services from time to time.

"Did you get to see everything you wanted to?" she asked her aunt and uncle, looking around the room.

"Yes, I think so," Stormy replied, standing up.

"Did you get one of these brochures they had by the door when you came in?" Ann opened the brochure in her hand and read from it. "It states the mission of this chapel as 'to inspire men and women to become leaders of character by providing spiritual care and facilitating the free exercise of religion'."

"Okay, folks, we'll be closing the Chapel in five minutes. Please see that you have all of your belongings before you leave," called out an elderly man from behind them, his long robes swishing as he walked by. He flashed them a big smile. "Thank you for visiting with us, and we hope to see you again soon."

"It's nice to know that the military sees the need for religion for its members," Lance said as he took Stormy's arm and steered her toward the exit sign over a nearby door. "I found it always made a big difference in the lives and views of the men and women under my command and how they treated one another."

"Yes, I'm grateful for that," Ann said, walking beside her aunt. "You will see an effort made to supply this at all the military bases around the world."

"That's wonderful," Stormy declared as they walked outside. "Thank you for showing us this magnificent building, Ann."

"I thought you two would enjoy it," Ann said, giving her aunt a hug.

"How about a burger and fries?" Lance suggested. "I'll even throw in a milk shake, although it's not on my diet." Raising his eyebrows, he looked hopefully at Stormy.

"Sounds great, Lance," Stormy agreed, "as long as you make mine a chocolate mint."

"I'll second that," Ann put in.

"Okay, you two wait here while I get the car," Lance said.

"They'll be closing this parking lot soon." Ann pointed toward the other side of the lot. "Just in case they do before you can bring the car around, we'll wait for you out there."

"Alright but be careful crossing that ice. I'll be back as quickly as I can." With that, Lance quickly headed back the way they had come along the trail.

"Aunt Stormy, I want to show you our classrooms before we head out across the parking lot. It'll just take a minute. Do you feel up to it?"

"Sure, I'd love to see it." Stormy followed Ann to the edge of the terrace and looked out over the wall and down to the open area below them. A few cadets were hurrying along the sidewalks below them, but other than that, the area looked quite empty. To the edges, there were buildings that held several classrooms, each with their doors closed.

"Those are the rooms where we study and take our training. You should see it when classes are in full session," Ann said, pride filling her voice. "Cadets are scurrying here and there, leaving no time for conversation. We must be in our places before the instructor begins or pay the price. That large cement area over there is for cadets to practice marching, and also for the band to play at times."

"I take it you're going to miss all of this when you leave for your new assignment next spring," Stormy said, placing an arm over her niece's shoulder.

"I never thought I would when I first came here. It was all so overwhelming then, but now, yes, I guess I will." Ann looked out over the campus for another few moments. "We'd better get going so we'll be in place when Uncle Lance brings the car around."

As they turned to leave, Stormy noticed a dark-haired man in a deep blue jogging suit looking at them from the staircase to the Chapel's lower floor. He held a blue-knit hat in one hand. When he noticed Stormy looking his way, he quickly turned and disappeared down the stairs.

"Where does that stairway lead to?" she asked her niece.

"I think it goes to some storerooms underneath the building. Why?" Ann replied, turning to look.

"Come on." Stormy grabbed Ann's arm and pulled her toward the stairs the man had just dashed down. "There was a man in jogger's clothes that was staring rather intently at us, and when he realized that I'd seen him, he fled down those stairs."

"Let's go see if we can find out what he's up to," Ann said. "Maybe he's the one that knocked us down." She took the lead and reached the door a moment before her aunt. Though her hands still smarted from the fall on the asphalt, she pulled the door back. Holding it open for her aunt, she followed behind.

A dimly lit passageway stretched out before them. At the far end, they spotted a door that was just closing, and they sprinted for it as quickly as Stormy's knee allowed her to go. Once there, Ann again pulled open the door, took a quick look inside and held it wide for her aunt until she could reach it.

"How's your knee doing?" she asked, as she walked beside her aunt.

"Better," Stormy replied. "Let's not lose him."

"Okay, but let me go first." Ann took the lead once again, looking back every few minutes to check on her aunt, only to find Stormy had no trouble keeping up.

The second door opened into a large room filled with metal folding chairs and long rectangular tables. Three large whiteboard panels ran the length of one side of the room and several rolling partitions were placed near the wall on the opposite side. A large metal desk had been positioned near the middle whiteboard, with a high-backed chair sitting behind it.

"Well, I don't see anyone in here," Ann said, her eyes scanning the room. "I guess we must've missed another door or passageway in our hurry."

"No, I checked all the walls as we went by, and this is the only way he could have come. Let's look around the room more closely."

The two of them made their way across the room, heading toward the whiteboards. Several colored markers filled the trays below and were accompanied by a few dry erasers in need of cleaning.

Ann approached the desk, circling around to where the chair sat. She pulled the chair out and peered beneath the desk. Stormy went around the other side and continued to scan the room.

"No one under here," Ann announced. She stood up and pushed the chair back underneath. Noticing that Stormy had continued across the room, she followed.

Stormy neared the rolling partitions, and as she did so, a small ping sounded from behind the nearest one. Stormy stopped, holding up a hand and motioning for her niece to do the same. When no other sound came to their ears, Stormy stepped forward to pull the partition away from the wall, and

Ann quickly came forward to help her. The only thing they found was a large vent in the wall behind it.

"Well, no one is behind here either," Ann said, releasing her pent-up breath, relieved that her aunt had not been in harm's way.

"No, but it seems that someone was here a few minutes ago." Stormy reached down beneath the wall vent and retrieved something from the floor. Standing up, she opened her hand to reveal a shiny metal clip. "Look here, Ann." Stormy bent forward as she examined the vent closer and pointed to the edging.

"Oh, I see. The vent covering is held in place by these clips." Ann leaned closer to get a better look.

Stormy ran her hand along the cold metal edges and touched one of the three remaining clips. It fell to the ground with a loud "ping".

"Check this out." She pointed to the floor beneath the vent. A partial, wet footprint was showing on the floor from the light overhead.

Stormy carefully removed each of the other two remaining clips from the vent cover and slipped it off the wall. The two women peered into the hole, but it was too dark for them to see anything. Opening her purse, Stormy withdrew a small flashlight, one she always carried with her. She shined the light into the deep recesses of the hole, but to their dismay, the passageway turned a sharp corner after only a few feet.

Resisting the temptation to follow the air shaft, Stormy shut off her flashlight, returning it to her purse.

"Here, help me close this vent back up. It's no use, we've lost him." She held the vent cover as Ann fastened the clips back into place.

"He obviously knows his way around here," Ann surmised. "We'd better leave before they secure the doors, and we get locked in for the night. Besides, Uncle Lance is probably wondering where we've are by now." Stormy agreed.

As they made their way back out of the building and up the stairs, Stormy's knee throbbed with pain. *If I ever got ahold of the man that ran us down . . . !*

Six

Lance was waiting for them as they made their way across the parking lot to the street beyond. A troubled expression played upon his face as the duo approached and opened the car doors.

"I was getting worried about the two of you. Where have you been? Most everyone has already left." Lance put the car in gear after they'd fastened their seat belts and headed the car back out onto the street.

Stormy and Ann took turns relating to Lance what they'd experienced as he drove through the east gate of the Air Force base.

"You shouldn't have followed him down there. It could've been dangerous if you'd cornered him," Lance said, shaking his head.

After a few miles, Lance turned off and drove across the overpass and into town. It was almost completely dark outside by then.

As they discussed the events of the day, Stormy's attention was drawn by a beam of light that continued to flash across her rear-view mirror.

Focusing on the mirror's reflection of the roadway behind them, she realized how closely the car behind them was following.

Wondering if the mirror's message, "Objects may be closer than they appear" might apply to this, she turned her head to have a better look. Staring past Ann and out the car's back window, she confirmed that it was not just a trick of the mirror; the car really was as close on their tail as it had looked to be.

"Lance, what's that car doing?" Stormy continued to stare behind them. "Why are they following so close? Are they drunk or something?" She looked over at Lance to find him looking back in the rear-view mirror.

"They've been following us ever since we exited the Air Force base," he replied, "but until now they've kept their distance. I'll try slowing down a little and see if that'll get them to pass us."

Lance slowed their car's speed down by another ten miles, now going beneath the posted speed limit, as he kept an eye on the vehicle behind. The car behind followed suit and continued at the same distance as before.

"It didn't work," Ann called from the back seat. "Maybe they're afraid to pass."

Lance attempted, for a second time, to annoy the driver enough to make them pass by slowing down yet another few miles. Being in the far-right lane of traffic gave him the opportunity to do this without causing too many problems to the other drivers on the road.

A few cars whizzed past them, disappearing down the roadway, but the car behind continued to follow their SUV.

"What kind of nut is driving that car anyway?" Ann asked, as she tried to see past the lights in an attempt to get a better view of the vehicle and its driver. "It looks like the car has heavily tinted windows and seems to be a late model black vehicle, but I can't tell the make of it."

As they approached the turn-off that would take them to the burger place, Lance put on his signal and steered the SUV over into the turn lane. The car behind followed as if it were interested in also acquiring something to eat and easily slipped in behind them.

"I hope they're just going the same way as we are," Stormy put in, "but something tells me that isn't the case this time."

"Hang on, ladies," Lance announced, determination filling his voice, "Let's see if we can shake them."

Stormy reached for the handgrip above the passenger's door as Ann grabbed hold of the back of Lance's seat. Lance steered their car down the ramp, flew under the highway's bridge, and headed toward the yellow light at the nearby intersection.

They followed a blue pickup truck through the intersection and, as they reached the middle of it, the stoplight changed to a solid red. The car behind them, ignoring the angry honks of the other driver's horns, shot on through the red light and continued the pursuit. One would have thought the two cars were connected to the bumpers; it followed Lance so closely.

"They must have lived here a while. They say you know you're a true Coloradoan when you're the third car through the red light," Ann quipped as she gripped the seatback.

"Good thing we believe in seatbelts." Stormy reached over and quickly pulled at hers, making it a little tighter as Lance zoomed past the blue truck.

He slowed only a margin to zip around the next corner and head down the street as quickly as traffic allowed, grateful for the unusually thin traffic on its surface. However, the dark vehicle behind continued the chase like a hound on the trail of a fleeing rabbit.

"Lance!" Stormy tightened her hold even more on the handgrip above her and braced herself against the dashboard with her other hand. "The car chasing us looks like the one that followed us for a short time last night."

"Yes, that's what I was just thinking," he murmured, taking another glance in his rear-view mirror as he tightened his grip on the steering wheel.

"You were followed last night as well?" a pale-faced Ann asked, looking back into the head lights of the pursuing car.

"Yes, but only for a short distance," Stormy answered. "Watch out, Lance!" she shouted. Her husband swerved the car just in time, barely avoiding a vehicle pulling out of a side street.

The vehicle behind took the opportunity to close in on its prey and rammed its front bumper hard into the back of the Winters' SUV. The jolt sent them all flying forward. Pain shot through Stormy's left leg as her knee impacted with the dashboard in front of her. Ann's head flew briefly between the two front seats, then to the back again, her seat belt barely holding her as she was tossed around.

Lance slammed down the gas petal, watching for an avenue of escape, trying to keep the car under control. Once again, the dark car slammed into their back bumper, but this time the trio was prepared, bracing themselves on whatever was handy.

Both cars' tires squealed around the next corner as Lance maneuvered into a quick turn and down a narrow lane. He pressed forward, a determined set to his jaw, only to notice too late that he'd turned onto a one-way street—and he was going the wrong way!

"No," Stormy yelled, as car lights bore down on them. "Get down on the seat, Ann. Brace yourself." She put her own arm over her head, prepared for the worst.

What happened next, they would only later be able to describe as a miracle. With the oncoming car only yards away from colliding with them, Lance managed to steer their car into the narrow parking lot entrance of a small convenience store, coming to an abrupt stop just a foot away from the store's front glass windows. The oncoming car brushed past them with only a few inches of space to spare. There was no sign of the once pursuing dark vehicle anywhere in sight.

The three of them sat speechless and in shock for some time. Finally, Lance opened his door and let out a sigh of relief.

"Are you both okay? Anyone get hurt?"

"I think so," Stormy replied, looking back at Ann. "Are you hurt?"

"A bit shook up, but I'm alright. What was that all about?" Ann looked back behind them to make sure the dark car was really gone. "That was a close call. What great driving, Uncle Lance!"

"I think I had a little help, Ann, for which I'm greatly thankful." Lance mumbled a quick prayer of thanks.

A tough, burly-looking man in a clerk's apron rushed from the store and approached the vehicle, staring in amazement at how come the car had come from sailing through his store's front window.

"Are you three okay? Anyone hurt?" he asked, scanning the occupants of the SUV. "Why were you going so fast down the one-way street? Did you lose control of your breaks?" He shook his head as he waited for Lance to respond.

"No, some maniac was chasing us, bent on doing us harm," Lance responded, his face turning from white to a shade of red. He rubbed his left arm as he spoke. "We're okay, by the grace of God."

"I'll go call the police so you can tell them what happened. Maybe they can catch the guy before he kills someone." Checking once again to see that they were alright, the man ran back toward the store doors yelling to his young assistant to take over for him while he summoned the police.

Before long, sirens could be heard as a police car arrived, followed by an unmarked vehicle containing a single occupant. As a police officer stepped from the squad car, a young man exited from the car behind. Stormy recognized the young man as Chris Jacobs, the news reporter from outside the bank. He no longer had his news vehicle and crew with him, but was driving a red, older model car.

Chris hailed the officer before he approached the Winters' car. After a brief conversation, the reporter came around and approached Stormy's window, the officer heading toward the driver's side.

"Oh, it's you again, Mrs. Winters," Chris said, surprised to see her sitting in the front passenger's seat. "What happened? Are you okay?"

"I think so, Chris, but how did you happen to be here so quickly?" She stared up into the boyish face from her seat in the car.

Lance continued to talk to the policeman on the other side of the car as he explained what they had all just gone through with the dark sedan.

"Well," Chris began. After a moments pause, he went on. "I was on my way home from the station and I heard it on the police scanner. I carry one around with me in case a possible story should develop. I like to get the scoop on anything that happens, if I can." He grinned and his face lit up, his eyes twinkling in the light from the storefront.

"Who are you talking to, Aunt Stormy?" Ann said, lowering her window. She had scooted across the car to just behind where her aunt sat. "Oh, hi there," she said, flashing Chris a big smile.

"Hi, and who might you be?" Chris smiled back, running a hand through his brown hair and stepping backward to get a better view.

"This is my niece, Ann," Stormy answered for her, turning around in her seat. "And this is Chris Jacobs, the news reporter I was telling you about from the bank robbery."

"Okay, nice to meet you, Chris." Ann reached her hand out of the window, offering it to him.

He took her hand and held it in his. "Same here." His smile widened across his face. "You look good . . . for what you've just been through, I mean."

"Thanks," Ann said, slowly withdrawing her hand from his.

"Stormy," Lance spoke into her ear, startling her. "This policeman wants to talk with you now about what happened."

"Okay," she said, turning to look in his direction. On the other side of him a uniformed police officer leaned over and peered into the car. "Sure, let me come around to your side of the car, Officer," she said, looking back at Chris and Ann. "You'll have to excuse me. I'm wanted by the police." She laughed, reaching for the inner door handle.

"Here, let me help you," Chris said as he reached over, opened it, and stepped back out of the way.

"Thanks, Chris." Stormy exited the car, closed the door, and headed around the front of the vehicle to where the policeman stood waiting for her. Glancing back, she saw that Chris had opened Ann's door for her as well, and she was climbing out to stand by him. Stormy chuckled to herself. Ann was quite a pretty young woman. At one time she would have been worried about her niece, but not anymore. She had a good head on her shoulders.

"Hello, Officer," Stormy said, coming to stand by the policeman.

"Are you okay, Mrs. Winters? Would you like to sit down as we talk?" The policeman pointed to the open passenger's front door of his patrol car.

"No, I'll be just fine here," she answered, leaning against the side of their Santa Fe in front of the driver's side door.

"I understand you had quite a ride there, Ma'am. Can you tell me in your own words what happened? I'll need a statement from each one of you," he continued, looking across the car to where Ann and Chris were chatting.

"Would you rather not have Ann talking to that news reporter just yet?" Stormy asked, looking over at the two on the other side of the car, following the officer's line of sight.

"No, it's okay," the officer replied. "Chris is a cool guy, so he'll know what not to say."

"I take it you know him then?"

"Yes, we've worked on many calls together and I've found he's got some pretty good insight into things."

"That's good to know," Stormy said, filing this tidbit of info away. "Now, Ma'am, back to what happened."

"Yes, well we were headed out to get something to eat when . . ." Stormy began.

After the police were done taking all three of their statements, they got back into their car. Chris had gotten permission from the officers to go ahead and file a news report on the incident. He was pleased and would file it with his station as soon as he had it ready. It would be a short piece, but he would scoop the other stations before they had a chance to report it.

"I hope your car hasn't had too much wear and tear on it," Chris said, closing Stormy's car door for her. "That was some smart maneuver turning as you did into such a small area and not flipping the car over." He looked back behind him at the parking lot's entrance, then back to Stormy.

"Yes, Lance is a good driver, and we were all very blessed indeed."

"I don't mean to scare you, but from what I overheard, and what your niece was telling me, I think you should keep a watch out for trouble wherever you go from now on." Chris's face filled with worry as he looked from Stormy back to where Ann sat in the back seat. "I hate to say it," Chris continued, "but it sounds like someone is out to get you, and they're pretty determined to succeed at it."

"Yes, I'm beginning to think that, too," Stormy said. "And I can't help but think it all goes back to the robbery. And maybe it even has something to do with that car I saw speeding out from behind the bank moments before I entered it. That young woman in the back seat looked frightened."

"What's this about a speeding car coming from the back of the bank?" Chris snapped to attention, the reporter in him taking back over. "And a frightened young woman in the back seat? You didn't say anything about that the other day, Mrs. Winters."

"No, I didn't, but I talked to you just after the robbery and hadn't had time to really think about it," she said, looking up at him from her seat in the car. "The two may not have anything to do with one another. But then, who knows?"

"It sounds suspicious to me." Chris stood there in thought, hands on his hips.

"Yes, it does. Have you heard anything about a kidnapped victim? And about how the bank manager is doing?" Stormy questioned the reporter.

"Yes, is he doing okay?" Lance called from the driver's seat. "That sounded like a nasty wound he received."

"I hope he's going to live," Ann added.

"I'm going to check on him tomorrow morning and do a report on how he's doing," Chris answered, pausing to tap out a few notes on the Android he'd pulled from his pocket. "And as far as I know, there's been no report of anyone being kidnapped, that I'm aware of. I check into it."

Stormy thought for a moment, a seed of a plan starting to take root in her mind.

"Chris," she said, a look of determination in her eyes.

"Yes?" he inquired, breaking his attention away from the droid.

"Would it be okay if I came with you in the morning to visit poor Mr. West in the hospital?"

"I guess it'd be alright." A smile crossed over his handsome face. "I'll just tell them that you're with me and the soundman. That should give us some interesting looks."

"I'd like to come along with you as well," Ann spoke up. "If that's alright, Chris, I mean?" A slight blush spread over her cheeks as she smiled at him, awaiting his response.

"Sure, I'd love to have you join us." The smile on Chris's face grew even wider. "We'd have a lot more lookers if you came along, too, Ann." The blush brightened even further across Ann's face. The two of them stood there smiling at one another, not saying a word.

"Well, I'm hungry, how about the rest of you?" Lance's voice boomed out, filling in the void of silence. "We'd better get going before it's all gone."

"I second that. Let's go," Stormy said. "But how about a change of plans? Why don't we go to the Golden Corral? I love their food, and we haven't been to one in a long time. And, as I remember it, they serve burgers there, too"

"Sounds good to me," Lance said. Turning, he called out to Ann, "What do you vote for, Ann?"

"Um, the Golden Corral sounds great to me, too," she answered, turning away from Chris to answer her uncle. "I like the food and will go anytime I get the chance."

"Would you like to join us, Chris?" Stormy asked the young reporter. "We'd love to have you come."

"I'd like to, but I already have a dinner appointment." Chris looked at the watch strapped to his wrist. "And I'd better get going before I'm any later."

"Oh." Ann frowned as disappointment filled her eyes.

"Okay, then we'll meet you at the hospital in the morning," Stormy said, reaching for her seatbelt. "About what time will you be there?" "I'm scheduled to meet the camera man there by 8:30," he answered, suddenly aware of the look on Ann's face. "We'll meet you two in the hospital lobby."

"Oh, which hospital is it?" Stormy asked, grabbing a tablet and pen from her purse.

"The Penrose Main Hospital on North Nevada," Chris responded, returning the Android to an inside coat pocket.

"Okay," Ann piped up. "I'll meet you both there at 8:30." She flashed Chris another big smile.

"Okay, it's a date then," he said, smiling back. "Um, I'll see you both there. We'll find out how Mr. West is doing. Have a great night." As he started to leave, then stopped and turned back to them. "Wait." Reaching into his pocket, he withdrew a leather wallet, opened it and produced a small business card. Taking out a pen from the same pocket, he scribbled on the back of the card. "Here," he said, handing it in through the open window to Ann. "In case you think of anything else, or need to get in touch with me, this is my cell number."

"Thanks, I'll let you know," she said, looking at the card he'd handed her, then back up at Chris. "I'll see you tomorrow."

"Great!" He turned and hurried over to his own car. A few minutes later, he'd turned into traffic and was out of sight.

"Nice young man," Stormy said as Lance started the car and backed it out.

"Yes, I thought so, too." Lance turned the car around and waited for the traffic to clear before heading out onto the street. "It's nice of you two to go and see how the bank manager is doing, Storm, but I sense there's more to your motive for going there than just the man's health." He glanced over at

Stormy, then focused back on the traffic. "Well, I've been thinking. Something seems very odd about the way the manager approached the gunman during the robbery."

"How so?" Ann asked, leaning forward in her seat in order to better hear.

"When the gunman turned to see who was talking to him, it was as if a look of recognition crossed his face for a minute there," Stormy said, stealing a quick glance in her side mirror.

"The man had a stocking over his face, but you think they'd met before?" Lance asked, scanning the buildings ahead for the turn-off to the restaurant.

"It looked that way from where I stood," she said. "Then there was also the way the manager kept stepping forward as if he felt safe in doing so."

"Maybe the gunman has an account there at that bank and has talked with the manager before," Ann suggested, holding onto the back of her aunt's seat with one hand.

"Well, that's possible," Stormy said over her shoulder, "and he realized who it was when he saw the man behind him."

"And it's possible that Mr. West is a bold man and thought he could press his luck with the gunman." Lance turned into the entrance to the Golden Corral. "Here we are, ladies."

"Great, I'm starved. And yes, he did press his luck," Stormy put in, as they opened their doors and stepped out onto the wet asphalt. She was grateful to the thoughtful souls that had taken the time to clear the parking lot of snow and ice, making it easier to navigate.

"Good thing he wasn't killed," Ann added. She closed her car door and joined her aunt and uncle as they headed towards the restaurant door.

"That's for sure," Stormy agreed, holding her walking stick in one hand as she took Lance's in her other one.

Seven

Despite the terrifying car chase of the previous evening, Stormy and Lance awoke well rested and ready to begin the new day.

"Lance, are you ready to go downstairs and eat?" Stormy inquired as she was putting on her shoes and locating her purse.

"Almost, dear, just let me finish this paragraph and save the file I've been working on. I'll be right with you. Now that you mention eating . . . why is it that when I'm working on the computer, I seem to get so very hungry?" Having said that Lance looked up at his wife with an expression that told her he could probably eat everything in the restaurant!

"It must be all those brain cells working so hard, using up your energy. A good breakfast will replenish that." Stormy chuckled as she retrieved the nail file from her purse and sat down to fix a broken nail while she waited.

Upon entering the Antlers Grille, the hostess greeted them with a nice warm smile.

"Good morning. A table for two, please." Lance requested, smiling back. Stormy noticed there were already several other people sitting down to delicious-looking food placed before them.

"Yes, and could you make it a booth please?" Stormy asked, as they followed behind the woman.

"Sure, we have a nice one over here," the hostess replied. "Come this way, please."

Stormy always preferred to sit in restaurant booths, feeling like it gave her a bit more privacy. She noticed that these particular booths were a lot taller and thicker padded than in most other restaurants, making them warm and inviting. They were constructed out of dark-finished wood covered with leather seat cushions. She loved the shade of the carpeting: blue with a lively gold pattern across it that fit nicely with the rest of the rich decor.

*   *   *   *

After a hearty breakfast of eggs and bacon, juice, bagels, and plenty of fruit, Stormy and her husband headed back upstairs to their room. Lance went to sit at the desk that held his laptop, while Stormy headed to the phone on the nightstand to make her call.

"Sure, we'd love to see you again," the woman's excited voice confirmed. "If you have a pen and paper handy, I'll give you instructions on how to get here. It's just off North Academy and not hard to find at all."

Stormy grabbed the tablet and black pen sitting on the table, preparing to jot down the instructions. "Go ahead, I'm ready."

After double-checking the directions she'd written down, and promising to be there after lunch, she returned the phone to its cradle. Quickly glancing in the room's full-length mirror, she gave her blue pants suit the once-over, then returned to where Lance sat typing away at his laptop.

"Well, I'm off to the hospital to meet with Ann and that news reporter, Chris. Oh, and the sisters said they'd be delighted if I could drop in after lunch." Stormy informed him. "I'll see you later, Lance. I'm sorry they had to call you in on the project while we're here on vacation." She leaned over him, hugged his neck and kissed him on the cheek.

"Me, too," he mumbled, staring at the screen.

"I'll be gone for a few hours, so don't worry. I hope we can do something together this evening."

Stormy ran her hands through Lance's hair, loving its soft feel against her fingertips.

"We'll have to play it by ear. I found that they have several problems to solve and it's going to take me some time on each one of them. You know these guys: they needed it completed by yesterday." He leaned back in his chair, pulled her into him, and gave her a lingering kiss before releasing her. "Don't forget to turn on your cell phone in case I need to get ahold of you. You know where I'll be . . . slaving over this keyboard."

Though retired from military duty, Lance did occasional work for one of their contracting firms. All had seemed to be running smoothly with the last project he'd helped them with, until bright and early this morning when Lance had received an urgent call from the project's manager, pleading for his help on several snags they'd run into. The man apologized for interrupting their vacation but explained that this project was due for review on Friday. Could Lance please help them out? Lance knew the project from the inside out, and it would need his expertise to work out all these bugs. He had no choice but to help them out.

"I already have it turned on," Stormy replied. "Don't forget to call room service and order in a sandwich if I'm not back by lunch time."

"Don't worry about me. Just take care and watch out yourself. You never know what some crazy nut might be up to!" He stretched out his arms high over his head, wiggled his fingers, and once again placed them back on the laptop's keyboard. "If anyone starts to follow you again, drive to the nearest police station. Then give me a call"

"I'll check on our GPS for the nearest police station and log it into the unit for quick retrieval," she teased Lance, chuckling to herself. Lance didn't notice this last statement as he was deep into his work.

Stormy pulled on her coat, grabbed her walking stick and purse, and walked out the door. She caught the elevator to the ground floor and headed out to the parking lot.

Stormy carefully watched around her as she unlocked the car and scanned the back seat. She climbed in and immediately locked the doors, fastened her seat belt, and started the vehicle.

Lance would be pleased to know that she'd followed these safety precautions that police departments all over the country recommended before getting into one's car.

As she drove down the street, the cell phone next to her rang.

I wonder who that could be? Stormy thought. *Maybe Ann's running late or Lance forgot to tell me something. Hopefully it's not one of those solicitor calls.*

Reaching for her cell phone, Stormy glanced at the caller ID. Relief filling her, she hit the speaker button as she answered, careful to keep her eyes on the road ahead as she did so.

"Hello, Will." She spoke loudly to be heard and awaited a response.

"Hi, Mom, what are you doing?" The young man's excited voice came through the phone loud and clear. It was as if he were sitting in the front seat next to her.

"I'm driving to a nearby hospital to meet up with your cousin, Ann, and a news reporter," she answered her son. "We're going to sit in on a news interview. But you sound excited. What's going on there?" She hoped he wouldn't question her any further as she hadn't told any of her children about being in the bank when it was robbed. They would just worry about her. She brought the car to a stop just before the crosswalk as the light ahead turned red.

"I am doing just great," Will declared. "We wanted you to be the first to know the good news." She could hear the mounting excitement in his voice.

"What good news is that?" Stormy suspected she could already guess what her son was about to tell her, but didn't want to ruin his big moment.

"Christy is expecting our second baby," Will proudly announced.

"That's wonderful, Will. How's she doing, and when is the baby due?" The traffic light changed, and Stormy proceeded forward.

"We just came from the doctor's office, and he said she's doing fine, but that it was important she get more fluids in her this time around," Will explained. "The doctor said the tests show that the baby will come in about six and a half months."

"Are you going to let this one be a surprise? Do you know if it's going to be a boy or a girl. Or will you have one of those tests to find out early?" Personally, Stormy thought it was much more fun to wait and find out what the baby was when it was born.

"Oh, Mom, everyone gets those tests done now days to find out ahead of time," Will proclaimed. "Why wait? This way you can be prepared and have everything all set up. And it saves on having to return gifts from baby showers."

"I suppose so." Stormy laughed. Reaching the hospital entrance, she pulled into the parking lot. "Will, I just arrived at the hospital, so I'll have to go. Give Christy my love and call your father. You know how he loves being a grandpa."

"Okay, will do. Talk with you later, Mom. Love ya, bye." He hung up before she'd gotten the chance to say goodbye. She laughed and, closing her phone, tucked it into a pocket of the purse on the seat beside her.

Stormy circled the hospital's parking lot a few times before a car backed out of a space near the street. Since the weather was a bit sunnier this morning, she didn't mind walking the distance across the pavement to the hospital's front entrance.

As she approached the door, a middle-aged doctor, dressed in surgical greens, a stethoscope hanging around his neck, exited the building. He stopped and held the door open for Stormy, asking her if she needed help in locating anything there at the hospital.

"I'd be more than happy to assist you," he offered, showing greater interest.

"No, but thank you anyway. I'm meeting some people in the lobby," she replied, pausing a moment.

"Well, I hope I see you here again. It's nice to have such pretty women around the place," he declared, extra-white teeth showing in the smile he gave her. "Have a good day now, ya hear?" He gave her one last look, turned around, and headed out across the lot.

"Uh, thank you," Stormy said, both surprised and rather pleased by his flirting comments. Lance often told her how beautiful she was, but she didn't usually feel that way about herself.

"There she is." Stormy heard a familiar voice call out from across the room as she entered the lobby. "We're over here." She looked ahead to the area around the reception desk and spotted Ann standing beside Chris and another man holding some electronic equipment in his arms.
Ann waved her over.

"I know I'm not late. I'm sure you said 8:30 and it's only," Stormy pulled back her sleeve and looked at the silver watch on her wrist, "just turning 8:25." Releasing her sleeve, it fell back into place, covering her watch once more.

"No, you're not, Mrs. Winters," Chris spoke up, chuckling. "I like to be places early just in case something happens that might change matters. And in the news business, that's most of the time." He laughed and the man next to him did so as well.

"Oh, Mrs. Winters . . ." Chris began.

"Why don't you call me Stormy, as we seem to keep running into each other," Stormy interrupted with a smile.

"Okay, Stormy, this is my sound man, Greg."

"Hi, it's nice to meet you," Greg said, bowing slightly.

"It's nice to meet you, too. Looks like you have quite an armful there." She tried to make out the items he held.

"Yes, Chris here sometimes thinks of me as his personal pack mule," he teased, shifting the items he held to get a better grip on them.

"Hey, that's what you get paid for. You wouldn't want me to hurt my nails, would you?" Chris teased as he inspected his hands in mock concern, a twinkle in his eyes. They all broke out laughing. "Here man, let's hand some of that stuff to the women."

Stormy gave him a questioning look, not sure if he was serious or not. Chris laughed again.

"But first, before I forget, here are a couple of passes for the two of you." He reached into his pocket, pulling out what looked like two pieces of paper sealed in plastic, a pin glued to the back of each one. "Pin these news tags to your shirts and follow my lead. Greg will hand you each a piece of equipment, which I want you to hold and look like you are busy using as I interview Mr. West."

The two women pinned the tags onto their shirts. Afterwards, Greg handed Stormy a medium-sized black machine and a two tightly-wrapped cords to throw over her shoulder. He gave Ann a meter box with a glass window on one side of it and several dials on top. He told her to hold it near him as he used his microphone to record the interview with the bank manager.

When they were ready, the group headed down a hall to their right. As they walked, Stormy glanced through some of the open doorways, noticing that most of the patients' rooms were occupied. There were two beds to each room. Some patients sat in chairs, a tray of half-eaten food in front of them, while others lay in bed watching T.V. or fast asleep, blankets pulled up to their necks. She felt sorry for the patients. She knew that being in the hospital was a necessary thing, but it was no fun at all. The smell of breakfast permeated throughout the hallway, and she thought it didn't smell too bad for 'hospital food'.

After navigating several turns down various hallways, they reached a half-closed door and stopped. Chris knocked and called out, "Mr. West, it's Chris Jacobs and my news team. May we come in, Sir?" "Yes, come on," a feeble voice called from within.

The group entered and saw that the patient, Mr. West, was in the bed on the far side of the room over by the window. The bed nearest the door was unoccupied. As they approached the man, Stormy noticed how pale and weak he appeared. His hair was in a terrible state of disarray and his left arm and shoulder were wrapped in several layers of bandages. An IV drip hung from a post attached to the top of the bed, fluid slowly dripping through a clear tube and making its way down and into the top of the man's right hand.

"Hello, Mr. West. As I said, I'm Chris Jacobs and this is Greg, Ann, and Stormy. Chris pulled out a small droid device from an inside coat pocket. Sliding a finger across the screen, he looked back up at the man "How are you doing today?"

"A little bit better than I felt yesterday, I'll tell you that," the man said in a feeble voice. He cleared his throat and winced as a pain shot through his shoulder.

Stormy noticed a rolling table holding a tray with a half-eaten meal upon it, a water container alongside. It had been pushed away from the side of the bed. A newer-looking pair of forest green slippers sat on the floor beneath, and a matching green bathrobe draped across a nearby chair.

Stormy stood at the foot of the bed holding the black machine in front of her, while Chris stood to the right of the bed, closer to the patient. Greg, along with Ann, stood to the left of the bed. Ann held the meter in her hand with a serious look across her face.

"Could you please tell us in your own words what happened to you two days ago at the bank?" Chris asked. "When were you first aware that a robbery was taking place in your bank?" he added, droid in hand.

"I was in my office with the door closed, trying to catch up on some work." The man started to cough, and they waited for him to stop. "Can I get you a glass of water?" Ann said.

"Yes, please," the man squeaked out as he continued to cough.

Ann handed the meter to Greg, reached around him, and grabbed the plastic pitcher of water and the nearby glass with the straw. She poured half a glass of the cool liquid and handed it to Mr. West. He took it from the young woman and drank deeply.

"Thank you, miss," the bank manager said as he handed Ann the glass. She replaced it on the table and stepped back around to the other side of Greg. Greg returned the meter to Ann.

"As I said, I was in my office catching up on some work when I heard a commotion outside in the bank's lobby," he continued, his voice a little stronger. "I'd been concentrating so deeply, it took me a minute or two to fully realize that it needed my attention."

"What did you do then?" Chris asked, tapping a few notes into his droid.

"I got up from behind my desk and went to see what was going on out there." The man winced and held his left arm with his right hand for a moment.

"Is that when you opened your office door and walked out?" The reporter looked over at Greg to see if the mic was close enough to pick up what the patient was saying. Seeing that is was, he focused his attention back on Mr. West.

"No, first I pulled the blinds back that cover my office window to check if I was really needed," the man answered, his eyes flashing with concern for a moment. "It looks out onto the lobby and teller counters."

"Then what did you do?" Chris glanced over in Stormy's direction with a look on his face she couldn't quite read.

"After assessing the situation and seeing that the bank was being robbed, I naturally had to think of the best course of action," the man answered, his eyes searching the reporter's.

"I understand that the only call placed to the police was after you were shot, Mr. West, and the gunman had already left the building," Chris said. "Why didn't you call them right away when you first saw the gunman from your office window? You do have a phone in your office, don't you?" Chris pressed him, then glanced once again in Stormy's direction before turning back to the patient.

"Of course I have a phone in my office, young man," the bank manager snapped at the reporter. "And I did try to call the police from my office, right after I saw what was going on, but the phone was dead."

"Interesting, then what happened?" Chris asked as he entered a few more notes.

"Well," the man paused, cleared his throat, then continued. "I wasn't going to have anyone hurt in my bank, so since that the gunman had his back to me, I carefully opened the door to my office and stepped out."

"Don't you think it was a little dangerous, calling out to him like that while he held a gun in his hand?" Stormy blurted out before she had a chance to think.

Chris gave her a surprised look, then a slight smile played across his face. He awaited the man's response.

"No, I guess I thought I could get him to calm down and leave," Mr. West replied, looking over at Stormy, a puzzled look on his face.

"You did seem rather calm about it all, I'd say," Stormy added, since there had been no objection to her question from Chris.

"Who told you about me and how I acted?" the man demanded, his face flushed with anger. "My assistant, Miss Grey? One of the tellers?"

"I don't think so, Mr. West," Chris answered for her. "Stormy was in your bank during the robbery and saw you herself."

The injured man gave Stormy a guarded look. "I don't remember seeing you at the bank." With narrowed eyes, he continued to stare at her, a concerned look on his face. "I guess I was too busy worrying about what the gunman would do."

"I'd stepped into the bank as the robbery was already in progress." Stormy explained. "When I saw what was going on, I hid behind that sign you have near your front doors. I watched what was happening from behind it and saw you come out from your office doorway." "Oh," the man said, still looking at her in bewilderment.

"Mr. West, isn't your bank equipped with alarms at each of the tellers' stations for just this kind of thing?" Chris asked the man, drawing the focus of attention back onto himself.

"Yes, of course it is," the man said, glaring once more at Chris. "And I suppose the next thing you're going to ask me is why didn't the tellers press the buttons then?" He pulled the edge of the cotton blanket up over his wounded arm in an effort to ward off a sudden chill.

"Yes, that was to be my next question." Chris smiled, raising an eyebrow.

"Miss Grey came to see me yesterday afternoon and I asked her that very question," the man said. "She told me they had tried to press them, several times in fact, but to no avail. A lot like my phone and the other ones in the bank, it appears."

"That's too bad," Chris said, considering his next question. "As you stepped toward the gunman, did he seem unstable to you. You seemed pretty sure of yourself, as I understand things."

Stormy shifted her weight onto her other foot as she awaited Mr. West's response. She had wondered why he'd kept stepping forward herself, being either very brave or very foolish.

"I guess I just thought I could get him to leave. I wasn't thinking about anything else but the safety of the tellers and customers in the bank at the time."

Another apparent pain shot through his arm, his face turning into a mask of pain.

"I guess it was a surprise when the gun went off and you realized that you'd been shot," Chris said, a bit more gently.

Before the man had a chance to respond, a nurse entered the room carrying a small paper cup filled with medicine.

"I think Mr. West has had enough visitors for now," the nurse announced. "It's time for his medication and he needs more rest to get better. I'm sorry, but you'll have to leave now."

Stormy noticed a look of relief spread across the man's face as he relaxed back into his soft pillows.

"Okay, we'll be going," Chris said to the nurse. "It's a wrap, Greg." He looked over at his assistant, then back at Mr. West. "Thank you for letting us interview you. We hope you get better quickly." Mr. West nodded and thanked the group for coming.

They filed out as the nurse retrieved the bed-side glass of water and handed the ailing man his medication.

"Sorry about that, Chris," Stormy said to the reporter as they headed back down the hall the way they'd come earlier. "I guess I spoke out of turn in there when I shouldn't have."

"No, that was quite alright, Stormy," Chris returned, smiling at her. "I didn't mind you asking that question, and it was a good point.
It seemed to make Mr. West a bit uncomfortable. Did you notice?"

"Yes, I did, though it might be from all the pain the poor man seems to be in." Stormy thought about this as they walked along the corridors of the hospital.

"Maybe, but he didn't seem to like it when you challenged him about the phone in his office or the teller's alarms either," Ann added from behind Stormy.

"No, he didn't, did he?" Chris stopped in the hallway and thought about this for a moment before continuing. "Maybe Stormy's right though. He is in a lot of pain right now."

The group walked in silence until they reached the hospital's lobby.

"I'll take that equipment from you ladies," Greg announced, indicating the machines and cables they held in their hands. In all the excitement of the interview, Stormy had forgotten about the objects she carried.

"Oh, right, here you go." She handed them back to Greg.

"And here's mine too," Ann said, handing her piece to the soundman.

"Thanks for letting us tag along, Chris," Stormy said, pulling at the collar of her shirt as she adjusted the purse on her shoulder. "That was a very interesting interview."

"I was happy to have you both along," he said, running his hand back through his short brown hair and looking from Stormy to Ann. "I'll need those badges back. I don't want to get in trouble back at the station."

"Oh, certainly," Stormy agreed. She and Ann removed the badges from their clothing and handed them over to Chris.

"Thanks. Hey, how about you two joining Greg and me for an early lunch, in say," Chris looked at his wristwatch, "about an hour from now? We have to head back to the station and file our report." He looked from one woman to the other as he awaited their reply.

"I'd love to," Ann said, smiling at Chris. "How about it, Aunt Stormy, can you come along?"

"Thanks, but I have a few errands to run, and I'd better get back to the hotel and make sure your uncle takes a break and gets something to eat. He forgets sometimes, when he's working away." Handing her purse and walking stick to Ann, Stormy pulled on her coat and buttoned it.

"Okay, where would you like me to meet you for lunch?" Ann asked as she handed her aunt her belongings. "I have a few errands I can run here in the downtown area while you file your report."

"See you all," Stormy called as she headed for the door, leaving the group to make their own lunch decisions.

"Goodbye. I'll call you later, Aunt Stormy, and see what your plans are," Ann called out to her. The other two called their good-byes to Stormy as well.

"Okay, do that," Stormy called back. Pushing open the door, she exited the building and headed out across the parking lot. Thinking back to her encounter with the doctor earlier, when she'd arrived at the hospital, made her chuckle. She decided he was just one of those big flirts. Still though, maybe she didn't look so bad after all.

Stormy stopped at a few stores on her way back to the hotel to see if they had some of the things she'd wanted to purchase. She ended up taking a little longer than she'd expected. She'd been looking for a charm for her bracelet as a reminder of their visit to Colorado, something she liked to collect from each area they visited throughout the country and the world.

Looking at her watch and finding it was a little past noon, she drove to a nearby Sonic and ordered food for both she and Lance, certain he'd probably not yet ordered any lunch for himself.

With the food safely on the passenger's seat, she drove the car back to the hotel and turned into the parking lot. By the time she had found a place to park the car, the wonderful aromas coming from the bag of burgers and fries had made her downright starving. Juggling the bag and drink carrier, along with her purse and walking stick, she made her way up to their room. She would return later for the few purchases she'd put in the car's trunk, one's she couldn't resist from the great sales she'd found here in the Springs.

"Are you hungry, Lance?" Stormy called out after she'd turned her key in the door of their room and entered in. "I don't suppose you've eaten anything yet, have you?" Placing her walking stick near the door, she set the food down on the small table placed to one side of the room. Removing her purse and coat, she continued to where Lance sat, busily typing on his laptop.

"Oh, hello dear. No, I didn't have anything to eat. I've been too busy to stop." Lance quit typing, leaned back in his chair, and looked up at Stormy. She leaned over him and gave him a kiss. "But I was just about to call downstairs for a sandwich."

"I'm sure you were," Stormy said, laughing. "Well, you won't have to after all. I stopped at Sonic and picked up some lunch. Come on." She headed back to the table.

Lance got up from the desk, stretched his body with his arms held high in the air, and joined her at the table. "Umm, it smells delicious. Thanks, Storm."

"They had one of their special shakes on sale, so I got us each a small one. It's peppermint cream." She set a shake in front of him, along with a burger and fries. She had opted for one of the chicken sandwiches for herself. Since the order only contained one of the little peppermint candies, Stormy gave it over to her husband.

"So, how did things go at the hospital?" Lance asked her. He took a big bite of his burger after the prayer, then reached for a napkin to catch the juice as it ran down his hand.

"It was interesting. Chris gave Ann and I each a news badge and we became part of his team." Taking another sip of her shake, Stormy set it down before continuing. She went on to relate what had taken place while they were interviewing the bank's manager. However, she left out the part about the flirtatious doctor at the front doors of the hospital. That would be her little secret for now.

"How convenient that the robber just happened to pick the day that the bank guard was out sick, and all the phone lines were down," Lance commented, after swallowing a fry. "I assume the police will check out the lines to see what was up with them."

"I would hope so," Stormy said. "After all, it does seem a bit too much of a coincidence that all these things came together just when the gunman held up the bank." She picked up her now empty sandwich wrapper, wadded it up, and placed it in the paper bag. "Well, I'd better get going. I told the sisters I'd be at their shop after lunch. It's now almost 1:30."

"Yes, and I'd better get back to work, myself." Lance stuffed his own empty wrappers into the bag with Stormy's, stood, and pushed his chair back under the table. "Drive carefully and give me a call on your cell before you start back for the hotel."

"Okay, I will," she promised. She put on her coat and retrieved her purse. Giving Lance a quick kiss, she headed for the door, grabbing her stick on the way out.

Eight

Stormy entered the northbound traffic on Academy and navigated her way through the other vehicles, vying in search of that better spot to get one more car ahead of the next guy.

Eventually she reached the address she'd scribbled down. Navigating a right turn off Academy, she turned into the parking lot and began scanning the signs above the shops until she spotted the one she was looking for.

Tucked neatly into the corner of the L-shaped strip mall, Stormy spotted the sister's shop: K & K Graphic Designs. The colorful letters on its sign creatively flowed, one into the next, in an easy-to-read, yet distinctive pattern.

Guiding the car into a vacant parking space in front of the store's entrance, she switched off the engine and reached for her purse. As she stepped from her vehicle, a movement caught her attention, causing her to turn her head and look in that direction.

Down at the end of the row of shops, Stormy noticed a young man loosely grasping a broom and half-heartedly sweeping the sidewalk in a slow back and forth motion in front of him. A pair of old blue jeans and a faded red t-shirt hung loosely on his thin frame, a pair of dirty white tennis shoes with loosely tied laces on his feet. His head hung low, as if deep in thought, as he worked. A sign above him read, "Other Side of the Ocean Imports."

What a lonely looking man, Stormy thought.

As she continued to study him, a large, muscular, dark-haired man appeared from inside the shop. He stepped out onto the walk, shouting words at the sweeper in a language Stormy was unfamiliar with. On first thought, it sounded a bit Slavic to her. Spinning on his heels, the larger man disappeared back through the door. The now-distraught employee quickly followed after him.

Turning away, Stormy continued towards her destination. Upon entering the design shop, she felt immediately at ease, its friendly atmosphere mixing business with pleasure. To the right of the door, pushed up against the wall as far as it would go, stood a large, healthy-looking green fern, its branches reaching out to greet her. Along the wall beyond, a cloth-covered table provided liquid refreshments in the form of a coffee maker, several bottles of power drink, and a large bottle of clear spring water. A stack of paper cups rested beside, inviting all who might be thirsty to partake.

To Stormy's left, two large leather chairs were placed in front of the shop's low-set windows. A small wooden table stood in between them, a few magazines artfully arranged upon its surface.

Proceeding forward, she approached the long counter that separated the rest of the shop from what looked to be the shop's work area beyond. An electronic cash register, five little nesting dolls in blue dresses and white aprons, a rose-colored vase of pens with fake flowers attached to the tops of them, and a small stand holding K & K Design business cards were creatively arranged along its surface.

The counter stretched two-thirds of the way across the width of the room, with a glass window covered with wooden blinds filling up the last third. A short, swinging panel was placed in between the two, providing a way through which to enter the area beyond. Fastened to the panel was a sign that read, "Employees Only."

"Hey, Kim, Stormy's here," shouted a middle-aged woman, stepping from an open door behind the counter. "It's great to see you again." She came forward, extending her right hand to Stormy.

"Hi, Stormy," a second voice chimed in behind Katie. "We're so glad you could come. Any more mysterious fires since we last saw you?"

"No, Kim, not since we all toured Austin anyway." Stormy replied, and the two women agreed that it was a good thing.

The three of them had met on a tour the previous fall in Austin, Texas, where several mysterious fires had baffled police and put the group in danger. If not for the astute detective reasoning and quick actions of Stormy, things may have turned out a lot worse than they had. She, herself, had almost lost her life to a deranged killer.

"I like the display you have on the wall. Are they yours, Kim?" Stormy pointed to a pair of long swords hanging on the back wall behind the counter. A battle axe hung to their right, along with a reindeer fur.

"Yes, I'm afraid so," Kim answered, looking up at the wall, "much to Katie's chagrin." She glanced over at her sister.

"They bothered me at first, but I've gotten used to them now." Katie smiled at her sister. "We're partners here after all."

"How is your business doing?" Stormy asked, looking around the room. "You have a wonderful shop here."

"Thank you," Kim said, glancing about her. "We're really doing well. We've had a lot of new customers this year, and a lot of very fun projects to create."

"Yes, I've really enjoyed the challenges we've faced," Katie added. "It's been good for us. How about you and Lance? He didn't want to come with you to see us?"

"He would have, but he got a last-minute call, and it looks like he may have to work the whole rest of the trip, I'm sorry to say." Stormy leaned against the counter as she talked.

"That's too bad. Why don't we sit down over in those chairs and chat for a while," Kim suggested. "I'll get us something to drink. What would you like, Stormy?"

"A little water would be great, please. Lance and I had lunch before I came over." Stormy made herself comfortable in one of the two large leather chairs.

"We received this wonderful box of chocolates from a client of ours yesterday when he came by to pick up the completed work we'd done for him." Katie reached back behind the counter and brought out a large box of assorted chocolates. "They're very fresh. You must try at least one, Stormy." She carried the box over as Kim returned with a cool glass of water for their guest.

Opening the box, Katie held it out for Stormy to choose a piece of the rich confections.

"Ooh, they do look good," Stormy said, lifting out a chocolate from the center of the box. "I guess one couldn't hurt." Stormy bit into the dark treat. "This is delicious. Thank you."

"So, you and Lance came here to watch the big game with your niece?" Kim said. "How did that go? I hear there was a big turn-out." She took a sip from her soda.

"Yes, Ann's parents couldn't attend as they're overseas, so they asked if we'd like to go in their place," Stormy replied. "The stadium was packed and, much to Lance's chagrin, the Army lost." She set her glass upon a coaster on the table next to her and noticed a copy of The Rocky Mountain News lying next to it.

The shop's phone rang, and Katie jumped up. She ran behind the desk and picked it up on the third ring.

"Yes," she answered, "I'm still looking for one. You do? Great, I'll be there in a bit. Thanks!" She hung up, a look of enthusiasm on her face. "They got some more of it in!" She headed back around the counter and rejoined them by the leather chairs.

"More of what is in?" Kim questioned. "And who was that call from?"

"Oh, sorry, that was from the import shop down the row here. They got some of those jars of Tsar's Red Caviar in their shipment this morning and they wanted to let me know." Katie looked past them and out the window down the row of stores.

"Are you talking about that shop just down at the end of the row?' Stormy asked, turning around in her chair to peer out the window. "The one called 'Other side of the Ocean Imports?'"

"Yes, that's the one," Kim answered, turning around to look as well. "We've been in there a few times to see their wares. They have some pretty interesting things on their shelves."

"And some rather odd people as well," Katie added, making a face.

"Odd? In what way do you mean?" Stormy turned around. She wondered at this strange comment from Katie.

"Well," Katie began, looking over at her sister, "I don't mean to speak ill of anyone, but some rather weird things go on there, and at the strangest times of night."

"What type of things?" Stormy asked. She wondered what this was all about.

"Things like fancy, dark-windowed cars pulling up in front of their shop," Kim answered for her sister.

"What's odd about that?" Stormy asked.

"For this neighborhood, it's usually SUV's and trucks, most of the time. But that's not the oddest thing," Kim related. "It's the people that get out of those cars that seem out of place to us."

"Like the ones with well-dressed drivers that alight from the front seats, then hold the doors for men attired in expensive-looking, well-tailored clothes that emerge from the rear." Katie glanced out the window once more.

"I guess they have some pretty rich clientele," Stormy observed. "I wonder what they import. Is this the only shop of its kind in the area?" She picked up her glass and took another sip.

"Care for another chocolate, Stormy?" Kim said, passing her the box.

"They are pretty good, but I'd better not, thanks," she responded, returning her glass to the table.

"No, there are a few other import shops around besides this one," Katie said, reaching out for the box. "I'll have another one of those." Kim extended the box to her sister and Katie chose a light chocolate one loaded down with nuts.

"Don't forget the saying, Katie," Kim teased, as her sister raised the chocolate to her mouth. "A minute on the lips, forever on the hips."

"You would have to say that and take the joy out of this treat," Katie glared at her sister. "Oh well, what's another inch or so." With that said, she took a bite out of the delicacy.

Stormy joined Kim as they laughed at the sisters' friendly banter. It was nice to see how well the two got along, especially since they ran a business together.

"What else has been going on at that shop?" Stormy's curiosity got the better of her.

"Many nights we have to stay late to work on a project in order to finish them in time for a deadline," Kim began. "There's always something to catch up on when running a business. We're talking late, well after the other stores have closed for the night and most of the proprietors have left. That's when we have noticed these activities."

"Yes," Katie chimed in. "Some vehicles pull up in front of the shop and drop off people in dark clothing."

"Maybe they're having meetings of the owners or something," Stormy suggested.

"We wondered about that at first, but it seems to happen two or three times a week from what we can tell," Kim said, leaning forward in her chair. "And when we notice them, and we do be careful that they can't see us watching, we find them acting in an odd way. They get out of their cars, look around as if to see if they are being followed or some such thing, and then practically run for the store's entrance. Well, at least at what you might call a very fast pace."

"We have both seen this happen many times. It's like they're afraid of something or someone, or have something to hide," Katie said. Taking a tissue from her pocket, she wiped a bit of chocolate from one corner of her mouth, then from her fingers. "It really has us curious."

"That does seem suspicious indeed," Stormy mumbled, thinking it over. "I wonder what they would be afraid of. Say, how about we go for that jar of caviar right now? I'd like to come with you and take a look at the place."

"Sure, that would be a good idea. And I think you might like looking at the items they carry in their store." Katie said.

"You take her, Katie. One of us had better stay here and watch the shop," Kim suggested. She rose from her chair. "Grab me one of those carrot-apple juices if you think of it, will you?"

"Sure thing." Katie went behind the shop's counter and through an office door beyond. Gone for only a moment, she reappeared with a purse over her shoulder. "Let's go take a look. Like spies on a mission." She laughed and headed for the door.

Stormy stood and followed her out, leaving Kim behind. The two of them headed out onto the sidewalk and strolled down to the end of the strip. Stormy glanced back at her car to make sure everything was okay.

As they approached the shop's door, they could hear loud music floating forth from the inside. It sounded like a rather joyous, lively tune to Stormy, and it made her smile.

They don't sound too strange to me, Stormy thought to herself as they entered through the open front doors of the import shop, the music feeling the air around them.

"Welcome, welcome," a colorfully dressed man called out in a thick foreign accent from behind a desk set to one side of the shop. "Come in. See what you might want to buy today. We have wonderful things for you." He smiled at them as he headed in their direction. "Come, I will show you around."

"Hello," Katie said over the loud music. "I've come to see about that caviar your assistant called me about."

"Oh yes, the best caviar in all of the world, it is," the man said. "I get it for you." Turning around, he bellowed toward the back of the store. "Turn that music down, boy." He turned back to the two women. "I am sorry for the loud music. In my country, we love 'our tunes' as you say."

"Yes, we can hear that," Stormy said, laughing. "It's quite lively." "I will get you that jar. Maybe two?" he asked, hopefully.

"No, I think one is all I can afford right now," Katie said.

"Okay, please wait. It is still in boxes in the back room." He spun on his heels and headed for a door in the back wall of the shop.

"Let's look around a little while he's gone," Katie suggested, turning toward a nearby rack of scarves, their patterns formed of many different and brilliant colors.

As Stormy wandered about the shop, she wondered where the young man with the broom was that she'd seen earlier when she drove up. "Oh, well," she mumbled to herself.

A shelf of colorful nesting dolls caught her interest, and she headed over in their direction. She was marveling at the many designs they came in when she spotted the young man over along one wall, unpacking some items of clothing. He seemed to be busy arranging several colors of socks and gloves onto shelves from one of the many boxes that surrounded him.

As she stood there staring in his direction, the young man happened to turn and look her way. He stopped and momentarily stared back, then turned quickly away to the shelves he'd been stocking, but not before she saw a look of what appeared to be fear cross his face. He continued to unload and shelve the items from each box, careful to no longer turn in her direction.

Maybe he's afraid of strangers, Stormy wondered. *Odd though, for such a young man.*

Stormy continued to browse the items around the shop, careful not to approach the shelves where the young man was working. She didn't want to stress him out any more than he already appeared to be.

The door in the back of the room opened and the proprietor headed their way, carrying a small jar in his hand.

"Here we go. A jar of the finest red caviar you will ever taste." He approached Katie, offering her the container. "Now, what else can I get for such beautiful women?" His smile broadened as he looked from one to the other in anticipation of a further sale.

"I think I'll take this scarf for my mother," Katie said, holding up the beautiful red paisley item in her other hand. "And three, no make that four, of that apple-carrot juice from the Ukraine that you carry. You must try it, Stormy. I'll send one for Lance, too. You'll both love it, I'm sure."

"Sounds interesting," Stormy replied. "I think we'd like to try it."

"Great choice, it's over there," the man said, pointing across the way to where the young man had finished emptying the last of the boxes. "Boy, bring me four of the apple-carrot juices," he called.

Stormy looked across the room as the boy slightly turned their way, yelled something back she didn't quite catch, and hurried for the door in the back. He pulled it open and quickly disappeared, slamming it behind him.

The shopkeeper's face grew red with embarrassment and anger, and shaking his head from side to side, he turned back to face the women. "It is hard to find good help these days, no? I will get it for you myself." He forced a smile onto his face and headed over to the rack.

"I wonder what that was all about," Katie said, turning to Stormy.

"I don't know, but that young man sure was acting peculiar." Stormy looked back over to where the young man had been stocking the shelves, then at the door he'd quickly exited through.

The shopkeeper returned with the bottles of juice. He rang the items up and Katie opened her wallet, reached inside for the money, and paid the man. The man put the items in a bag and wished them a happy day.

"Come back again soon," he shouted as they exited the shop. "We have more to offer."

Nine

"Hope you guys like the juice," Kim exclaimed to Stormy. "It's one of our favorites. We don't have time to run down there and grab some up as often as we'd like, even though it's just down the way from us." She picked up two of the bottles and took them back behind the counter, leaving the other two beside Stormy.

"It looks pretty good," Stormy commented, examining the label. "I'm sure we will. What made you give it a try in the first place?" She stood up and approached the counter.

"We first tried it when we were overseas on a trip with our husbands. They helped to bring medical supplies to the Georgian people. We were also in Russia, Moscow to be exact, for a few days." Katie rose from where she'd been sitting and walked over to join them at the counter alongside Stormy. "It was an exciting time, but also one of much learning and even a little sadness."

"What do you mean?" Stormy asked, looking from one sister to the other.

"We were able to see most of the tourist sites in Moscow, the ones that everyone goes there to see, and that was exciting. But then we got a close-up look at how the average, or should I say poor, people live their lives each day when we were in Georgia," Katie explained. "Those poor souls work very hard and have little to show for it. Many must struggle day to day just to be able to have anything to eat for their families. We came away feeling quite sorry for them."

"Yes," Stormy agreed, her thoughts taking her back over the years. "There are many in need all over this earth. Lance and I have met them throughout our travels as we've moved around with the military. I'm not sure that many of us Americans realize just how lucky we are to have the things that we have. And how lucky we are to have all the freedoms we enjoy in this country."

"From the things that I've heard, both in the news and in person, I think a lot of people don't understand how really good they have it here," Kim put in, shaking her head. "There seem to be quite a number of spoiled, belly-achers around, doesn't there?"

"Kim and I have given to a charity that helps provide food and medical supplies for the people of Georgia ever since we were over there. Hopefully the government will take a more active role in helping their people." Katie went through the swinging panel and around to the other side of the counter to where Kim stood. "By the way, don't forget that tomorrow the garbage truck comes to empty up the dumpster."

"Yes, that had crossed my mind earlier this morning," Kim answered her sister, reaching underneath the counter to retrieve a small trash container. "This one's stuffed to the brim and there are several boxes in the back that have to go out, too."

A phone in a back room began to ring. "I'll help you in a minute with those boxes, Kim. I've been expecting a call about that project I'm working on." With that she turned and disappeared into a nearby doorway, closing the door behind her.

"I can help you," Stormy volunteered. "What should I carry?" She looked expectantly at Kim.

"Thank you. I could really use your help. Katie will most likely be on the phone with that client for a while." Pulling the garbage bag out of the trash can, she spun it around a few times, then secured a tie around the top. "Come behind the counter and we'll go to the back." She waved a hand for Stormy to follow.

Stormy tread on Kim's heals as she entered through a doorway that led to a short hall. Three more doors lined the hallway; two on their right, a third on their left.

"In case you need it," Kim said, pointing to the first door on their right, "the bathroom's in there. The one on our left leads to a small kitchenette where we keep our lunches and other snacks. And this one is where we're going to go." She reached for the second door to the right, and turning the knob, she threw it open. "This is our supply room," Kim proudly announced.

Stormy followed behind Kim and paused to examine their surroundings. Along two sides of the room sat tall shelves that filled each wall from floor to ceiling. She noticed that one of the shelves held a large variety of colored paper, boxes of ink replacement cartridges for printers, and canisters of ink powder for the copy machines. The other shelves held what looked to be cleaning supplies and old rags on the bottom, with various assorted-sized boxes adorned with small, unreadable labels from where she stood, placed through the rest of them. A small space heater stood nearby.

A third wall was occupied by a long wooden workbench strewn with scissors, pens and pencils, stacks of paper, rulers, drawing equipment, and an array of lights with an overhead magnifying glass attached to the end of a thin metal swing-arm. A silver laptop rested to one end of the clutter. The fourth wall held a large pile of empty boxes, one of which caught Stormy's eye due to the writing on it being in what she perceived as a form of the Russian language. A solid door with a peep hole at about eye level stood in the back wall.

"We need to take out these two trash bags," Kim said, setting down the bag she'd carried from the front counter and pulling a second one from the plastic can that sat beside the workbench. She tied a twisty tightly to it. "If you want to grab some of those boxes, we'll take them out to the dumpster behind the shops." Carrying the two garbage bags, Kim headed for the outside door. Setting them down, she unlocked the door and opened it, revealing an icy alleyway beyond.

"Let's see how many of these I can carry at once." Stormy approached the pile of boxes and began piling them together for easier carrying.

"Don't take too many. We can always come back for more," Kim warned.

Taking a stack in her arms, including the one with the Russian writing, Stormy followed Kim out the back door onto the wet asphalt beyond. It was apparent that the city, or someone, had been there that morning, as a thin layer of sand had been spread over the ice and snow that had fallen the day before. The sand had caused the ice to begin to melt in some areas, and the two women carefully picked their way across to the dumpster.

Stormy now wished she'd listened and taken a smaller pile of boxes to allow her to carry her walking stick in her hand instead of it dangling from its' strap. It would have afforded her the extra balance she needed over the slippery surface.

Reaching the dumpster ahead of Stormy, Kim tossed the bags over the edge of the container.

"I'll go get the rest of the boxes while you go around the front and slide those in the opening," Kim said, pointing in the direction that Stormy should go.

"It'll be easier to put them in there than try to toss them over the side."

Kim carefully walked back over the slippery surface to disappear into the shop's back door as Stormy slowly made her way around the side of the large metal container.

"Okay, I see what she's talking about now," Stormy mumbled as she spotted a large, hinged door set into the wall of the trash bin. She lowered the boxes down onto the snow and tugged at the door. At first, she couldn't budge the frozen metal, but eventually it gave way and creaked open. Picking up the boxes, one at a time, she tossed them inside. When she came to the box with the foreign writing along each side, she paused to examine it closer. She could make out little of its writing and made a mental note to ask Kim about it. "I'd better leave this door open so Kim will have an easier time with her pile of boxes. I wonder what's taking her so long?"

Stormy made her way around the heavy, metal dumpster to check on her friend. As she rounded its' corner, she spotted Kim emerging from the shop's back door with a pile of boxes in her arms, the stack well above her head.

"That was very thoughtful of her," Stormy whispered to herself. "She must be worried about me making a second trip."

I'd better help her with some of those boxes so she can see where she's going or she might slip on the ice, she thought as she stepped forward.

Kim was halfway across the asphalt when Stormy called over an offer of help. As she did so, a car's engine gunned to life and came barreling toward them. Turning in the direction of the sound, Stormy saw a frightening scene: a large, dark sedan was closing in on them at a high rate of speed. Stormy's heart leapt to her throat as she realized Kim was out in the middle of the alley, in harm's way.

"Kim, look out!" Stormy shouted. "Drop the boxes and run. That car, it's speeding your way and it doesn't look like it's going to stop. Run!" Stormy pointed in the direction of the oncoming vehicle.

"What was that?" Kim shouted back, as she tried to adjust the boxes to order to see what Stormy was going on about.

Kim managed to move the boxes in her arms just enough to see the car. Holding tightly to the boxes, she hurried across the pavement in the direction of the dumpster.

"Drop the boxes," Stormy yelled, holding her stick out in front of her as if she could somehow whisk them away.

Kim attempted to hurry across when her foot hit an icy patch. A loud scream escaped Kim's throat as she fell to the ground, arms splayed out in front of her, boxes covering her form. The dark sedan sped by barely missing Kim's sprawled legs by only inches.

The car fish tailed as it hit an icy patch of its own. As it reached the far end of the shops, it entered the road, swung left, and disappeared from sight.

Stormy carefully made her way over to where Kim lay in the snow, anxious to know of her condition. At the same time, Katie appeared in the shop's back door.

"What's going on out here? I thought I heard someone scream." Katie inquired. It took her a moment before she noticed that Stormy was bent over a still form on the ground, covered partially in cardboard boxes. It took her another moment to realize that it was Kim lying on the ground. "What in heaven's name happened?" she shouted, a look of horror filling her face.

She made her way as quickly as she could across the ice and snow. Once there, she bent down over her sister and helped Stormy remove the boxes.

"Is she okay?" Katie franticly questioned as she brushed back the damp hair from Kim's face.

"I don't think the car actually hit her. I think she just passed out from fright and the hard fall," Stormy answered as she checked Kim's pulse.

"What car? Where and who was driving?" Katie looked quickly around the alley way, bewilderment showing on her face.

"Oooh, my arm, what happened?" Kim moaned. She tried to sit up, pushing a box off her arm.

"Don't get up too quickly," Stormy cautioned. Taking hold of Kim under one shoulder, with Katie grasping the other, they helped her into a sitting position. "Just sit there for a minute. You had quite a close call with that nut hurrying too fast down the alley like that. They could've hit you, and they didn't even stop to find out if you were okay."

"Maybe I'd better call an ambulance," Katie said, starting to rise. "And notify the police as well."

"No, that won't be necessary, Katie, I'll be okay," Kim insisted. "Give me a minute or two to catch my breath."

Kim sat there waiting for the fog in her head to clear, thanking the heavens above that she'd landed on a flattened box to lessen the effects of the cold pavement and ice beneath it.

"Do you think you're able to walk now?" Stormy asked after a few minutes, still holding onto one of Kim's arms in support. "We should get you out of this cold, wet snow and ice and back inside where it's a bit warmer."

"Yes, that's a good idea," Katie agreed, surveying the alley once more. "Think you can stand up now, Sis?"

"Yes, I think so" Kim said, looking a bit sheepish. "I'm feeling better. However, I do feel a little foolish about fainting like that. That hasn't happened to me in years. Not since I had that piece of wood stuck in my foot and tried to pull it out too quickly, without first sitting down." Her mouth turned down at the memory.

"Oh yes, I remember you telling me about that," Katie said, once again grabbing hold of her sister's other arm. "Here, let us help you up. Then we'll walk you back inside. Let's take it slow and easy."

Through their combined efforts, Stormy and Katie managed to get Kim to her feet, then made their way back across the ice and into the shop's warm interior. Stormy used her stick to help steady them as they walked along. Tightly securing the door behind them, they sat Kim down on one of the chairs beside the long workbench.

"Do you have a blanket or throw of some kind that we could put over Kim?" Stormy asked Katie. "We'd better get her warmed up before she catches a cold."

"Yes, we each keep one in our offices, as the winters can get pretty cold around here," Katie replied, rubbing her sister's arms in an attempt to bring heat back into her frozen limbs. "I'll go get yours," she told Kim, "and turn up the heat on the way by. I think it would be good to lock up the front door and put the closed sign out, too. I'll be back in a few moments." Katie dashed from the room and out into the hallway.

"Stormy, would you please . . . ma . . . make us . . . some hot chocolate?" Kim managed through her chattering teeth. "There's a pot of hot water . . . on . . . on the stove in the . . . kitchen and some boxes . . . of cocoa on the counter nearby. I'd like . . . the . . . the raspberry flavored one . . . please. Have whatever kind . . . you want." She wrapped her arms tightly around her body in an effort to get warmer.

"Sure, I'll make you a cup. I don't want anything. Just stay where you are until Katie comes back," Stormy ordered as she headed for the door, then paused and turned. "Are you sure you don't want to report this to the police? That driver shouldn't be on the road."

"Not right now," Kim replied. "Maybe later, if I see that car again." She briskly rubbed her hands along each arm.

"Okay, that's your choice."

Upon entering the small room, Stormy headed for the stovetop set into a cream-colored counter with oak cabinets hanging above. She noticed that a copper kettle full of water sat on one of the burners. Carefully feeling the side of the kettle, and finding it to be only a tad warm, she reached over and turned on the burner.

"Better warm this up a bit more," Stormy mumbled to herself. While the kettle was heating, she scoured the kitchen to discover where the sisters kept their cups.

After opening a few of the overhead cabinets, Stormy located a shelf containing several sturdy looking ceramic mugs with animal figurines painted on the sides of each one. Pulling down a mug with a cheerful kitten batting at a butterfly, she set it on the counter next to the stove. In a nearby drawer, Stormy found a stack of assorted teaspoons to choose from. Selecting a package of raspberry-flavored cocoa from a box on the counter and emptying it into the mug, she poured steaming hot water over it and briskly stirred to dissolve the powder.

Stormy lifted the mug of steaming chocolate and headed back across the hall to the supply room. She found that Katie had returned and was sitting beside her sister, engaged in quiet conversation. Kim appeared to be much warmer wrapped in a thick, red and green plaid blanket, a space heater pouring out warmth beside her.

"Here you go, Kim." Stormy handed her the cup. "Be careful, it's quite hot. Katie, can I get you some?"

"Oh, I think the chocolate mint sounds good to me," Katie answered, "but you sit down. I'll get it myself."

Stormy took a seat in a wooden chair on the other side of Kim. "These are adorable mugs," she remarked, gesturing to the mug in Kim's hand.

"How are you feeling now?" Concern filled her eyes as she awaited a response.

"I'm much better now, thanks," Kim replied, taking a sip of the hot drink. "We love to collect things like this. It brings a bit of sunshine into our lives." A brief smile lit her face before taking on a more serious look. "Katie and I were just discussing what terrible drivers there are these days. That nut out there was definitely going way too fast down the alley."

"Yes, and we're going to keep a better eye out when we go out back from now on," Katie called from the hallway. "If we find out who owns that car, they're going to hear a thing or two about our opinion on how they drive. They could end up killing someone for sure." Katie walked into the room and settled into a third chair beside her sister. "Didn't either one of you see who the driver was?"

"No, I had too many boxes in the way," Kim said, taking another sip of cocoa from her mug.

"I was too worried about Kim to get a good look. All I really saw was a dark sedan barreling down on her," Stormy replied, sharing in the warmth of the space heater. "By the way, Kim, why were you carrying so many boxes?"

"I was concerned that you might fall and hurt yourself if you carried anymore," Kim explained as a small grimace appeared on her face. "I guess I should have taken my own advice."

"Yes, but that was very thoughtful of you," Stormy said. Turning in her chair, she glanced up at the clock on the wall above the worktable. "Oh, look at the time. I really must be going. It's later than I'd realized it was, and Lance will be expecting me back." She stood up, reaching for her stick. "Can I do anything for either of you before I leave?"

"No, I don't think so, Stormy," Katie said, rising to her feet. "I'll see that Kim gets home safely after we close here. Let me put my mug in the kitchen, and I'll walk you to the door."

"If you don't mind, I'll just stay here," Kim said adjusting the blanket around her. "Thanks so much for coming to see us. I guess it turned out to be a more exciting visit than we'd planned. And thanks again for your help."

"I loved seeing the both of you, too. I'm sorry you fell. Make sure you rest up and see your doctor if you get to feeling any worse. And remember, you're always welcome to visit Lance and me if you two are ever in Phoenix." Stormy headed out to the hall and waited for Katie to return from the kitchen.

"We sure plan to," Kim called out. "See ya! Have a good visit."

Katie reappeared, and walking to the front of the shop, she unlocked the door and let Stormy out. After goodbyes and promises to see each other again, Stormy headed for her car, aware of the shop's door locking behind her.

Ten

Stormy unlocked the Santa Fe driver's side door, and as she did so, felt as if eyes watched her every move. She quickly vaulted into the vehicle and locked the doors. Glancing about, she was sure she'd seen a shadow duck around the corner at the end of the row of shops. As she scanned the area, her cell phone rang from inside her purse, startling her.

"Hello," Stormy said, after she had retrieved and flipped her phone open. "Oh hi, Ann. What's going on? Did you enjoy your lunch with the guys?"

After a few moments' conversation, Stormy replied, "Yes, I'd love to. Let me check with Lance and see if he'll be free to join us as well. I promised I'd call him when I left here anyway. I'll call you back in a few minutes and let you know."

Pushing the button on her cell phone to end the call, Stormy pulled up her contacts list and scrolled down to Lance's name. Lance answered on the third ring.

"Hello, this is Lance Winters." Lance's voice came over her phone.

"Hi, Lance. You sound so formal." Stormy chuckled. "How's it going with the work?"

"Oh, sorry, Stormy. Okay, I guess. I didn't look at the screen to see who was calling. How are the sisters doing?" he inquired.

"They're doing pretty good. I'll tell you all about it when I see you. I'm just about to leave here." She thought it was best to wait and tell him about what had happened with Kim and the speeding car in person. "Listen, Ann just called and since she has the day off, she was wondering if we would like to spend some time with her touring the Garden of the Gods and the gift shops there. Can you get away for a while?"

"I'd love to, Storm, but I'm right in the middle of a rather intense part of this project and I'm working over the phone and internet with one of the guys who's out in Virginia. But why don't you go with Ann and have some fun looking around?" Lance told her.

"Are you sure? We could wait until tomorrow and go then?" Stormy wanted to give him every opportunity, as she knew how he'd looked forward to this trip and to visiting these places as much as she had. Too bad this project had to be done right now.

"No, I don't know what tomorrow will bring," Lance responded, "Go and have a fun time. And don't forget to look for a new charm from here for your bracelet. If you find one you love, buy it, okay?"

"Okay, thanks. I'll see what they have. Ann said she's going to take me to two gift shops, so hopefully I'll find something I like. I'll call Ann back and see where I can meet up with her. Love ya."

"I love you. Oh, and watch yourselves," he warned. "There seem to be an awful bunch of nuts out there these days."

"I will, but don't worry, we'll be fine. See you later. Bye," she said.

"Bye, dear," Lance returned, before he hung up.

Stormy pushed the end button, then pressed the menu button on the phone and chose her address book. Scrolling down, she located Ann's cell number and gave her a call. The two of them agreed to meet at the Visitor and Nature Center located just outside the Garden of the Gods' entrance.

As Stormy drove her SUV along the roads of Colorado Springs, she marveled at the beauty of the place. The day had been a pretty clear one, but clouds had blown in to cover the sky once again and more snow could be on the way. Even with that possibility, Stormy enjoyed the drive.

She pulled into the parking lot and spotted Ann's red sports car. Conveniently, there was an open space next to it. She jumped out and went around the back to join Ann, who was walking towards her.

"Hi, Aunt Stormy, just look at this view out here," Ann said, gesturing toward the majestic scene displayed out in front of them. "Isn't it just gorgeous?"

"Yes, it is wonderful," Stormy replied, breathing in the fresh air. She looked out over the red rocks in their various shapes and then to the tall mountains beyond. She loved the way that Pikes Peak stood out so proudly, deeply covered in snow, behind the others. "Hopefully Lance and I will be able to go up the COG railway to the Peak tomorrow. And I hope you'll get to join us, Ann." She turned toward her niece, awaiting her response.

"Yes, I think I can come along," Ann said, turning away from the view and facing her aunt. "I have been able to get most of this week off while you're here. I just have to check in and do a little light duty is all."

"That's great, Ann. I am really looking forward to seeing the view from up there. And maybe Chris can come, too. Well, shall we go into the center and have a look around?"

"Maybe he can." Ann laughed as a slight blush filled her face. "Let's get going. We have a lot to see, and I think you'll love it." Arm in arm, Ann led the way, with her aunt keeping in step.

As they entered the front doors of the center, Stormy thought she saw a person coming in behind her, but when she turned to hold the door for them, no one was there.

"That's weird," Stormy muttered. She released her hold on the door, a puzzled look upon her face.

"What's weird, Aunt Stormy?" Ann asked, unbuttoning her coat and looking back at her aunt. She noticed that something was bothering her. "Is anything wrong?"

"I could have sworn that there was someone behind me, but when I looked back to hold the door for them, there was no one in sight," she explained. "I guess my eyes were just playing a trick on me." She looked out through the glass doors in search of anyone. No one was in the entire parking lot. "Maybe I'm becoming paranoid."

"Don't worry about it," Ann said, smiling at her aunt. "That kind of thing happens to all of us."

"I guess so," Stormy said, slowly shaking her head. As she unbuttoned her coat, she looked at the entry room they'd just stepped into. "Will you look at that? What a big creature!"

In the lobby stood a huge buffalo on display, standing amongst red rocks, cliffs, and prairie grass. In front of them on the floor was another large buffalo lying down. To one side of the display was a sign with information concerning the Plains Buffalo and the Indians that hunted them, known as the Red Rock Peoples.

"Would you like me to take a picture of you two ladies in front of the display?" a pleasant looking man asked as he stepped through the door of the nearby gift shop. "Many people have their picture taken in front of the buffalo. It makes a memorable photo of your trip here." He stood there with a big smile on his face, awaiting their answer.

"Sure, that would be great," Stormy answered. Reaching into her coat pocket, she pulled out her small digital camera. "I haven't taken as many pictures on this trip as I'd planned to." She handed the camera over to the man and stepped back beside her niece. "I'm sure your parents would love to receive a few of the two of us having a fun time together."

"I know they would, and we'll have to remedy that. There are many shots in the Garden that will make for the most wonderful pictures. You'll love it here." Ann put her arm around her aunt's shoulder and they both smiled at the man as he took a couple of shots of the two of them.

"Yes, you must take plenty of pictures while you're here," the man eagerly agreed, handing Stormy's camera back to her. "I think you will find that this is one of the wonders of the area. There is much to see, and many famous people have visited here over the years and loved it."

"Why don't we start upstairs and then come back and see what they have in this gift shop?" Ann suggested pointing toward the staircase. "They have a lot of displays and information on the area up there."

"Sounds great," Stormy said. "I will definitely want to take a look around your shop," she assured the man. "I want to find a silver charm for my bracelet."

"We have many nice charms so please do stop in before you leave. I'll be here to help you find anything you want." The man smiled at the ladies, turned and went back into the gift shop just as a man and woman bustled through the shop's door. "If I can help you with anything just let me know," they heard him say to the couple as they started up the stairs to the second level.

Once there, the two went from display to display, reading about the area and its interesting plants, animals, and early civilizations. Stormy found it all very fascinating. She wished that Lance could be with them, as she knew he would love looking at all these things. She leaned over and pressed a button on the display in front of her.

"During the winter months," a voice began, "the Garden of the Gods Visitor and Nature Center brings you a wonderful series of talks featuring a variety of topics centered around the geological and cultural history of the Colorado Springs area. In August of 1859 two surveyors started out from Denver City to form a town site. It would be called Colorado City. While exploring nearby locations, they came to a beautiful area of sandstone formations. M. S. Beach suggested that it would be a 'capital place for a beer garden' when the country grew up. His companion, Rufus Cable, a young, poetic man exclaimed, 'A beer garden! Why it's a place for the Gods to assemble. We'll call it the Garden of the Gods.' It has been so called ever since."

"By the 1870's," the narration continued "the railroads had forged their way west. In 1871, General William Jackson Palmer founded Colorado Springs while extending the lines of his Denver and Rio Grande Railroad. In 1879, General Palmer repeatedly urged his friend, Charles Elliott Perkins, the head of the Burlington Railroad, to establish a home in the Garden of the Gods and to build his railroad from Chicago to Colorado Springs. The Burlington never reached Colorado Springs, but Perkins did purchase two-hundred and forty acres in the Garden of the Gods for a summer home in 1879. He later purchased more land and decided to leave it in its natural state for the enjoyment of the public. Perkins died in 1907 before he'd made arrangements for the land to become a public park. In 1909, Perkins' children, knowing their father's feeling for the Garden of the Gods, conveyed his four-hundred eighty acres to the City of Colorado Springs. It was to be called the Garden of the Gods and remain free to the public. No intoxicating liquors could be manufactured, sold, or dispensed there and no building or structure was to be erected except those necessary to care for, protect, and maintain the park."

"I think I'd better use the ladies' room," Stormy told her niece as the presentation came to an end. "I see the restroom sign over there. I'll only be a few moments."

"Okay, I'll be over there in the food area," Ann said, pointing in the opposite direction. "I think I'll get us a couple of large hot pretzels and some juice. You want some? And I'll get us a table by the window so we can look at the view of the Gardens area while we eat."

"Yes, that sounds good to me." Stormy headed off to the restroom as Ann went to get the food.

Upon reaching the door, she paused and read a large sign on the wall. It told of one Katharine Lee Bates, a professor from Wellesley College in Massachusetts. It said that in 1893 she came out to Colorado to lecture at Colorado College. While there, she went up to the top of Pikes Peak with several others. She was so taken by its beauty that she just had to write a poem about it. Later this became the words to "America the Beautiful."

The words to the song ran through Stormy's mind, all eight verses of them, as she entered the restroom. She'd learned the song in high school music class under the direction of Miss Peterson. Her teacher was a stickler for having her classes memorize the names of those who wrote the lyrics and music to the songs they sang. She would always remember that the words were by Katharine Lee Bates and the melody was by Samuel Ward.

Stormy couldn't help but sing the song in her head.

"O beautiful for spacious skies,
For amber waves of grain,
For   purple
mountain
majesties,
Above   the
fruited plain!
America! America! God shed his grace on thee,
And crown thy good with
brotherhood,

From   sea   to
shining sea!"

"Wow, I still remember them," Stormy mumbled to herself as she washed her hands and dried them on a paper towel.

Upon exiting the ladies' room, Stormy started back through the displays, then came to an abrupt stop and pretended to examine one about how the Native Americans thrived on a bean grown in the area called "Anasazi Beans." It was one she had found quite interesting and had looked at with Ann, but what made her stop once again at this display was not to re-read the information on the attached sign. It was the man she'd seen exit the rest room at the same time she had.

This in itself was nothing out of the ordinary, but it was the expression on his face and the way he reacted when he had seen her that was what had made her think twice about him. When he saw her, she noticed that he stopped in his tracks, a look of fear crossing his face like one might expect of a cornered rat or a child caught with his hand in the cookie jar. Then he'd abruptly spun around on his heels and disappeared back through the restroom doors, trying to hide his face with one hand as he went.

Stormy thought she would just stand at the display and wait a few minutes to see if she could get a better look at the man when he once again exited the men's rest room.

"He has to come out some time," she mumbled under her breath. Choosing the display she was standing at to deliberately make sure she couldn't be easily seen from the men's room, she waited. This might make the strange man think she'd left the area and that it was safe for him to finally come out.

After several minutes of waiting, Stormy was about to give up her vigil and head over to where Ann would be waiting for her, when the men's room door cracked open a tiny bit, a small sliver of light coming from beyond. After a long pause, the door opened wider and a black-haired, roughly bearded man carefully stuck his head out of the door and slowly peered around the area outside of the restroom.

Stormy ducked further back behind the display and waited for the man to decide that it was okay to leave the safety of the men's room. As she peered past a corner of the display, she noticed that the man's skin was of an olive tone, and judging from his face, he appeared to be in his mid-thirties.

Apparently deciding that it was safe to come out, the strange man quickly exited through the door and hurried toward a nearby rack of brochures. He proceeded to browse through them as if all was right with the world after all.

Stormy observed that the man was dressed from head to toe in black clothing. Maybe he was the 'shadow' she'd been seeing out of the corner of her eye.

He's acting so odd, Stormy thought. *I wonder what he's up to and, more so, why he seems to be afraid of me.*

The olive-skinned man nervously picked out several of the brochures before looking quickly around. He proceeded over to the entrance of the movie room where the history of this area was being shown and quickly slipped inside. The door closed behind, blocking him from her view.

"Now that is down-right odd," Stormy murmured. "What is he up to anyway? Oh, well." Stormy shrugged her shoulders. "I'd better go and meet up with Ann before she thinks I got flushed down the toilet or something."

Stormy turned around and headed over to the food area, where she spotted Ann sitting at a table, anxiously looking about. As she approached the table, Ann saw her coming and a look of relief spread over Ann's face.

"There you are," Ann said. "I was getting a little concerned about you. I wasn't sure if maybe you fell or got sick in there, or what. And I couldn't just get up and look around for you as I had already bought all of this food." Ann motioned to the hot pretzels and cold drinks that sat in front of her on the table. "Are you okay then?"

"Yes, I am, and I'm so sorry to have worried you that way." Stormy sat down in the seat across from her niece, setting her walking stick against the window side of the table and placing her purse in her lap. "I had a rather odd thing happen to me when I left the restroom."

"What was that?" Ann took a bite of her pretzel, a sprinkle of salt falling onto a napkin below.

Stormy proceeded to explain to her niece about the man hiding in the men's room and taking his time to come out.

"That does seem very odd for sure, Aunt Stormy." Ann's eyes searched the room for a black-haired man dressed in all black clothing. Seeing no one matching his description, she turned back to her aunt. "Do you think he's been following us and didn't want to be seen then?"

"Yes, I believe so, at least that's the way it seems to me," Stormy answered. She took a sip of the juice her niece had bought for her. "I think we'd better keep our eyes open as we tour the gardens."

"I think you're right."

The two of them enjoyed the view of the Garden of the Gods through the window by their table as they ate the delicious hot pretzels and drank the bottles of juice. Each was absorbed in their own thoughts.

When they were finished and had looked around at the beautiful things the top floor areas had to offer, including each of them picking out a pair of animal earrings, they headed back down to the gift shop on the first floor.

"Oh, you are back again!" the man exclaimed that had taken their picture with Stormy's camera earlier. "What would you like me to help you find?" He ushered them into his shop with a small bow. "Come this way, ladies."

"I was hoping to see some of those silver charms you told us about," Stormy said. She followed the man across the store as Ann went to browse the various shelves of earrings.

"Ah, yes, right overhear, ma'am." The salesman led Stormy to a small display at one of the shop's counters and pointed out what they had in silver charms.

Stormy looked them over and found two silver charms that she liked. It was hard to decide which one she liked best, but she finally made her choice. It would be the one made of two silver braided circles with the name 'Pikes Peak' in capital letters split into two words, with 'Pikes' at the top and 'Peak' at the bottom. In the center of the charm was a design that appeared to be a snake-type river running through tall pine trees. Attached to it was a silver chili pepper.

"I'll take this one, please," Stormy said handing it to the salesman.

"Nice choice. I'll wrap it up for you," the man said. He took the charm and turned to grab some tissue paper from behind him.

"Did you find a charm for your bracelet?" Ann asked her aunt, coming to join her at the counter.

"Yes, I did. It's perfect. I'll show it to you later."

Stormy paid the man for the charm, and she and Ann headed out to their cars.

"Why don't we take my car, and I'll show you around the park?" Ann suggested. "You can leave yours here and pick it up later on the way out."

"Sounds like a good plan to me."

As soon as Ann had unlocked her vehicle, Stormy placed her walking stick in the back seat and climbed into the front passenger's side. They were soon driving through the entrance to the Garden.

Eleven

Stormy marveled that many of the trees in the park still showed plenty of green on them for so late in the season. She loved how patches of snow wound their way here and there throughout the area as she and Ann slowly drove along the narrow asphalt road through the Garden.

"Take a look over to our left, Aunt Stormy." Ann pointed to a tall rock formation across a small parking area. "Let's stop here for a minute."

Pulling the car into a space alongside a red minivan, the two women exited and stood on the nearby path. Ann pointed to a small group of people at the base of the rock formation.

"What are they doing with all of that gear strapped to them?" Stormy inquired. She watched as a tall, muscular-looking man with sandy-colored hair went from one person to the next checking their equipment, pulling on a strap here and there before proceeding to the next. She could hear the man speaking to the group but couldn't quite make out what he was saying. However, even from where she stood, she could feel the excitement of the group as they got ready.

As Ann stood observing the preparations, she explained, "Many groups obtain permission to come here throughout the year to challenge their skills at climbing. It's a fun way to get exercise, and what better place than here in this beautiful park? I've been here a few times myself with a group of friends from the Academy."

"It sounds like a lot of fun," Stormy said, shielding her eyes from the suns' rays with her hand as she watched the group. "I would have liked to try it myself when I was younger, but just never had the chance to." They watched for a few more minutes before climbing in the car and continuing along the roadway. As they came around one of the many bends in the road, Stormy marveled at the gorgeous view before them through the car's front windshield. She took in a deep breath. "Oh, this is truly one of God's great creations! There's no doubt about it."

"I never tire of coming here," Ann said as she slowly steered the car along the asphalt. "Sometimes Darlene and I grab sub sandwiches and eat lunch here, usually in the warmer months. A few times, Jeff and Mark have even joined us."

"This would be a good place to sit and relax for a while." Stormy thought how she could have used a place like this to come to when the stress of raising a family had gotten to be overwhelming at times.

"Here's the turn off to the Trading Post," Ann told her aunt, "but before we go there you have to see this formation up ahead of us." She drove the car past the turn off as Stormy studied a sign pointing straight ahead of them.

It read 'Balanced Rock', followed by 'Steamboat Rock.'

"That sounds interesting," Stormy voiced, peering out the windshield to get a better look at what lie ahead.

"Oh, it is. Wait and see." Ann smiled at seeing the excitement fill her aunt.

Just around the next bend, Stormy could see that the paved road narrowed as it ran right between two of the most unusual red rock formations she'd ever seen.

"Will you look at that," Stormy remarked, her attention drawn to a formation on her left. "It looks as if a giant ship ran aground before turning into stone."

"Look to your right," Ann suggested, pointing a finger in that direction.

A huge, oddly formed, many-layered rock rested precariously atop a ledge of sedimentary stone. It appeared from where Stormy sat in the car that the huge boulder could at any moment break away and roll down onto the road below, crushing all in its path.

"Wow, I want to get some pictures of this to show Lance." Stormy continued to marvel at the majestic artistry of nature.

A small parking lot lined either side of the roadway with several cars already filling many of the spaces. Ann spotted an empty slot and skillfully slipped her car in between a black pickup truck with a California license plate and a lime-green Volkswagen, an orange ball hanging from its radio antenna.

"Let's get out and take a closer picture of them." Ann opened her door and climbed out as Stormy followed suit. Stormy reached for her walking stick in view of the steep look of the terrain.

The two women headed along the sidewalk, then up the side of a small hill where it appeared to be an easier climb. Once on top of the hill, they made their way around to approach the huge bolder, the 'Balanced Rock.'

Upon closer inspection, Stormy observed that the bottom of the boulder actually sat upon a much smaller rock beneath it, and in fact, one could look under the huge rock and see clear to the other side. The only exception to this, and what seemed to hold the boulder in place, was a section under the very center of the rock and one outer corner that touched the surface of the hill.

"It's a wonder that this huge rock stays where it is at all," Stormy observed as she bent over, staring under the boulder. She marveled that she could see through to the people standing on the other side of such a formation.

"How about a picture of you in front of 'Balanced Rock', Aunt Stormy? Everyone that comes here to visit the Garden loves to get their picture taken next to it."

"Okay, that would be fun and then I could show it to Lance when I get back to the hotel." Stormy withdrew her camera from a coat pocket and held it out to Ann as the clouds parted and sunrays beamed down upon them. "Heavenly intervention?"

"It looks like it. Stay where you are, and I'll go down to the bottom for a better shot." Ann took the camera and turned away from her aunt and headed back down the way they had come.

Once at the bottom, Ann found the perfect spot and took a moment to adjust the distance on the digital camera. She took several shots of a smiling Stormy posing by the rock. After they had finished, Stormy took one last look at the base of the rock and then carefully made her way down to the bottom to join her niece. She found that her stick had indeed come in handy, especially for the descent.

The two of them crossed the road to have a closer look at its sister formation, Steamboat Rock, and take some more pictures, this time making sure to have Ann in several of them. A kindly old woman approached and asked if they would like her to take a few shots of the two of them together. Stormy appreciated the offer.

Making their way back to Ann's car, she unlocked it and they settled into the seats. Ann turned the car around and headed back to the turnoff that led to the Trading Post, a short distance down the road. On the ride there, Stormy scanned through the pictures on her camera, checking to see how the shots had turned out.

"Oh, my goodness!" she exclaimed as she stared down at the image that filled the small display.

"What's the matter? Is something wrong with your camera?" Ann questioned, alarmed that she might have broken it somehow.

"I don't think so, but there's that odd man again. The one I saw at the Visitor's Center. And he's standing right behind me in this picture you took of me at Balanced Rock." Stormy continued to stare at the photo, attempting a closer look at the man's features.

"The one that was afraid to come out of the men's room?" Ann asked as they approached the parking lot of the Trading Post. The Post sat nestled back in amongst several tall evergreens, appearing very rustic in its design.

"That's the one," Stormy confirmed. "I wonder what he's doing there, and right behind me no less."

"Do you think he followed us there on purpose?" Ann glanced into her rear-view mirror to see if any cars were shadowing them. She released her pent-up breath. The road was clear behind. Turning into the parking lot, she found a spot just opposite the

Trading Post's front doors and pulled to a stop, facing the woods out beyond the paved area.

"It certainly looks that way. But for what reason, I'm not sure." Stormy continued to look closer at the picture on her camera's screen, and then handed the camera over to Ann. "He came out a little fuzzy, as if he started to turn away as you snapped the picture."

"Yes, I see what you mean. Perhaps at the last minute, he realized that he might get into the shot and decided he'd better move away."

"It looks that way," Stormy agreed. "Let's keep an eye out for him in case he shows up again." She took the camera from her niece, turned it off, and placed it into her coat pocket.

Upon entering the shop, Stormy realized that the building was much bigger than she'd first thought, judging by its outside exterior. The saying, 'appearances can be deceiving', ran through her head. In front of her were several glass counters. Jewelry-filled turntables rested upon their surfaces with enclosed display cases beneath. Several artfully arranged presentations, with various styles and stones of jewelry pieces, caught her eye. Jewelry had always been a passion in her life, even as a young girl; that and shoes, of course.

After a few moments perusing, she turned to her left and spotted several racks of clothing and other similar articles further down the length of the shop. But before heading that way, she turned to discover many more items worth checking out further along in that direction as well. Which way to headfirst? she wondered as her niece's voice cut through her thoughts.

"What do you think?" Ann inquired, a gleam in her eye, knowing of her aunt's love for such places.

"Wow, what a nice place. Look at all these wonderful things," she answered, looking around the store. "I can see we'll be here for a while."

"Yes, I love coming here any chance I get, but I have to watch myself or I find too many things I want to buy." Ann laughed. "Though, I really don't get to come here as often as I'd like to with my duties and all." She shrugged out of her jacket and draped it over one arm. Her aunt followed suit.

Stormy stepped back to a jewelry counter displaying several turquoise necklaces and matching earrings to take a closer look. "Nice turquoise," she mumbled, looking them over.

"I'll be right back, Aunt Stormy." Ann stepped away and disappeared around a tall, freestanding display of silver earrings.

"May I help you find something?" A smiling, middle-aged woman appeared from behind the counter in front of Stormy.

"Not yet, thank you. I'm just looking right now," Stormy answered, returning the smile.

"Well, we have plenty to look at," the woman remarked, gesturing around her with open arms. "Just let me know if you would like to examine anything more closely and I'll bring it out of the case for you."

"Okay, I'll do that," Stormy assured her as the woman moved on to a young couple looking over a display of rings that appeared to be wedding band sets. She overheard the young man ask the saleswoman to pull a set out of the display for them, confirming her thoughts. She watched them for a moment, noticing how the young woman oohed and awed over the rings while the young man next to her beamed with pleasure at his bride-to-be. Stormy smiled to herself as it brought back memories of when she and Lance had chosen their own rings, years before. They'd had little money in those days but were able to find nice rings at a good price. She often wondered if the jeweler, a sweet old man, had given them a discount. He'd explained that the rings were on a special sale that day, but there hadn't been a sales sign in sight anywhere near the ring counter.

Bringing her attention back to the present, and the case in front of her, Stormy examined the various shades of stones and silver work put into each design of the many pieces displayed. After a few minutes, she headed toward an array of jars filled with various types of jams and jellies touted to be from the Colorado Springs area. She'd briefly noticed them upon entering the store and was considering taking some back as a gift for their house-sitter, when she heard Ann call out her name.

"Here you are. You've got to try a bite of this," Ann exclaimed, coming up behind her aunt. She handed Stormy a piece of paper with a small piece of layered fudge resting upon it. Lifting it to her mouth, Stormy sampled the delicacy.

"This is absolutely delicious!" she exclaimed, crumbling up the paper and looking for a place to discard it. "Where did you get this from?" "They make a variety of fudge here, each with its own unique flavor. Come and take a look . . ." Grabbing her aunt by the arm, Ann led her back to the confectioners' aisle.

Stormy savored a few more samples of the various flavors of fudge offered to her by the young, blonde-haired man behind the counter before deciding to purchase three different kinds to surprise Lance with when she returned back to the hotel. She couldn't help but notice the man's appreciating glances at her niece. She smiled to herself as Ann continued, seeming to be unaware.

"I always buy some when I'm here," Ann said. "I can't help myself." She held up a package to prove her point, and the two women laughed out loud together.

The twosome spent the next hour moving from one section to the next, each one filled with an abundance of fascinating items to browse through.

Before leaving the shop, Stormy had purchased several post cards, a pair of turquoise earrings for herself, and two matching t-shirts embossed with wild horses running across an Indian dream catcher for she and Lance to wear back home.

When they were all done shopping, the two women exited the Trading Post and went out into the parking lot. They crossed to Ann's car and were about to get in when Stormy spotted movement in the trees across the parking lot to one side of them. Spinning around in that direction, she was surprised to find two beautiful does coming out of the trees. A few steps behind followed a young fawn, trailing in their footsteps across the pavement.

"What lovely deer," Stormy remarked. "And look at that cute baby back behind them. They don't seem terribly worried about us standing here."

"These are mule deer and there are quite a number of them here in the Garden." Ann watched along with Stormy as the three deer continued across the length of the parking lot, heading for the forest and trees on the other side. "Even though they roam freely here, they've grown up amongst the care takers and the many visitors to the park. They aren't as concerned about being around people as most deer that live totally separate from mankind out in the wilderness."

After watching the deer vanish behind the trees, the two climbed back into Ann's car and headed through the rest of the Garden of the Gods before returning to the Visitor's Center. Ann pulled up beside Stormy's car in the lot.

"Let me see what Lance has to do tomorrow, and we can make plans for a trip on the COG up to Pikes Peak." Stormy unlocked her car as she spoke, placing her packages on the passenger's seat.

"Okay, that sounds like it'll be a very fun day," Ann replied through the car's open window. "See you tomorrow and be safe."

"You, too." Stormy got into her car and started the ignition. She backed out of the parking space, followed Ann's car out of the Visitor Center, and onto the street. Soon she was back at the hotel and the room she shared with Lance.

"Hi, Stormy, how's it going? Did you have a nice time?" Lance inquired. He lay on the sofa, his feet propped up on a pillow, a book in one hand.

"You sure look more rested," Stormy observed. She put her purse and bags down on a small table, threw her coat over a wooden chair, and plopped down into the comfortable, over-stuffed chair next to him. "We had a great time. Ann is a pleasure to go around with, and we had fun shopping at the Trading Post. But we both missed you not being along with us. Can you join us to ride the COG train and visit Pikes Peak tomorrow? I hear that Chris Jacobs might be coming along."

"Yes, as a matter of fact I can." Lance sat up to face Stormy as they conversed.

"Great, it will be so much fun having you along with us. I'm glad you won't have to miss out on this." Stormy smiled, sinking further back into the chair as she relaxed from the day's events.

"I can't wait to go. We finally finished this phase of the project about an hour ago. Now it goes on to the next team, so I'm free for the rest of our trip here to do whatever we want to do." Lance smiled back at his wife, wiggling his bare toes and placing his hands back behind his head.

"That's great. Ann will be happy, too." Stormy leaned forward, removed her shoes, and pulled the foot stool closer to prop her feet up on. She extended an arm to the table beside her and retrieved her digital camera from her purse. "Lance, I wanted to talk to you about the odd things that have been happening to us since we got here to the Springs."

Lance sat straight up, bringing his arms in front of him, a look of concern crossing his otherwise handsome face. "Did something else happen today? Are you and Ann alright?"

"Yes, sort of," Stormy said, turning on her camera. "And yes, we're just fine."

"Good." Lance's shoulders relaxed. "What do you mean, sort of?" Lance asked, moving closer to the end of the sofa nearest Stormy.

"Well, when we were in the Garden of the Gods Visitor Center, there was a man that was acting rather odd." Stormy related the incident to her husband. "Then we saw that same man again at the Balanced Rock. Look here." Stormy handed the camera over to Lance. "We caught him in one of the photos that Ann was taking of me beside the rock. See, he's standing right there behind me. And I didn't even sense or notice him back there."

Lance scanned the photo on the camera's small screen. He carefully studied the man dressed in all black clothing before asking, "Did he also show up at the Trading Post while you were there?"

"No, not that we could see, though we half expected him to." She brought one hand under her chin, her elbow resting on the chair's arm. "I guess he could have been somewhere around the area, maybe even outside, but kept himself better hidden this time."

Stormy sat there in thought for a minute as Lance browsed through the rest of the pictures that she and Ann had taken of their outing.

"It looks like the two of you had a lot of fun. These are great photos."

"We did," Stormy began, then paused before continuing, "but I think someone has been following us around . . . well, possibly me anyway, ever since I walked in on that bank robbery the first day we were here in the Springs."

"Yes, I can see what you mean. There certainly have been a lot of weird things happening since then," Lance agreed, shutting down the camera. "Like the cars that have been following behind us, and the one that ended up chasing us down the one-way street, going the wrong way."

"And include to that list the jogger that just happened to knock you and Ann down on the path to the Chapel on the Air Force Base, and then the someone that was spying on you two near the Chapel," Lance added, shaking his head. "Just coincidence?"

"No, I don't think so," Stormy replied, dropping her arm into her lap. "Now what?"

"I know, Storm. Stay there." Lance got up from the sofa and made his way over to the desk and his waiting laptop. He sat down and positioned his fingers on the keyboard. "Let's make a list of all the things that have happened to any of us, including Ann, since we've been here. Then we can see it all down in black and white, so to speak. Now, let's put down what we've already discussed so far."

Stormy repeated the items one by one as Lance's fingers flew over the laptop's keyboard. They made sure they added the few other things they had noticed as well.

"Okay, now come over here and see what we have," Lance requested, sitting back in his chair.

Stormy rose from the chair she'd been reclining in, grabbed one of the wooden chairs from the nearby dining table, and dragged it to where Lance sat at the desk. Placing it next to him and sitting down, she leaned over and read the words on the screen.

"Yes," Stormy said after reading the list. "You can see it even more clearly now. Someone, or several someones, seems to have taken great interest in us over the past few days."

"But why would someone single you out from all of those other people that were there at the bank during the robbery?" Lance stared at the screen in front of him before turning to his wife.

"I don't know. I've been wondering about that as well." Stormy leaned back in her chair and folded her arms over her chest. "I don't think I saw anything different than any of the others did at the time, though I wasn't with my nose to the floor. Though neither were the tellers." She paused before continuing. "I believe most all of us saw the gunman at one moment or another. And we saw or heard him shoot the bank manager, yell out, and then flee the scene through the bank's front doors. I just don't know what it could be about the robbery that would have anyone worried about me or what I could've witnessed differently at the time." She shook her head as if to emphasize the point.

"Do you think that you saw things more clearly or differently from your vantage point behind that sign than those on the floor or behind the counters might have seen?" Lance asked, his eyebrows slightly lifting as he spoke.

"No, probably not enough to make any difference, though I was the only one he ran down in his hurry to escape." Stormy continued to play through her mind about what had happened inside the bank and what she'd seen. Then a forgotten scene slowly pushed its way forward and surfaced into her thoughts, making her sit up and take notice. "Wait a minute. I wonder if it could have anything to do with what I saw before I entered the bank."

"What do you mean?" Lance asked, turning in his chair, awaiting her answer.

"Remember when I told you the other night about the wild driver and the car skidding onto the icy street just before I reached the bank?" A face filled Stormy's mind.

"Yes, I do, now that you mention it," Lance said. "How does that fit in with the bank robbery?" He turned around and typed a few more notes into his laptop, then looked back at Stormy.

"As the car came closer to where I was walking along the sidewalk, a woman leaned forward and pressed her face against the window of the speeding car," Stormy explained. "I remember thinking how she had what looked to be an expression of fear on her face. At the time, I thought it was probably due to the crazy driver behind the wheel of the car."

"But now you don't?" Lance questioned, clasping his fingers across his stomach, elbows resting on the arms of the chair. The chair squeaked as he turned it back and forth, thinking about what his wife had just said.

"I wonder why she even looked my way. If I was in a car going that fast, I would sit back and hang on to something for dear life. Maybe to the man that was sitting in the back seat with me."

"There was a man in the back seat with her? Did you get a good look at him?" Lance asked her as he typed in what she'd just told him.

"No, not a real good look. He reached forward and grabbed her shoulder, pulling her back from the window," Stormy recounted, scratching the side of her head. "However, come to think of it, I did notice in that brief moment that he had a rather crooked nose."

"Those are pretty good powers of observation, Stormy." Lance grinned at his wife, always impressed with her never-ending abundance of talents. Of course, he was her biggest fan after all.

"Now I wish I'd seen him more clearly," Stormy lamented. "And the driver in the front seat as well."

"I wonder who she was, and about the others with her?" The chair protested loudly as Lance leaned back in it. "I think they need to oil this chair."

"I think so," Stormy agreed, laughing. "I don't know, but I think it might be a good idea to visit the bank again tomorrow after we come back from Pikes

Peak and see if I can get in to see the bank manager for a few minutes," Stormy suggested. "He might be able to shed some light on all of this."

"He might have some ideas as to who they were since they seemed to be coming from behind his bank, but do be careful, okay?" Lance cautioned her. "Is that all for our list then?"

"I will," she promised, raising her hand as if to take a pledge. "Yes, I believe that's all. And I think you had a great idea to write it all down like this. It puts it into perspective much better this way. Now, how about joining me for some dinner downstairs in the restaurant?" She started to rise when Lance put a hand on her arm.

"I have a better idea," Lance said, closing the cover of his laptop and turning in her direction. "Why don't we order room service and watch a movie on pay-per-view while we eat? I checked to see what was on tonight and surprisingly, there are three different choices for us to choose from."

"I like that idea. What are you hungry for?" Stormy retrieved the hotel's menu from where it sat on the dining table and bought it over to Lance.

Lance wiggled his eyebrows and started to speak. Stormy playfully placed a hand over his mouth.

"We can see about that after we eat some food." Stormy laughed before lowering her hand.

"Okay, later then. As for the food, I'll let you decide, but something big. I'm hungry as a bear," Lance said, growling loudly to prove his point.

Stormy broke into laughter as she reached for the room's phone.

Twelve

"I hope we'll be able to see from on top of the Peak," Stormy said, shielding her eyes with one hand from the sun's rays reflecting off of a bank of clouds as she gazed upward. Even with her sunglasses, the sun's glare was intense.

"I hope so, too." Lance started the car and soon they were on their way to the COG railway station. They'd agreed to meet Ann and reporter, Chris, there at 9am.

"That was nice of Ann to invite Chris to join us today," Lance said as he changed lanes to comply with the signs announcing road work ahead. It seemed they were always doing some kind of road repair around the city at any given time of the year.

"I think it's more than her just being nice," Stormy said, a sparkle in her eyes. "I think she really likes him. And what's more, I think he really likes her, too."

"Yes, they did seem to be having fun talking together," Lance had to agree.

They arrived at their destination in Manitou Springs, and it took a little bit of searching for them to find a parking space. Finally spotting one, Lance parked the car. As they approached the COG station, they spotted Ann waving to them from an outside table. Chris sat next to her, smiling their way.

"Looks like the two of them made it here okay." Stormy smiled and waved back. Using her walking stick and holding onto Lance's arm, the pair made their way across the ice-filled street and onto the sidewalk. "Hi, Ann." Lance embraced her in a hug before turning to Chris. "Nice to see you again, Chris." He reached out and gripped the young man's hand in a firm handshake.

"You, too, Mr. Winters," Chris responded, looking Lance in the eye.

"Good morning, dear," Stormy said, giving her niece a hug and a kiss on the cheek. "And good morning to you, too, Chris. It's great that you could join us." She reached over to touch his arm.

"Morning and thank you for inviting me along with your beautiful niece." Chris grinned and looked in Ann's direction.

Blushing, Ann turned back to the table and reached for a couple of Styrofoam cups. Stormy noticed steam rising from each of them.

"Here, we got you something hot to drink before we board the train. We already finished ours." Ann handed one cup to her aunt, the other to her uncle. "It can get cold on the trip up, and also once we're at the top. This will help to warm you up a bit."

"Thank you, Ann." Stormy took a sip of the hot liquid. "This is delicious. You know how much I love chocolate, especially hot cocoa. And I see you even remembered the marshmallows."

"No hot chocolate is complete without marshmallows," Ann declared, laughing.

"Great apple cider," Lance remarked. "I see you remembered that I prefer cider over chocolate."

"Well, we wouldn't want you sneezing the whole way up the mountain." She smiled warmly at him, remembering the first time she'd witnessed his sensitivity to chocolate. "By the way, Chris has an assignment he'll be working on today as well."

"Oh, and what might that be, if it's okay to ask, that is?" Stormy studied the handsome young man. His brown hair moved slightly in the breeze as his face lit up.

"Of course it's okay," Chris replied, pleased to share the details of his assignment with them. "The station is sending me to interview the head ranger at the top of Pikes Peak. We want to know how he likes working up there at such a high altitude, and other things like that. So I guess this way I can, as they say, 'kill two birds with one stone.' It should be a fun day."

A long, shrill whistle sounded, followed by a pleasant voice instructing all passengers to get aboard the train for the journey to the top of the mountain.

"I guess that means us," Stormy said. "Here, give me your cup, Lance, and I'll get rid of it."

"Thank you, dear." Lance handed her the cup before reaching inside his coat. "I'll get the tickets out."

Stormy walked over to a nearby trash can and disposed of the two cups. She looked around the parking lot to see if anyone was watching them. Hopefully nobody would be following them today and ruin their trip.

The foursome chose the car nearest the front of the train and climbed aboard. They sat down near the window, with Stormy and Lance sharing one seat and Ann and Chris in the seat across from them.

Soon the train was filled with the energy of excited passengers as they started away from the station on their journey to the top of the Peak.

Microphone in hand, a middle-aged man in jeans and a blue shirt ran his hands through his short, sandy-colored hair as he cleared his throat and smiled at the seated passengers. "Good morning, folks, my name's Pete and I'll be your guide for our trip up this here grand mountain. As you waited for the train," he paused, looking from face to face, before continuing, "you may have noticed that our tracks here are laid out a bit different than a conventional set."

Several passengers attempted to look out their windows at the tracks below them. A few smiled smugly and nodded, obviously aware of this fact beforehand and wanting the other passengers to know that they already knew this tidbit of information.

"Your average tracks, called adhesions," the guide continued, "provide for only up to a six percent climbing grade—in some cases to a nine percent grade, but only on a short run—whereas with a COG, or rack train, we can climb up to a forty-eight percent grade. And as you have seen, the ascent to the top of Pikes Peak is quite steep." He waved his hand toward the windows facing the front of the train's engine. As before, many of the passengers attempted to look out their windows at the front of the train.

"Are we going way up there, Mommy?" asked a small, blond-haired boy across the aisle from where Lance and Stormy sat. With his small hands up against the windowpane, he stared out, trying to get a better look.

"Yes, dear," his mother patiently answered as she checked the contents of her purse.

"Whoopee!" the boy exclaimed as he bounced up and down in his seat.

"Quiet down now," the woman cautioned, "we want the other passengers to be able to hear this nice man." She reached over and adjusted the small coat around him. The boy stopped, looked around at the other passengers, many looking back at him, and shyly slid down in his seat, leaning up against his mother.

"Okay," the guide said, smiling at the child, "this promises to be an exciting trip."

As the engine chugged its way up the mountain, Stormy looked out of the window beside her. She loved sitting in the window seat of most any vehicle she traveled in, be it a bus, plane, or train, and Lance was kind enough to always offer her first choice of the prized seat.

"You might be interested to know that the founder of the Simmons Beautyrest Mattress company, a man by the name of Zalmon Simmons, helped to bring this railway to a reality," the guide explained. "On a visit to the area in 1880, he fell in love with the Peak and wanted all to have a chance to see it. After several setbacks, the railway finally opened in June of 1891. Since then, people from around the world have made their way here to ride the COG and visit the top of Pikes Peak. The tracks stretch for eight point nine miles and the entire round trip will take us a little over three hours. I promise you'll love every minute of it."

As they chugged their way to the top of the Peak, the guide continued a running dialogue of the different areas they passed through, including pointing out several of the area's interesting plant and wildlife. Near an area the guide called Minnehaha Falls, another COG train tooted its' whistle as it passed by on its way down the mountain.

Stormy marveled at the beauty of the landscape, sharing its wonders with Lance, and asking their guide further questions as he paused in his narration.

Drawing close to the top of the Peak, the guide reminded the passengers: "Don't forget, stay nearby and don't wander off too far. You'll only have about 40 minutes before we leave for the trip back down. This is due to the fact that most people will start to feel the effects of the altitude up this high, things like headaches and dizziness, and so on. So grab a hot drink and a doughnut or two . . . . they sell out quickly . . . . and enjoy the view."

The train came to a halt and the foursome waited until the others had disembarked before making their way to the door and down the stairs to the platform.

"Feel that fresh air," Stormy said, taking a deep breath in through her nose. "It's so refreshing and invigorating, don't you think?"

"Yes, it's great up here," Lance agreed, taking Stormy's hand in his. Chris and Ann stood off to one side as Chris pointed out a structure several yards away, their conversation inaudible to the others.

Lance led Stormy over to the edge of the nearby railing in hopes of seeing the valley below. The Peak had been covered with low-lying clouds, but it was as if the heavens knew of their desire to see the wonders that were laid before them. As if on cue, the wind picked up and the clouds parted to make way for the spectacular scene. Chris and Ann joined them, and they all stood spellbound for several moments without speaking a word.

Stormy broke the spell by withdrawing her phone from her coat pocket. They took turns snapping photos of each other near the rail with the beautiful scenes beyond.

"These will be great pictures to show our family and friends back home." Stormy thumbed through the pictures on her screen before placing her phone back into her pocket. She drew her coat more tightly about her with her gloved hands as a cool wind continued to blow across the mountain's top.

"This really is beautiful, and you can sure see a long way out across the valley," Lance commented as his stomach growled loudly. "But I would like to go get those doughnuts our guide was telling us about. It sounds like they are to die for, and since I overheard on the train that they only serve them for the first few minutes after we arrive,
I think we'd best hotfoot it over to the stand and get in line."

"Yes, and I had better get over there and get my interview done before the train heads back down the mountain." Chris took a digital recorder from one of his coat pockets and a press tag from another. He pinned the tag to the outside of his coat and started toward a building on the far side of the snack area. "I'll catch up with you guys in a little while. And grab me one of those doughnuts, if you would please," he called back over his shoulder.

"We will," Ann promised him, adjusting the wool scarf more tightly about her neck. Turning to her aunt and uncle she said, "Let's go see what they have left."

"Why don't you and Lance go buy some?" Stormy suggested to Ann. "And see if they have a chocolate one for me." She smiled as she turned back to look over the valley below, then beyond to the neighboring mountain ranges. "We're not going to have much time left before the train leaves after standing in that line, and I would like to take in as much of this gorgeous view as I possibly can before we head back down."

"Okay, but don't go far from this area so we can find you when we get back," Lance said, a twinkle forming in his brown eyes. "If you're not here when we return, I'll have to eat your doughnut for you." Lance teased. He'd been doing it for all their married life. In fact, his sense of humor, besides his good looks, was one of the things that had attracted Stormy to him in the first place.

"Don't worry. I'll guard it for you, Aunt Stormy." Ann laughed as she took hold of her uncle's arm and led him away.

"See that you do," Stormy called after them. "I'll be good and hungry when you get back."

Looking around for a place to sit, Stormy noticed that some thoughtful person had placed a large carved-out boulder, most likely with the help of a crane, a few yards to her left where one could sit down and still take advantage of the scenes around them.

Stormy approached the rock and ran a gloved hand along its smooth surface. She momentarily paused to study the rays of sunlight as they brought out tiny sparkles in its texture. Propping her walking stick against one side, she tucked her coat beneath her for added warmth against the certain coldness of the stone and sat down, resting against the tall backing. She'd sat on many rock surfaces before but found this one to be surprisingly comfortable.

"What I would give to be able to sit here each day and look out over this beautiful place," she mumbled as she breathed in the crisp air and surveyed the scene before her. Stormy knew she would thoroughly enjoy the peace it would bring to one's soul to have a home with a view like this. And even though she would always love her home in northern Phoenix, she secretly wished they could afford a second one nestled here in the Rocky Mountains.

As she sat admiring the view and daydreamed, she caught a movement out of the corner of her left eye. This startled her, as no one else had been around when she'd sat down. Thinking to acknowledge whomever it was, she turned and was surprised to find no one there. Curious as to what she'd seen, she leaned forward, attempting to get a better look. The area was void of any life, but her own.

"I guess it must have been a bird swooping by", Stormy mused. "Or just my eyes playing tricks on me." This made her realize that it'd been some time since she, or Lance for that matter, had been in for an eye checkup. She made a mental note to remedy this as soon as they returned to Phoenix.

She focused her attention back on the scenery before her, thankful that the fog had lifted enough for her to be blessed to witness such a breathtaking view as this one. There was no doubt in her mind that God had created this beautiful planet for mankind to dwell upon; it was not some chance happening of the universe.

Stormy marveled at how, from this height, the tall red rocks of the famed Garden of the Gods looked like the tiny pebbles that Lance placed throughout his rose gardens back home to keep the neighbors' cats from using the freshly turned soil as a litter box.

What a difference perspective can make at how one sees things, she marveled.

After a few moments, she again caught movement out of the corner of her eye. She quickly turned her head. She was in luck. She spotted what appeared to be a deer's hind foot disappearing behind a large scrub oak several yards from where she sat.

Stormy jumped to her feet and hurried in the direction of the foliage. Pulling her camera from her coat pocket in hopes of snapping a picture of the deer before it completely vanished. She wondered if there might even be others for her to photograph hidden beyond; possibly a whole herd of them.

"Now where did you go?" Stormy moved further into the brush, attempting to avoid any undue noise that might scare the deer into bolting away.

She noticed that the hard-packed ground held a small path running ahead of her that slowly descended, disappearing into more brush and trees beyond. Small rocks, concealed by a dusting of snow, covered a good portion of the ground. Stormy realized she'd have to watch her step. Looking back toward the rock she'd been sitting on and seeing that Lance and Ann had not yet returned, she decided to go ahead. If only she hadn't been in such a hurry and remembered to grab her stick.

Oh well, I don't have time to go back for it now, she chided herself. She'd only go a short way and be back in her seat before they had a chance to miss her. She moved around a small evergreen and carefully navigated the narrow pathway.

The path continued to wind in and out of the brush. Stormy followed it before halting in front of a large bush. Its thick branches stretched across the path, obscuring the way before her. Only then did she realize she'd come further than she'd intended to.

"Maybe I'd better turn back and forget about the deer," Stormy mumbled. "Lance will be worried if he can't find me." She turned to retrace her steps when a noise sounded from the other side of the bush. Wondering if it might be the object of her search, she decided that a few more feet wouldn't hurt before heading back.

Stepping off the path, she skirted around the tree, only to find another wall of bushes partially blocking her way.

"Well, I've come this far," she rationalized. "I might at least check the other side of these before I go back."

Stormy proceeded to push her way through the branches when she came to an abrupt halt. A shock, akin to lightning, ran down her spine and adhered her feet in place as the realization hit her like a brick wall. Slowly, she turned her head to the right to face the reality; that she stood only a few yards from the edge of a cliff.

The ground roughly sloped away and down over a sheer drop off. Her eyes were drawn to the small rocks that rolled with the muddy dirt and leaves out over the edge, kicked loose by the movement of her feet. She was barely aware of holding her breath as her heart beat wildly in her chest.

Stormy stood there, frozen in place as if part of the mountain itself, not daring to move another step. With sheer will power, she forced herself to slowly release her breath, hoping to calm her run-away heart.

"Whoa, ole girl," she told herself, "calm yourself down. You're going to be okay." She wasn't sure she believed this, but she'd always heard it worked best if you said things out loud for your own ears to hear. This was confirmed when she felt her heart begin to slow.

As she stood there mulling over her situation, forcing herself to relax, Stormy heard a rustle in the branches behind her.

The deer? she wondered.

Her feet firmly planted; she twisted her upper body to take a look. The head of a young doe peered through the brush, and Stormy found herself staring into the most inquisitive deep brown eyes she'd ever encountered. They held her spellbound, and for a few brief moments she forgot about her predicament. She was amazed that the doe would come this close to a human. It must have been as curious about her as she was about it.

Stormy suddenly remembered the camera she held in her hand, and feeling more secure of her position, heartbeat almost back to normal, she slowly raised it to her eye. *After all*, she told herself, *isn't this why I'm out here in the first place?*

Oh, what a great picture this will make. Stormy imagined the look on her best friend's face back home when she related the adventure . . .. "Yes, I climbed to the edge of a cliff just to snap this amazing photo." But before she could take the shot, the deer jerked its head to the right. A look of fear momentarily crossed its face, and it quickly disappeared from sight.

"Oh, crumb, there goes my moment of fame," Stormy mumbled, lowering her hand. "I wonder what spooked it?"

It would have been the perfect shot, a shot that her friends back home would have been talking about for some time to come. She and her friends were always comparing their latest photos from this outing or that recent trip.

Oh well, another time, she mused, putting the camera back into her pocket.

Focusing back on her situation, she slowly turned and looked once more in the direction of the mountain's edge. Being so close to the rim of such a high mountain definitely unnerved her. Where others got their thrills standing on swinging bridges looking down at the deep gorges below, or bungee jumping off the famous dam sites across the West, she couldn't understand this herself. Even the high rising thrill rides at amusement parks were a little too much for her tastes.

Reaching a decision, Stormy carefully took a step backwards and extended one arm behind her in an attempt to grab hold of a large branch. She was confident that with the help of the bush, she could then retrace her steps back up the narrow path from whence she'd come.

She felt the tips of the branch brush up against her fingers. If she could reach just a bit more, she was sure she could get a good hold on it.

"Come on, you can do it," she urged herself. "Just a little bit further, that's all."

Stretching as far as she could, she grasped onto the branch and held it tightly. When she was sure her body was stable enough, she slowly turned and tugged at the branch to see if it would support her weight.

It will. Relief flowed through her body as she carefully made her way up toward the shrub.

"Good," Stormy said aloud, pleased with herself as she planted another foot in front of her.

She reached the thick foliage and was about to make her way around to the other side, when a loud snapping noise resounded from deep within the brush. Before Stormy's mind could process the sound, the bush began to violently shake back and forth. She attempted to tighten her hold on the branch as the swaying intensified.

"Hey!" Stormy yelled, astonished at what was happening. She realized she was fast losing her grip.

As the branch slipped through her hands, the unmistakable sound of a snake shaking its rattles sounded in her ears. It was well known, at least by her family and close friends, that Stormy did not like snakes. Not even the ones at the zoo enclosed in those aquariums.

Fear shot through her body, causing her palms to become sweaty. She lost what little grip she had left, and in an effort to step back away from the rattler, she lost her footing and fell backwards. Air was forced from her lungs as she dropped heavily to the ground. Gasping, she was unaware that her purse had flung from her shoulder and was headed down in the direction of the cliff's edge.

Confusion filled Stormy's mind following the fall's hard impact, but as her brain began to clear, the shocking realization of her predicament hit her like a slap on the face. She found herself slipping sideways through the dirt and rocks, following the path of her purse, heading ever closer to the edge.

"Help!" she tried, the word catching in her throat.

Thirteen

With a frantic prayer on her lips, Stormy wildly grasped for anything she could find to break her fall as the cliff's edge came ever closer.

As her body neared the edge of the cliff, she smacked up against a large, thick root protruding in a loop from out of the ground. Smarting from the impact, she clung onto it with both hands and held tight with all the strength she could muster.

Stormy lay there with her eyes tightly shut, her heart beating wildly in her chest. She attempted to take a deep breath but found instead that her lungs were invaded by dirt-filled oxygen. This sent her into a brief coughing fit, forcing her eyes open. To her horror, she found herself peering down at the last few feet of ground as the words of the guide ran through her mind: "bottomless pit."

She tried to force herself not to look, but her eyes were drawn out over the edge. She found herself peering out upon full-sized pine trees that, from this height, looked like tiny twigs amongst jagged red rocks, covered in a fresh dusting of white. Her heart raced till she was sure it would explode from her chest as she imagined what it would feel like falling the vast distance to the bottom and onto those rocks below.

My heart will most likely give out before I reach the bottom, her mind summed up.

With immense effort, she forced her eyes away and on to the root. She was surprised at just how large it was and how it came up out of the ground in one spot only to bend and plunge back in again. Funny how she hadn't noticed such a pronounced object like this when she'd looked down from where she'd stood by the bush only moments before.

As she lay there, she thought of how foolish she'd been. What had she been thinking, charging into the brush after a deer like that with no thought to watch her step more closely? After all, she was on top of a mountain: Pikes Peak, no less!

"Okay," Stormy said aloud, in hopes of reassuring herself. "I'll be okay. I can do this. Please, Lord." She silently prayed once again for His help and strength to get herself out of this life-threatening situation.

Sweat ran into her eyes, causing them to burn and making it harder for her to focus. She thought about screaming, but Lance and Ann would never be able to hear her from where she lay. No one would. They wouldn't even know which way she'd gone or where to begin looking for her. What could she do?

If you can get onto your knees, you can make it out of this, she heard in a soft whisper.

"If I get to my knees . . ." Stormy processed the words. "Okay, I'll give it a try." Even though her body trembled, she knew that she must try to pull herself up before she lost the strength in her arms.

More of nature's debris broke loose and spilled over the edge of the cliff with each movement she made. As she slowly moved one leg, she spoke again in a stronger voice, as if to command her shaking body on what it needed to do. "If I can get my knees under me, I can crawl back up this slope."

Stormy slowly pulled one knee up to her chest as drops of sweat ran down her cold face. It took much of her strength to accomplish this.

She finally managed it, though the movement sent several more showers of dirt and rocks flowing beneath her and out over the edge.

Good thing I spend all those hours exercising each week, she thought, bringing some relief.

"Okay, that's one," she murmured.

Stormy slowly attempted the task of pulling her other knee up to her chest.

"Did it!" She congratulated herself.

She paused to make sure of her position before proceeding. She would now have to push herself up onto her knees, she realized, while still holding fast to the root and avoid slipping from the cliff. It was the only option she had to make her way back to the safety of the bushes.

Steeling her nerves, she hoisted herself up onto her knees, her hands clinging tightly to the root. The sweat continued to drip from her face and onto the ground beneath, mixing with the dirt to form trails of mud.

So far, so good. Stormy told herself, paying little attention to the stinging pain emanating from her legs.

Now came a much harder task. She realized she must let go of the safety of her handhold if she was to make her way back up the slope.

Carefully, Stormy removed one gloved hand from the root and pressed it into the dirt beside her. She was aware of how cold and stiff her hands had become. What she'd give for some hand warmers about now.

She attempted to move one knee forward. This proved to be a mistake as the ground beneath her shifted and roared to life. Back onto her knees she went, sliding downward. Thankfully, she still clutched the large root with the other hand, thus stopping her from slipping further and plunging over of the cliff.

She hung there, her heart once again thumping in her chest.

What am I going to do now?

Cold and wet, and close to sobbing, she realized it would do her no good. She must keep it together if she was to survive.

Painstakingly, she proceeded once more to bring her knees up under her, one knee at a time. After careful movements, she was once again on all fours.

As Stormy knelt there, trying desperately to decide how to proceed forward without slipping, she heard movement above her. Peering upward, she was astounded to find a man in a heavy coat, hands shoved deep into his pockets, a dark hat pulled low over his face, staring down at her from beside the bush that had held the snake.

"Please help me," Stormy cried out, her voice raspy from the dirt in her throat and nose. "I need your help!"

She held tightly onto the root, hoping that her frozen hands would continue to hold her weight. She could feel her strength giving out bit by bit and knew she couldn't hold on much longer.

Thank goodness help has arrived, Stormy thought, hope filling her heart.

The man stood there another moment before turning around and disappearing behind the bushes, speaking not a word.

"Wait, help me, please," she called again, disbelief filling her mind. "No. Don't leave me here! What's wrong with you?" Stormy cried out louder. Was this man heartless?

Then a ray of hope entered her mind. Maybe he was hurrying to get some help for her. Maybe he didn't have the strength, proper gear, or knowledge to assist her and wanted to find someone to help. There must be rangers stationed here at the top of Pikes Peak. Certainly, the man would alert them of her situation.

Stormy spirits brightened as she clung as tightly as she dared to the root, her knees shaking beneath her. She hoped she could hang on for as long as needed until help arrived. Surely it would come. She would be alright and laugh about her stupidity later with the others, her narrow escape from death at the top of Pikes Peak in Colorado. She could even take some pictures once she was safely back at the top of the slope. Yes, that's what she would do. After all, her camera was still safely tucked into her pocket where she'd placed it earlier.

Stormy's neck ached and she lowered her head as she waited. Her ear was close by the watch and she became aware of its ticking as it counted each passing second. The seconds turned into minutes as she hung there.

She looked back up, hoping she'd see the welcome faces of the rangers, and hopefully Lance's as well, coming to her aid with their ropes and other gear. Maybe they would even send a helicopter to aid with her rescue.

No, that would be a little much for this situation, her thoughts rambled on as she nervously chuckled to herself. A cold wind nipped at her face, sending a shiver through her body. *Good thing I have my heavy coat on.*

Oh, why hadn't I waited to explore until after they'd brought back the doughnuts? Lance is going to have some words for me, and I don't blame him.

"Please, Lord, give me the strength to hang on until help arrives," she called out.

Time continued to tick by, and Stormy saw no signs of help on the way. She decided that maybe the man had just panicked and was not getting help after all. Maybe he even had thought she was mountain climbing and didn't realize that she'd needed help after all, although any idiot could've seen that this was not the case. She'd even yelled at him to help her. He must have heard her cries. She was certain of it.

Hopelessness settled over her. *Is this how my life is to end,* She wondered, *falling from this majestic mountain? Will they be able to recover my body, or will it be lost forever between the crags below?*

Stop it, she commanded herself. *You can do this. Just concentrate.*

Stormy knew she had to try once more to climb to safety.

"Okay, let's try this again," she told herself out loud.

Letting go of the root, she placed her hand out. Taking a deep breath, she slid a knee through the mud, followed by the second one. This time around, she was pleased to see there were no longer showers of dirt or rocks for her to slip in. The ground had become much firmer.

She took a deep breath. Gathering her courage. she let go of the safety of the root with her other hand.

Scouring the landscape above her for anything she might grab onto, she discovered the tips of several rocks protruding from the ground.

Odd. She'd not noticed them on her way down. *Maybe all that dirt that broke loose? It must have uncovered these.* Reaching for one of the rocks, she spotted her purse lying in the dirt a short way from her.

"My purse!" she exclaimed, remembering her cell phone. "If I can just reach you," she told the purse, "I'm as good as saved."

As she reached out to retrieve it, she heard the faint sound of music emanating from within.

"Lance!" she shouted. "He must be calling to see where I am." Her heart leapt with joy at the thought of her husband, causing her to hurry in her attempt to reach it before it went to voicemail.

After a few more rings, she managed to get hold of the purse and unsnap the small outside pocket where she kept her phone, all the while continuing to brace herself against the mountainside. As she did so, the phone slipped from her fingertips and onto the ground beside her.

"Oh great," she murmured.

Stormy reached out to retrieve it but accidentally pushed it further away. Down the slope it went, coming to a rest below her foot, as it continued to play "Ode to Joy".

Why'd I ever choose that ring? she thought in frustration.

Stormy extended a foot over to where the phone rested. She carefully slid it upward with the toe of her boot as far as she could without losing her balance. But to her horror, the ground beneath the phone suddenly broke loose, taking the phone with it over the edge.

"Noooo!" Stormy cried out as she helplessly watched her phone disappear.

Faint echoes of the object hitting the rocks below brought tears to her eyes. But the thought came to her to be grateful that it was the phone, and not her, that had smashed against them.

"I hope that the phones warranty covers falls off of cliffs in the Rocky Mountains," she quipped to lighten her mood.

Okay, plan C, or was this D? she thought as she tried to decide what was next. *Well, maybe it's back to plan A. Or was that plan B? It didn't matter*, she chided herself. The rocks were there, and she would use them.

Pulling her purse strap over her neck to keep her hands free, Stormy continued the slow process of going from rock to rock as she crawled up the mountain.

When she drew closer to the bushes, she was dismayed to discover that there were no more rocks to which she could hold onto.

*Now what? sh*e wondered, her legs shaking from the effort, her body cold and tired. *I've gotten this far only to be stopped?*

Stormy noticed a small scrub oak not far from her. There must be some way she could reach one of its branches. Then she remembered that her purse had a long strap.

With renewed spirit, she removed it from around her neck and pulled the strap out with one hand as far as it would go. She threw it out at arm's length toward the scrub, but it fell short of its destination. She tried several more times, but it simply wasn't long enough to reach.

Now what?" She felt deflated with no more strength left.

Stormy was startled by a loud thud off to her right, accompanied by a small rock which stung the side of her cheek. Jerking her head toward the sound, she was astonished to find a thickly twisted hemp rope lying beside her on the ground. She quickly looked up the slope, expecting to see her rescuer, but was puzzled. No one was in sight.

"Hello," she managed to call out, her voice weakened by fatigue. "Who's up there?"

There was no response to her words, no one stepping up to take credit for her rescue.

"Okay, that's weird," Stormy muttered. Grateful for any help, she grabbed the rope. The sound of a train whistle filled the air. *"Oh no, that must be our train warning whistle. I'll never make it in time."*

Giving the thick rope a tug, she found it to be anchored. She grabbed onto the hemp with both hands, slowly crawling upward. She made it to flat land and nestled herself in amongst the bushes. She sat there for a time as great relief washed over her, thankful for being alive.

Unsure of how long she'd sat there, she realized that her name was being called out repeatedly. Joy flooded her heart as she recognized the voices of Lance and Ann coming from the bushes beyond. They were taking turns calling her name.

"I'm over here," she called back, her voice catching on the last word.

"Stormy, where are you?" Lance barreled his way through the brush, Ann right behind him, holding Stormy's walking stick.

"Watch your step," Stormy cautioned.

"Aunt Stormy!" Ann cried out as she looked down at where her aunt sat in the foliage.

"Stormy, I'm so glad we finally found you," Lance uttered, relief filling his voice. "We've been looking all over the area." Noticing the rope in her hands and the scratches on her arms, his face filled with deeper concern. "Isn't it a little cold to be out mountain climbing?" he asked, one eyebrow rising upward.

"Well, you know me, always up for an adventure." Stormy chuckled as her husband reached down to help her up.

Stormy rose to her feet, every muscle in her body screaming out with pain.

Pulling her tightly against him, Lance supported her weight as he asked her what had happened.

"Get me away from this cliff and I'll tell you," she said, hands shaking as she dropped the rope. "I guess we missed our train. Sorry about that."

"Don't worry," Lance assured her, as he attempted to warm her body against his. "There'll be another one. What matters is that you're safe."

"Hopefully they won't mind if we're up here a bit longer than planned," Stormy voiced.

"Don't worry about that right now, Aunt Stormy. Where'd you find that rope? Was it just hanging from a tree?" Ann asked, handing Stormy the walking stick as she took her aunt's other arm.

"Someone threw it down to me a few minutes ago." Stormy was aware of how much her arms and legs felt like wet noodles as they stood there. "But wait a minute." She withdrew the digital camera from her pocket and turning around, snapped a few pictures of the slope below. "Okay, now we can go."

A bewildered Lance glanced over to Ann and back again but held his tongue. He knew Stormy would fill him in as soon as she was ready.

The three of them made it back up the path and were making their way to the stone chair when Chris came into sight.

"There you all are. I'm afraid we missed our train, but we'll catch the next one," Chris assured them. "Did you save me that doughnut? I'm starved."

The trio broke out in laughter.

"What did I say that was so funny?" Chris asked, puzzled by their reaction. Only then did he become aware of the scrapes and mud on Stormy's hands and clothing, and the fact that Lance and Ann were supporting her. His expression immediately turned to one of concern. "What happened to you? Do you need medical help?"

"No, I'll be okay. I'll tell you after I rest a bit," Stormy answered. An involuntary shutter ran down her body at the thought of reliving the ordeal in the telling of it.

After some hot chocolate and doughnuts, they boarded the next train. Lance helped Stormy to a seat, with Chris and Ann sitting across from them.

As the others listened intently, Stormy quietly related what had happened to her. She told them of the shaking bush, the snake sounds, and her subsequent fall. She explained how she'd lost her cell phone and of the strange man who'd looked down at her, then walked away, never to be seen by her again.

"Did you see such a man, hat pulled low?" Stormy looked around, hoping to spot him amongst the passengers. "He may have come up on the same train as us." Even though there were several people crowded into the coach waiting for the train to begin its decent down the mountain side, she did not spot her rescuer.

"No, I didn't see anyone fitting that description around the area," Chris answered, his eyes sweeping the crowded car. Neither of the other two had seen him either. Chris pulled out his recorder from an inside coat pocket. "Don't forget that there's a road, a rather steep one that you can drive up here on. He may have come by car and not on the train."

"Please, Chris, don't report this in the news," Stormy pleaded. "I was just being careless, and I'd be so embarrassed if you did."

"Okay, I promise I won't. I wouldn't want to embarrass a great person like you." He replaced the recorder back into his coat pocket.

"I wonder who would throw you down a rope and just walk away, leaving you there to fend for yourself," Lance demanded, a trace of anger filling his voice. He had to admit he was grateful to whoever it was but upset that they would then turn their back and not offer further assistance.

"I don't know, but all I can think of is that they didn't want me to see who they were," Stormy surmised. She shifted in her seat to find a more comfortable position.

"Maybe they didn't want any of the credit for helping to rescue you," Ann suggested, shrugging her shoulders. "Do you think maybe it was that same man you saw up at the top of the slope before?"

"That's exactly what I was wondering, Ann. I just wish I could find him and thank him for his help. I don't think I could have hung there much longer." Stormy shivered, but not from the cold.

"I'm just glad you will be accompanying us down the mountain by train and not by freefalling," Lance said, drawing her closer to him. "I'm so glad

I didn't lose you, Storm." He gave her another big hug, accompanied by a kiss on her forehead.

Fourteen

"Let's go back to the hotel and grab a bite to eat," Lance began, a grave look showing on his face, "and then I think you'd better take a hot bath and lie down for a while."

"I think you're right," Stormy agreed. "Sorry guys, I guess we'll have to forgo the lunch plans." She pulled her coat more tightly about her, brushing off a few remaining leaves left over from her ordeal on the peak. "Maybe we'll catch up to you later."

"Go rest, Aunt Stormy." Ann gave her a worried look, then shared a brief glance with Chris.

"Maybe you'd better have a talk with that detective about what's been happening," Chris suggested. "It sounds like someone either means to scare you, hurt you, or even get rid of you."

"I'll think about it, Chris, but for now I'll be just fine back at the hotel with Lance." Holding onto Lance's arm, she made her way to their vehicle.

As they entered traffic, Stormy brought up the subject of her lost cell phone. "After lunch and a short rest, how about we go to the cell phone store and see about getting me a replacement?"

"I guess we could do that; if you feel well enough, that is." Lance glanced over at his wife, then back to the road ahead of him. "It'll be interesting to see if it's covered under our phone insurance plan." He chuckled at the thought of how they were going to explain how the phone had gone missing.

"I think I'd better fudge on the incident just a bit," Stormy suggested, "or it's going to sound a bit far-fetched to them." She leaned back in her seat and rested her eyes as they traveled.

"Or call the police in," Lance told her. He let up on the gas as he approached a slower moving vehicle and signaled to change lanes. "Maybe Chris is right, Storm. Maybe we should visit the police and tell them all that's been happening." He glanced over at her again and she saw the concern in his eyes.

"Maybe," Stormy held her breath, then slowly let it out. "But I think I'd like to wait just a little longer, until we can sort this out and have something more concrete to tell them."

"Okay," Lance conceded. "But if anything else happens it's off to the station we go," he stated firmly.

"Alright," Stormy reluctantly agreed, knowing she'd rather figure this out for herself.

After a quick lunch and a few hours' rest, Stormy was anxious to get to the phone store and get her cell replaced. Seeing that she was doing better, Lance agreed to drive her there. He wasn't about to let her out of his sight so soon after what had happened that morning.

Once in the store, Stormy, with a few words thrown in from Lance, explained to the short, brown-haired saleswoman that her phone had slipped from her hand and fallen down the mountain on their visit that morning to Pikes Peak. She didn't expound on how and why it had happened but inquired as to if it was covered under the insurance plan they'd purchased when they'd originally bought her phone.

"Yes," the amused clerk answered, after looking up the Winters' account. "It's covered in the event of being lost or stolen, no matter what the cause. Though I must admit, this is the first time I've heard of anyone losing it off of the Peak."

"When Stormy does something," Lance chimed in, "she does it in a big way." He laughed as Stormy let out a small sigh, retrieving her purse from off the counter before them.

"Come over here and we'll see what we can find." The woman led the way to a group of cell phones that Stormy recognized as being like the one she'd lost, only newer looking models.

"Now," the woman began, "we will gladly replace your phone with one of these, but I noticed that you are due for an upgrade." She smiled as she turned and led them to a nearby display.

"These are excellent phones. I have one myself and just love it." The woman picked up one of the models and handed it to Stormy. "Take a look at this one."

"It's a good time for you to step into the future, my dear," Lance told her. He reached past Stormy and picked up one of the phones. "As you know, I really love mine." He ran his finger across the top of the one he held as Stormy watched one screen slide into another.

"It's easier to search the internet, check your e-mail, and even read a book or play a whole slew of games while waiting to be called at the doctor's office."

The woman showed Stormy how to work some of the features on the phone, then handed it over to try for herself.

Stormy clicked on several of the icons.

"You'll get used to it in no time. Give it a chance." He withdrew his own phone to demonstrate how easy it was for him to use.

"Well," Stormy hesitated, looking around the store at the various other models around them. She handed the phone back to the saleswoman. "Okay. I'll take it. Do you have it in blue?"

"No, but we have many different covers so you can personalize it," explained the woman, tucking a strand of hair behind her ear. She walked them over to the accessory aisle. "You can have a color for almost every day of the week, depending on how you feel that day."

"Okay," Stormy chuckled. "I'll get the blue cover for now."

"Great, I think you'll love it. I'll be right back, and we'll get it all set up for you." The woman headed for the back of the store and disappeared through a door.

Lance led the way to the sales counter. "They have a two-week trial period in case you want to exchange it."

"Good," Stormy said as they reached the counter, wondering if she'd made the right choice. *Well, I do like adventure,* she reminded herself.

After the cell phone store, Stormy suggested that they go and see the bank manager.

"I think I had better go with you," Lance remarked, starting up the SUV's engine. "Just in case you need some help, or maybe as a guard or something. I am not going to let you out of my sight all day, unless it's to go to the bathroom." Lance smiled over at his wife, but she knew he was serious. He would stick with her like glue.

"Okay, Lance," Stormy agreed, fastening her seatbelt. "It will be good to have your company. I hope the bank manager is well enough to see us when we get there. They said he'd gone home when I called the hospital. When I phoned the bank to ask about this, they said he would be in for a few hours this afternoon to catch up on some paperwork."

"So why is it that you want to see him?" Lance sat there, his eyes holding Stormy's with a look of curiosity. "It's not just to see how he's feeling, is it?"

"Well, I would like to find that out, but, no, it's not just that." Stormy expression became more serious as she told Lance what she suspected. "I have been thinking about what I saw while I was hiding behind that sign during the bank robbery and things just don't add up."

"In what way do you mean?" Lance shut off the engine and sat back in his seat, eager to hear what was bothering Stormy about the events of the robbery.

"When the bank manager, Mr. West, came out of that office door and approached the gunman like he did, it was as if he was certain the gunman would do what he was asking of him," Stormy explained. "It was as if he knew the gunman, as if the bank manager had talked with him before and this was all just an act of some kind."

"Well, that sheds a different light on things, doesn't it?" Lance placed his hands on the steering wheel as he thought this over. "So, this is why you want to go and see him this afternoon?"

"Yes, and the fact that when I accompanied Chris and Ann to see him in the hospital, he seemed nervous, as if he was holding something back. He claimed that the reason he couldn't call the police when he realized that the bank was being robbed was that his phone was not working. And then when Chris asked him about the alarm buttons near the tellers not working, he claimed he did not know why that happened."

"Don't you think that the gunman might have had something to do with that?" Lance asked, shifting in his seat, the leather complaining as he did so.

"Yes, he may have been able to disarm them, but from what I saw of him that day, I don't really think he was capable of it. I think he may have had an accomplice take care of that."

"Maybe so."

"Then there was that speeding car I mentioned," Stormy continued. She stopped to take a sip from the water bottle she held. "After all, that car was coming from behind the bank as I was walking toward it. That woman seemed to want to tell me something."

"I see what you are getting at," Lance said. "Maybe she knew the robbery was taking place and wanted to warn you about it."

"Or get help to stop it?" Stormy replaced the cap back on the bottle and set it in one of the two cup holders between the seats.

"And she may have been in trouble and was trying in some way to get your attention without it being too obvious to her companion," Lance suggested.

"Maybe so," Stormy replied. "I just wish we knew for sure. It seems to me that it was more than just a simple robbery."

"Let's go see if we can get some answers," Lance remarked. He turned on the vehicle and put it in reverse.

Fifteen

Leaving the SUV parked at their hotel parking lot, Lance and Stormy walked the short distance to the bank.

When they arrived, Stormy approached the secretary and asked to see the manager. Stormy gave her their names and said that she thought she might know something concerning what had happened the day of the robbery.

The secretary told them to wait while she checked to see if the manager was available. She returned shortly and said that he would see them now, then ushered them to the door and announced them. Mr. West rose as they entered the room. Looking pale and nervous, his arm in a sling and a bandage on his forehead, he greeted the Winters and gestured toward two sturdy leather chairs. They each took a seat as Mr. West sat down behind his desk.

"My secretary, Miss Jenkins, told me that you might know something concerning the day of the robbery." He paused, looking more closely at Stormy. "Oh, I remember you. You were with the news team when they interviewed me at the hospital weren't you?"

"Yes, Mr. West, I was," Stormy replied, setting her purse beside her on the plush carpeting. "And how are you feeling today? I was really surprised to learn that you'd already been released."

"I insisted upon it. I felt that I must get back to the bank and make sure that everything was running smoothly . . . at least as smoothly as is possible after a bank robbery." He sighed and rested his bandaged arm on his desktop. "My tellers are really nervous now and I'm hoping my presence will make them feel better." He absent-mindedly tapped a pencil on the desk with his good hand before glancing over at his computer and quickly pressed a button to close the screen and the contents on it.

Stormy couldn't help but wonder if he had something to hide or was it just bank policy when a customer was in his office. Probably the later, she decided.

"My housekeeper was really upset with me about leaving the house so soon, but no one can run this bank as well as I can!"

As Mr. West continued, Stormy scanned the pictures behind his desk. She was startled to find that one of the pictures looked a lot like a photo of the woman she'd seen in the car that had sped away from the bank while the robbery was taking place.

"Oh, that's a beautiful woman you're standing with. Is she your wife?"

He glanced behind him, then replied, "Yes, that's her."

"I see she's a golfer," Stormy surmised, studying the photo. "Where does she play? My husband and I love to golf, but we don't know which are the best courses here in the Springs." Stormy gave Lance a quick look before returning to the manager. This wasn't quite the truth, but she felt a little fudging was needed in this situation.

"She plays at the Country Club. They have a new golf pro there, and she says he's an excellent instructor." He shuffled a few papers around on his desk. "I'm sorry, but I have a lot of work to do so I must cut this interview short. What did you have to tell me?"

"When I was approaching the bank the day of the robbery, I noticed a car speeding out of the alleyway from behind the bank. The car was really careening around the corner and as the vehicle passed me, I saw a man and a woman in the back seat. The woman looked very frightened," Stormy told him, closely watching his expression. "Little did I know that a bank robbery was taking place at that very moment. I was shocked when I realized what was happening as I stepped into the bank."

"Thank you for coming in." Mr. West abruptly stood, walked to his office door, and opened it. "I will check it out right away. My secretary will get in touch if we find out anything."

"Okay," Stormy agreed, bewildered by his behavior. Looking to Lance, she could see he felt the same way. She noticed his hands were slightly shaking as Mr. West shut the door behind them.

"Now that was strange," Stormy whispered to Lance as they walked back down the hallway.

"Yes, that definitely was," Lance agreed, steering them in the direction of the outside doors.

Stormy and Lance further discussed the conversation and what they should do as they walked down the sidewalk, careful to watch where they stepped on its icy surface. They decided that a visit to the golf course would be a good idea. They wanted to talk to the new golf pro and see what he could tell them about Mrs. West.

Just then, Stormy's cell phone rang. She retrieved it from her purse and ran a finger down its screen. She was proud of the way she was getting the hang of this new device.

"Hello, this is Stormy," she said into the phone. Holding onto Lance's arm they continued to walk, skirting around a pile of slush on the sidewalk.

"Oh, hi, Chris, how are you doing?" Stormy asked the caller.

"I'm doing okay, Stormy. Are you feeling better?" Chris inquired.

"Much better, thank you," Stormy replied.

"That's good. I was following up on a lead for a story that we may air later on, and I just came from the guard's home that worked at First Bank. His . . ."

"What do you mean by 'worked,' he doesn't work there anymore?" she asked, slowing her steps, Lance matching pace beside her.

"Yes and no. It seems that the bank manager got upset with him for being sick the day of the robbery and insisted that he take a two-week vacation without pay, effective immediately," Chris answered.

"Chris, let me put you on speaker so Lance can hear, too." She handed Lance her phone as they momentarily paused on the sidewalk. "Would you turn the speaker on, dear? I haven't figured that one out yet."

"No problem," Lance said, taking her phone in hand and skillfully running his finger across the screen before pressing several icons. "There you go. Can you hear us, Chris?"

"Hi, Lance. Sure can," Chris responded.

"Wow, that doesn't sound good about the guard." Stormy picked up the conversation where they'd left off. "Can he do that, I mean without pay and all?"

"I guess so, and he also told the man that it was due to his shoddy performance. His wife tells me he is just crushed over it, as he has always been a very conscientious employee. He has worked for the bank for over a year now and has only taken one other sick day when a bad flu swept through the area."

"Where was the guard when you talked with his wife?" Stormy asked as she followed Lance across the hotel's parking lot.

"He was at the store picking up some groceries," Chris told her. "And listen to this, his wife says that their doctor thinks her husband may have had food poisoning."

"Do they know what from?" Stormy climbed into the front seat of their Santa Fe and Lance shut the door. He walked around to the other side of the vehicle, slipping in behind the wheel as the conversation continued.

"They believe it may have been from a tuna sandwich he had for lunch. His wife claims they rarely ever go out to eat and that she packs her husband a fresh lunch each morning for him to take to the bank. She said he assured her he put the sack in the fridge in the break room just after he clocked in, as he always does. He was a little late getting his lunch break that day, and claims he's never had any trouble with the food going bad before. By late afternoon he started feeling sick and was very ill by evening time."

"Hmmm. So, anyone could go into the fridge, at any time, and get whatever they want to?" Stormy asked. "In other words, is it kept locked, or is it used by everyone at the bank?" Lance steered the vehicle out of the parking space, listening intently to the ongoing conversation.

"It's used by all of the employees there at the bank, it seems."

"Interesting, so anyone could have tampered with it," Stormy concluded.

"Yes, I wondered about that as well," Chris said. "And how convenient that he just happened to have food poisoning on that day."

"Yes, indeed." Stormy mulled over this new information for a moment before continuing. "Chris, do you know anything about the Country Club golf course here in the Springs?"

"As a matter of fact, I do. Why, are you going golfing right now? Wasn't the episode on the Peak enough exercise for one day?" He obviously meant it as a joke, but Stormy could hear it was laced with concern.

"Well, it's more like a fishing expedition, you might say," Stormy said, laughing into the phone. "We're not going to do any golfing. The bank's manager, Mr. Peters, said his wife was taking lessons from the new pro there at the Country Club's course. I happened to see her picture on his office wall when we talked to him a while ago, and she looked a lot like the woman I saw through the window of the speeding car outside of the bank the day of the robbery."

"You were in the bank manager's office today? You mean he's not recovering at home where he belongs?" Chris asked, surprise filling in his voice. "I heard he'd been released from the hospital this morning. I guess I'd just assumed her went on home."

Stormy filled him in on the interview she and Lance had done and what they had learned from the manager.

"He definitely was very nervous and seemed to be hiding something," she said.

"Actually, I'm not too far from the Country Club right now. Why don't I meet you there in about fifteen minutes? The man at the front desk is a friend of mine and he can get us a table there and tell us about this new pro," Chris suggested.

"That sounds great," she said, excitedly. "What about it, Lance?"

"We'll be there," Lance assured him as he steered the vehicle through some road construction.

"Okay, see you in a few."

Stormy touched the screen, disconnecting the call, and placed it back into her purse.

"Let's go see what we can find out," Lance said, changing lanes and turning at the corner.

A few minutes later, they were pulling into the Country Club's parking lot.

Sixteen

"Hey, man, how have you been?" A tall, dark-skinned man, his head close-shaved, came over to greet the trio as they entered the clubhouse, often referred to as the '19th hole.' His tan slacks and a light blue polo shirt fit his toned body well. His face lit into a smile as he held out his hand to Chris. "Here to play a little golf?"

"Hey, Brian, I was thinking about it. Maybe this weekend," Chris responded, clasping the man's hand and giving it a firm shake. "These are two of my friends from Phoenix visiting their niece here." Chris gestured toward Lance and Stormy, introducing them in turn. "You wouldn't have a few minutes to sit down and discuss some things with us, would you?"

"Sure." Brian looked around the room, then pointed toward a table by a window overlooking the golf course. "Let's sit over there. There's a great view of the 19th hole." He turned and led the way.

Brian pulled out a chair for Stormy. She thanked him as she took the proffered seat. Lance sat down in the chair next to her and the other two men sat across the table.

"Would you like something to drink?" Brian offered. "It's on the house. And no arguments, Chris." He held up a hand, palm forward. "You've helped me out more than one time before." Brian gave Chris a look that told him he'd better not refuse the offer.

"Sure, I'd love one, man," Chris answered, smiling. "Make mine a lemon-lime with a couple of cherries on the side."

"And how about you two? What can I get for you?" Brian waved over the waitress at the bar.

"I'd like a root beer, if you have it, please," Stormy said, leaning her walking stick against the window and hanging her purse on her chair's back.

"I'll take the same, thanks." Lance removed his coat and hung it on the back of his chair.

"How about a root beer float? Fred makes a mean one. You'll love it." "Sounds delicious," Stormy agreed.

"I won't turn that down," Lance put in, grinning at Stormy.

"Great!" Brian placed the orders, adding a cola for himself. "And I think we should add a couple of orders of Kristy's award-winning cheese rolls with that," Brian told the waitress. "She makes the best in town, probably in all of Colorado. Right, Melva?"

"Sure thing, Mr. Sutherland," the waitress agreed. She headed to the kitchen beyond the bar to place the orders.

"So, what can I do for you?" Brian asked, looking over at the newsman.

"We've heard that you have a new pro out here," Chris began, gesturing out the window toward the course outside. "How long has he been working for you?"

"Yes, you must mean Aleksandre. He's been with us for the past couple of months," Brian answered. "I hear he's pretty good. He has a number of the women here signed up with him for lessons. Not that most of them really need the lessons, but he's one of those cool characters with a foreign accent, the kind women love." Brian laughed. "Maybe I should start talking with one of those British accents. You know, 'cheerio and all that sort of thin'.'"

"It might improve your dating record," Chris teased, his face taking on a mischievous look.

The group broke out laughing as the waitress headed in the direction of their table carrying a large tray.

"Here you go," Melva said. "Careful, the rolls are right out of the oven and are still quite hot. I brought you some butter, but you may want to try them first without it." She set down a steaming plate of cheese rolls in the middle of the table, along with a bowl of little packets of butter. She passed out their beverage glasses before setting a small plate in front of each of them. She placed a couple of butter knives beside the plate of rolls. "Enjoy," she said, smiling as she turned to leave.

"Thanks, Melva," Brian said. The others chimed in their thanks as well.

"So, why are you interested in Alek, as we call him?" Brian took a sip from his cola before reaching for a roll. "Are you thinking of lessons?" He looked around the group, awaiting a response.

"We were wondering where he's from," Chris responded, reaching for a cheese roll.

"And what you might know about him?" Stormy asked. She placed a roll on the plate in front of her as Lance passed her a pad of butter.

"Well, I know he's been in this country for about a year," Brian explained after wiping at his mouth with a napkin. "Alek came here from a small city in upper-state New York, but I believe he said he originally hails from Russia, no maybe it was Georgia. One of those countries over there, anyways. Is there some problem concerning him that I should be aware of?" He turned his attention to Chris, questioning him with a raise of his eyebrows.

Chris swallowed the bite of roll he was chewing on before answering. "I've just been following up on a story I'm working on and one of the men said his wife took lessons from the new pro here."

"What's her name, if you don't mind me asking?" Brian inquired.

"A Mrs. West," Chris answered. He took a swig from the glass in front of him, then reached for another cheese roll. "You're right, these are very good."

"I told you, man." Brian looked pleased. "They're the best in the state. We're fortunate to have Kristy working for us." Brian smiled as he continued, "Yes, I know Mrs. West. She's been golfing here at the club for some time now, but like several of the others, she took one look at Alek and immediately signed up for lessons with him." Brian chuckled, half to himself.

"Didn't that worry her husband?" Lance chimed in.

"I don't really know. Mr. West used to come play more often with his wife, but like many of the husbands here," Brian remarked with a slight downturn of his mouth, "he seems to have gotten rather busy of late, so the wives come without them. Though I have noticed that the men get together now and then on weekends without their wives to play."

"So, this Alek kind of takes over as the wives' partner, so to speak," Stormy suggested, setting down her glass.

"Yes, you might say that," Brian answered, raising his eyebrows again. "Lives of the rich . . . and the bored." He grimaced, then added, "But I guess that's one of the things that keeps us going here. Thank goodness though, that we have many other types of golfers that make up our club here as well."

"How often does Mrs. West take lessons from Alek?" Stormy asked, looking out the window at a young woman lining up a shot on the nearest green, as two other women stood quietly behind her.

"Oh, I'd say twice a week." he replied, following Stormy's gaze out the window as the golfer on the green skillfully placed her ball into the hole as her friends' cheered.

"Can we talk to Alek?" Chris asked, leaning forward in his seat.

"I'm afraid he's not here today," Brian answered. "He called in for a personal day but should be back tomorrow. You might swing by in the late afternoon, after his lessons are through."

"Okay, will do." Chris rose from his chair. "If you'll all excuse me, I've got to get back to work. Got to pay the bills, you know."

"We'd better be on our way, too," Lance said, scooting his chair backward and standing up.

"Yes, we'd better. I've got an outing with my niece, Ann, to visit Miramont Castle this afternoon." Stormy stood up, then pushed her chair in. "Thank you for the rolls and drinks, Brian. It was nice talking with you."

"Thank you all for coming. Have fun at the Castle. You'll love it there but watch out for spooks." Brian grinned, his straight white teeth showing. He accompanied them to the club's outer door. "Hey, wait up a minute." Reaching behind the bar's counter, he brought forth a small stack of cards. "Here's a free pass for each of you to look the course over and get in a little golfing, if you have the time." He passed them each a cream-colored card. "It's been a pleasure meeting you, Mr. and Mrs. Winters. I hope I'll see you both again. And see you soon, Chris." He shook each of their hands as they left the club.

"You know, if we hadn't seen those people playing golf in the snow up in Montana," Stormy remarked, "I'd think these players were nuts." She turned to watch the distant figure of a man swing his golf club, sending the ball flying down the fairway.

"You just need to dress a bit warmer, is all," Chris quipped.

"I guess so," Stormy agreed.

"Interesting about Mrs. West and the golf pro," Lance mused as he guided Stormy around a large puddle of melted snow on the asphalt. "Not really needing any lessons but taking them anyway shows how charming and persuasive some people can be." The three continued their discussion as they headed in the direction of their parked cars in the club's lot.

"It certainly does," Stormy concurred as they approached their car. "Interesting that he's originally from the area of Russia, or possibly Georgia." The three stood beside the couple's SUV. "It seems we keep running into people lately from that area of the world, or who have visited there in the not-so-distant past." She thought of what the two sisters had told her about their trip to the area with their husbands.

"I find it interesting that he called in for personal days now, around the time of the robbery," Chris remarked, leaning back against his car, arms folded across his chest.

"Yes, now that you mention it, I do, too." Stormy wondered if it was just a coincidence. Was there a connection between the golf pro and the robbery? And what about the strange way the man acted at the import store? Were the two sisters possibly involved in this? After all, she'd only met them on the tour in Austin and hadn't spoken to them again until just yesterday. She hoped this was not the case. She liked the two women.

"Well, I'd better be getting back to work. I'll catch you guys later," Chris said, glancing at his watch. He hurried around his vehicle to the driver's side.

"Okay, nice seeing you again, Chris," Stormy called out. "Thanks for your help."

"See you later," Lance added, holding the car door for Stormy.

With a quick wave in their direction, Chris started his car and headed out of the lot and out onto the street.

Lance got behind the driver's wheel and buckled his seat belt.

"Wish you were coming to Miramont with us," Stormy commented as they entered the street. She pulled back her sleeve and glanced at her watch. "Ann will be picking me up in about fifteen minutes. You'll miss a lot of fun."

"I really wish I could, but I must complete those designs by tonight," Lance replied, pressing down on the gas petal as he merged with traffic.

"Take a lot of pictures so I can at least enjoy it through your eyes." "I'll do that." Stormy reached over to rub Lance's shoulder.

Seventeen

"Ann, where did you go?" Stormy called out, turning away from the register book and glancing about the small reception area. Ann had been standing right behind her when she'd leaned over to sign the guest register of the historic Miramont Castle. She unzipped the jacket she'd thrown over her red and green-striped blouse and dark pants. The room was quite warm, the thick walls sheltering its occupants from the cold winds outside.

They'd both been enthusiastically discussing the decor surrounding them: the chocolate-colored stone walls; an old gramophone resting in the corner; the carpet—a deep shade of burgundy with flowers of pink and white woven in, but giving the appearance of having been strewn across it; the arched, stained-glass window in the corner of the stairs, situated to bring light to the otherwise dark steps; and the carpeted stairs themselves—the finely polished steps and railings attesting to the excellent care that was shown them by the Castle's staff.

They'd both agreed that the outside of the historical structure with its cut-stone finish, rounded turrets, and many windows was a spectacular sight to behold, and were sure they would find a wonderland, just waiting for them to discover.

Stormy's eyes came to rest on the set of stairs that led to the upper rooms. "I guess Ann couldn't wait to see what's up there." Stormy chuckled. It was just how Ann was as a child-always dashing ahead of everyone to get there first.

The young woman manning the front desk had been called away to an area on the lower level which she'd mentioned held a large collection of dollhouses, leaving Stormy alone. There was no one else in the room and the air held an almost eerie atmosphere, sending a shiver down the length of Stormy's spine.

"I'd better catch up to Ann," Stormy murmured as she ascended the stairway to the second floor. She found the steps easy to ascend so she carried her walking stick in her hand, her purse pressed close to her body.

Halfway up the staircase, Stormy met a young couple holding hands as they descended from the floor above. The man wore a pair of tan slacks and a light-colored polo shirt, with a navy-blue cardigan tied loosely about his neck. The woman sported a black pantsuit and attractive black boots. Several gold chains hung around her neck, a silver-colored sweater draped over one arm.

"Hello," Stormy greeted them as she traversed the steps. The man acknowledged her with a slight nod, the woman continuing to gaze lovingly up at the young man, unaware of the greeting. Stormy smiled and continued upward.

Arriving at the top, she looked around. Which way had Ann gone? Stormy decided she would continue straight ahead, looking in the various doors along the way.

After checking through a few of the ornately decorated, old-fashioned rooms that led off the hallway, she decided that her niece must have doubled back and headed down in search of her.

As Stormy turned back in the direction of the staircase, she came to a standstill, listening intently. What was it she'd heard? A low moaning sounded again faintly from somewhere up ahead of her.

Slowly edging closer to the next doorway that opened off the hall, she held her walking stick at the ready. Abruptly, a figure sprang from the doorway yelling out "boo", a scary expression playing across its face. Stormy gasped, raising her stick high, ready to swing. The realization that the figure was her niece sank in and she lowered her stick as her other hand pressed against her chest.

"It's a good thing I wasn't closer to you than I am," Stormy declared, laughing as her racing heart began to slow. "If you'd been, I'm afraid I'd have decked you with my stick." She raised her walking stick and brought it down hard as if hitting an imaginary person.

"Well, I'm glad I wasn't," Ann responded, shifting her blue coat to her other arm and stepping forward to hug her aunt. "I would have had one nasty bump on my head." She laughed along with her aunt. "Sorry, I couldn't resist the temptation. Come and look at these wonderful old rooms with me. They're fantastic and filled with so much history." Dressed in blue jeans and a hunter-green turtleneck sweater, she took her aunt's elbow and led her through the nearest doorway.

The two women made their way from room to room, pointing out objects of interest. They marveled at the Victorian-era furniture in various patterns, fabrics, and colors. They commented on how the colors of the walls changed from one room to the next, some in dark hues of reds, others wall-papered in flowers, stripes, or Swiss-style dots. They took turns reading the strategically placed signs in each one.

The dining room was set as if for the arrival of guests, with fine chinaware, silver place settings, and crystal stemware. Several china cabinets and chests of drawers around the room displayed various pieces.

Upon examining the kitchen, Stormy was surprised at how small it was compared to the rest of the house.

"I wonder how they could work in such a tiny space?" Ann exclaimed. "Our kitchen back home was at least three times this big." She noticed how close the old iron stove was to the sink, piled with pots and pans.

"Yes, it's quite small at that," Stormy agreed, leaning slightly on her stick, before stepping to a nearby sign. "This says that when the priest lived here, the Sisters of Mercy would fix ample amounts of food, then bring baskets of it along the tunnels to the kitchen to be warmed up as needed. I guess there must have been an entrance that has since been boarded up." She scanned the floorboards around here.

"I guess so. I don't see evidence of it anywhere though." Ann surveyed the room, before proceeding on to the next.

"Definitely a wealthy family to have had all these luxurious items," Stormy exclaimed, examining an ornate vase on a low wooden table before her.

"It seems that this Jean Baptiste Francolon, a Catholic priest from France," Ann read from the sign in front of her, "was sent here to Manitou due to a stomach ailment around 1892. It was thought that the mineral waters here would help him. He first built a framed structure to reside in, then later had this castle built for him exactly to his specifications." Ann looked up at her Aunt, who was studying a photo on a nearby wall. "It does say he came from a wealthy family. His father was a diplomat, and he built this place for his mother to come here and live with him. Eventually, he gave his first home to the Sisters of Mercy for a sanitarium."

Stormy stepped over beside Ann and perused the sign as her niece continued to read, "The priest played the piano and loved music. I guess that accounts for there being gramophones and pianos throughout the castle."

"Yes, probably so." Stormy headed over to study a Victorian-style dress, admiring its rich brown fabric and the many, beige-colored flowers imprinted down its length as it hung on the upright mannequin. "I wouldn't mind wearing a dress like this, though I don't have the trim figure the woman who wore this must have had."

Ann turned to look at the dress her aunt was appraising. "Yes, that is a nice piece. I think it would look rather dashing on you. And I think you look good just the way you are." She smiled at her aunt before turning back to the placard before her.

"Thanks, dear. It's also interesting to note that the Sisters of Mercy were eventually allowed to take over the castle to operate their sanitarium, then later this place became a retreat. After the war, it was turned into family apartments until the historical society took it over."

"What a history this place has," Ann declared, joining her aunt in a more plainly furnished bedroom.

"This is what they believe the priest's bedroom looked like at the time he resided here," Stormy commented. "He preferred a simpler taste for his quarters; it seems in keeping with his order of the times." She walked to a nearby window and studied the scene beyond.

"This is a wonderful old castle and they've really done a great job of restoring and keeping it in marvelous shape, haven't they?" Stormy continued, looking around her. "I really like the way they made sure that most of the rooms had a lot of space in them when they built the place. I would've loved living in a place like this when I was growing up."

"Yes, me too, but I would not have loved keeping all of this clean," Ann emphasized, gesturing around her. "Can you imagine what it would have entailed? You wouldn't have time to do anything but clean!"

"I imagine that is why they had servants back then to do most of the chores that needed to be done. I know it's been a big help when we've occasionally hired in help to assist us around our home back in Phoenix."

"I'd like that," Ann said, walking behind her aunt and out into the hallway, "but they would frown upon it in the quarters. At the Academy we have to do all of our own cleaning and then have it inspected to make sure we've done it right. Though I will have to say that it has been good for all of us in many ways."

"Yes, I remember the inspections we had to go through when Lance was in the Army." Stormy halted before another plaque not far from a window at the end of the hallway and began to study it. "Interesting," she mumbled.

"What is?" Ann asked, coming to stand beside her.

"It says here that a young "half-breed" man met his death at this very window. And that his spirit has been seen roaming this hallway by many guests and staff members since." The hair on the back of Stormy's neck became electrified as she unexpectedly felt the presence of someone behind her. Spinning around, she scanned the room for signs of life. The distinct creaking of a floorboard from across the hall reached her ears. "Come on," she whispered to her niece, a finger pressed to her lips, as she sprang into action.

Reaching the doorway, she dashed through it and into the room beyond, a puzzled Ann close behind. A quick search of the room revealed that they were alone.

"What's going on?" Ann quietly asked, looking side to side, then back to her aunt.

"I'm sure I heard someone's footfalls from this room," Stormy quietly explained to her bewildered niece. "It felt like someone was watching us from this doorway."

"I would think it was your imagination from reading about that young man," Ann suggested, keeping her voice low, "but I know you have the gift of seeing spirits, so maybe it was his ghost walking around in here. After all, we were talking about him."

"It could have been, but this felt like it was a real person spying on us, not someone's spirit." Stormy checked the next room, but found it empty as well. "Okay, must have been my imagination, I guess. I'm getting hungry. How about a piece a pie in that dining room we heard all about? My treat."

"Sounds good to me," Ann agreed. "Lead the way."

After a generous helping of fresh apple pie á la mode, Stormy and Ann continued their tour of the castle.

A sign pointing the way to a gift shop on the next level, led to a steep flight of stairs. Ann led the way, with Stormy close behind.

"Welcome to the gift shop, ladies," a kindly older woman, attired in a long grey skirt and starched white blouse, greeted them as they reached the top of the stairs. "Look around at all the wonderful things and if you have any questions, feel free to ask me." She set aside the book she'd been reading, giving them a warm smile.

"Thank you, we will," Stormy replied as she studied the inventory. "Look at all of the marvelous items they have up here, Ann. Come and look at these dolls attired in various dresses from that period."

"Maybe we can find you something to take back with you to Phoenix."

"Be sure and continue back through that doorway when you've seen all that we have in this room," the older woman called. "We have many other fascinating things back in there. You might be interested in knowing that this used to be where the servants lived when they were not downstairs attending to chores or laboring outside."

The woman stepped from behind the counter, headed their way, and continued past them to a small doorway. "You'll see that their rooms were so small that they barely had the space to turn around in. It is thought that this was due to the small amount of time that the servants spent up here. It was mainly just a place for sleeping," the woman added.

"Wow, these rooms are very tiny," Ann called to her aunt, standing before one of the rooms. "I would hate to live up here."

Stormy agreed as she joined her niece in looking over the quarters.

"Yes, these would barely hold a small bed for the servants to lie down on. I guess they didn't really have as many belongings to worry about then as we do today. Maybe we as a society should take a hint from them," Stormy turned away from the room and walked down the small hall to see what else was on display.

"Yes, being in the Academy can help with that," Ann remarked, arriving at the far end of the servant's hallway. "Hey, Aunt Stormy, look at this small replica of the castle." Ann pointed out a small porcelain piece that was an exact duplicate of Miramont Castle. "What do you think of this?"

"I like it." Stormy looked it over and noticed the price on the tag that hung from one of its towers. "Yes, I think this is just the right thing. Sold." She and Ann broke out laughing as they turned to head back into the room where the older woman waited. "Can I get you a little something, Ann?"

"I would love to have something from here, but since I will soon be heading out for my assignment, I'd better not accumulate anything else for now." She stood beside a rack containing postcards of the castle and surrounding area.

"How about if I split a book of these cards with you?" Stormy offered, reaching over to remove a packet from the stand. "They're easy to pack with you and then we would both have something to remember this time we've had together here."

"Thank you, that would be great." Ann smiled at the thought. "Too bad Uncle Lance couldn't have come with us."

"Yes, I miss him, too," Stormy replied, "He would have loved to be here with us."

"I would like to buy these items, please," Stormy said, setting the items down. Opening her purse, she removed her wallet, catching it on a silver nail file that tried to come out with it. She showed the file back inside her purse.

"These are wonderful choices to remember your visit to Miramont," the older woman declared as she punched the purchases into her calculator.

Stormy handed over her debit card to the saleswoman. The elderly clerk slid the card through the reader before handing it back. Stormy returned the card to the folds of her wallet and zipped it securely into her purse.

The woman carefully wrapped the castle in several sheets of soft tissue paper and placed the whole thing into a white paper bag. She slipped the packet of postcards in beside the castle and handed the bag to Stormy.

"Thank you and I hope you will visit us again," the woman said, a smile warming her face.

Stormy and Ann headed back down the stairs to the floor below. They turned at the bottom of the stairs and headed back down the hallway, glancing in the doors of the various rooms as they passed by. Upon reaching the next staircase, Ann stopped.

"Would you mind if we took a few minutes and looked around a bit more at these rooms before we go?" Ann inquired of her aunt. "I would like to have another look at that dining area and the rooms beyond. I think my friend, Darlene, would love coming here and I'd like to take a few more photos to show her."

"Sure, I could stay here all day. I'm really enjoying myself," Stormy replied, donning more lip balm, then replacing it back into her purse. "I'd like another look at that bathroom with the old-fashioned bathtub, and maybe a bedroom or two. I'll take a few more pictures to show Lance, but let's not take too long or he'll start worrying that I've gotten myself into trouble again." She laughed at the idea. Lance worried too much.

"Well, we certainly wouldn't want to cause Uncle Lance any anxiety," Ann agreed, smiling at her aunt. "I'll only be a few minutes."

The two women wandered off in separate directions. Stormy meandered throughout the various rooms, taking a few more snapshots. After admiring the old-fashioned bathtub, sink, and oval mirror in a bathroom, she moved on to examine the wooden-framed bed, accented by a plain, but beautifully hand-sewn quilt, in Father Francolon's adjoining bedroom. A hand-carved wooden cross hung prominently on the wall over the headboard.

She found the room to have a simple, but pleasing feel about it. As she stood gazing out of one of the room's windows to the snow-covered trees beyond, she unexpectedly experienced goosebumps run down both of her forearms. This made her pause, wondering at the source of this reaction. Was there someone, or something, in the room with her? Whirling around, she quickly scrutinized the area, finding herself alone.

"What was that all about?" Stormy mumbled, continuing to examine the room as she ran a hand up and down one arm.

Walking to the doorway, she peered out and scanned the hallway. It was void of any signs of life. In re-examining her arms, Stormy found that the bumps had subsided. Turning back to the room, she shrugged and dismissed it, chalking it up to a possible draft often felt in castles and older buildings, or maybe standing too close to the room's window. Lifting her camera, she snapped a few shots before moving on.

As she continued on to another of the castle's bedrooms, once again a feeling came over her that she was not alone. It felt like she was being followed, shadowed in her every move; as if a dark silhouette lurked beyond each door, crouched behind a winged-back chair, or stood observing her from behind a drape. When she walked, it followed, when she stopped, it held still. But no matter how many times Stormy whirled around in an attempt to catch a glimpse of it, nothing was there.

"Am I going crazy?" Stormy muttered, scanning the bedroom a second time. Deciding she'd had enough, she set out to find Ann before heading down to the next level.

She went in the direction of the dining room, fully expecting to find Ann there, examining the china.

No such luck.

Stormy called out as she searched room after room, but to no avail. Ann just wasn't there.

*Oh, not again, Stor*my thought, *I think one scare in an outing is enough.*

Turning around, she retraced her steps, all the while expecting Ann to jump out at her. She went through the kitchen and back into the dining room.

"Okay, Ann, come on," Stormy called. "We really had better be going now. I think you've scared me enough for today, you silly girl. So like your father you are." She laughed out loud as she continued to scour the area.

Stormy was investigating the adjoining room, when she heard a small creaking noise behind her.

Ah, there she is. I'll have some fun with this. She would get her this time.

Stormy stopped and stood still. She would wait just long enough for her niece to get a little bit closer, then she'd quickly turn around and give her a scare of her own. As she stood there a moment longer, and no sound came again, she wondered just how close Ann had actually come. She'd have to hope it was close enough to do the trick.

Stormy spun around on her heels to face her niece. Coming to a halt, ready with a roaring "boo" of her own, the sound caught in her throat. Confusion briefly filled her mind. This was not Ann, but a young man's dark eyes she found herself staring into.

As her mind began to clear, the realization came to her that she'd seen him before. Yes, the young man that she'd seen sweeping the sidewalk in front of the import store, and then again stocking shelves when she and Katie had entered that same store near the sisters' shop. Now he stood before her, a nervous grin playing across his face.

Before Stormy had time to say anything, or react in any way, an arm reached around from behind and grabbed her roughly around the waist, pulling her against a muscular form. A second hand came up from the other side and tightly covered her mouth with a cloth that reeked with the strong scent of ammonia.

The room began to spin, and Stormy became extremely lightheaded. Her knees buckled and as she started to fall toward the floor, great concern passed through her mind for her niece. Where was she? As she was being drawn across the floor, the cloth momentarily slipped from her face and she attempted to call out a warning, but her voice sounded so very far away, as if she had whispered.

The movement stopped and a pair of arms helped cushion her fall, the cloth once again held tightly over her face, as she slid to the hardwood floor beneath. She was aware of her camera hitting the floor and felt her purse slip from her shoulder.

The last thing she saw before she lapsed into oblivion was the young man reaching down beside the iron stove. He lifted a door in the wooden floor, and as he did so, his pant legs hiked up, revealing bright orange socks and dirty tennis shoes.

Eighteen

Lance leaned back in the chair and looked once again at his watch, then down at the cell phone beside his open laptop. Having put the finishing touches on his project's designs, he'd zipped the package together and punched the send button. His hard work had taken flight, streaking across the internet to the inbox of an anxious client.

"What's taking you so long, Stormy?" he said out loud, as if she could hear him. Rising from the chair, he paced the room, barely avoiding a fall over the ottoman in his concern.

He'd expected his wife's return well over two hours ago, but there was no call to tell him she'd be late or the reason for it.

This isn't like her, he thought, as he continued to pace, stopping to check his watch every few steps. If Stormy found that she'd be late, even for a hair appointment, she'd call ahead and let them know. And she always made sure Lance knew, concerned that he might worry needlessly.

Having tried Stormy's cell phone several times, Lance had begun to agonize when she hadn't answered. And to make matters worse, Stormy's phone had rung repeatedly the first time he'd called, but each subsequent time he'd speed-dialed her number, her phone went straight to messaging. Even his attempts to get ahold of Ann had failed. Her cell, too, had gone directly to her messaging.

"Maybe the storm's blocking her reception," Lance mumbled out loud. He trod over to the window and pulled back the heavy drapes. The sun had now fully set, and a light snow had begun to fall. "I'll try her phone one more time."

As he walked over to the desk to retrieve his cell, he was startled by its ringing. A wave of elation and relief flowed over him as he picked it up, but his hopes plummeted as he read the caller ID. The call was not from his wife as he'd hoped but read "Chris Jacobs."

"Hi, Chris," Lance answered, trying to keep the disappointment from his voice, but falling short.

"Hi, Lance," Chris began, "I was wondering if . . ." He paused in mid-sentence. "Is something wrong?"

"Maybe," Lance said, pausing before he continued. "As you know, Stormy and Ann went together to visit Miramont Castle this afternoon," he expounded. "The place closes at four o'clock in the wintertime. I double-checked this on the internet. It's now almost six-thirty and I haven't heard from Stormy. In fact, I can't reach either one of them on their cells." He paused again, before admitting, "I'm worried, Chris."

"Yes, I am, too," Chris said, clearing his throat. "Even more so now. Ann and I had a dinner date for six, but she has yet to show up. I've tried to reach her cell, but it seems to be turned off. I was calling to see if Stormy knew anything, but I guess that's out of the question."

"That's strange," Lance uttered, continuing to pace across the hotel room. "Stormy's cell seems to be off, too." He stopped in front of the sofa. He needed to sit down and think. "Ann didn't happen to mention that she was going to stop any place before coming to dinner, did she?"

"No, I don't think so," Chris answered, after a moment's thought, "but then I haven't talked to her since around noon today. Maybe something came up."

"Maybe, but it still isn't like Stormy not to call me with any change of plans," Lance explained. He absent-mindedly drummed his fingers on the edge of the sofa's arm. "And it's starting to snow. I think I'll go out to the Castle and see if I can track her down. I don't know where else to start."

"Mind if I tag along?" Chris asked.

"I'd like that," Lance affirmed. "Give me your address and I'll pick you up."

Lance quickly jotted down the address and directions. Assuring Chris he was on his way, he grabbed his coat and headed out the door.

* * * *

"It doesn't look like anyone's still here," Chris said, peering through an arched window on the main floor of Miramont Castle. "I guess they've all gone home for the night."

"Yes, it seems locked up pretty tight." Lance paused alongside Chris and studied the small room beyond the windowpane. A single lamp, sitting upon a wooden table, had been left on for the night. It offered subdued lighting and made for a poorly lit room, leaving an array of shadows for one's imagination to play with.

"If it makes you feel better, we didn't get any reports of accidents this evening," Chris announced, craning his neck to look up at a window on the second floor. "I know it makes me feel better."

"Yes," Lance responded, the tension in his shoulders relaxing a little, "that is good news." He led the way down a short flight of stairs as they continued around the building, peering into various windows in hopes of spotting a person working late or a clue to the whereabouts of the two women.

After the brisk hike up to the Castle's rear entrance parking area, the two men scoured the stretch in hopes of finding Ann's small car waiting there. They were disappointed to be met by a single vehicle, a white van. As they approached it, they found it was cold to the touch and vacant of any signs of life.

"Well, that was a bust," Chris said, disappointment feeling his voice as he turned to examine the back of the Castle. "Maybe it's time to call in the police." He looked over at Lance, worry showing clearly in his eyes.

"Not yet. Let's give them a little longer," Lance suggested, praying for inspiration. Raising his arm and sliding up his sleeve, he punched a button on his watch, illuminating the dial. "It's seven-thirty now. Let's go back down to the car and then we'll decide what to do next."

"Okay, but I have a few friends on the force if you want me to call them." Chris fell in step beside Lance.

"We might just need to do that."

The two men had reached the edge of the parking area, when the sound of a door opening, followed by voices, made them look back over their shoulders. There, in the illumination of a solitary light bulb, a man and a woman, in matching outfits of grey pants and shirts, emerged from an open door in the Castle. Lance noticed the man's curly black hair and neatly trimmed mustache and the fact that he carried a large trash bag in either hand. The woman was slight of figure, with waist-length black hair, and was gripping a bucket of supplies with her left hand, a mop in her right.

Lance and Chris hurried toward the couple, intent on inquiring if they could speak with them for a moment. Spotting the two approaching men, the dark-haired man dropped the trash bags, grabbed the mop from the startled woman, and placed himself in front of her. Holding the implement in club-like fashion, a determined look upon his face, the man commanded the approaching men to come no closer.

"It's okay, we're not here to cause trouble," Chris assured them, slowing his steps and carefully reaching into his coat pocket. "I'm Chris Jacobs from News 1 Radio and this is Lance. We're here checking on two women who were visiting the Castle earlier this afternoon." He took a step closer to the man as he held out his news credentials with picture ID. Lance withdrew his wallet and followed suit showing his own retired military ID.

The man leaned forward, still holding the mop at the ready, and scanned the identifications. Finding them satisfactory and noticing the News 1 logo on the pocket of Chris's dark jacket, he relaxed and let down the mop.

"They look okay, Neli," he said over his shoulder to the woman. "Sorry. We must protect ourselves, no?" he explained in a clipped accent. "I am George and this is my wife, Neli."

"Hi," the woman uttered in a barely audible voice peering from behind her husband.

"Hey. I understand about being careful," Chris agreed, his thoughts filling with a story he'd recently covered with a not-so-happy ending. "As I said, we're looking for two women that were here this afternoon. His wife," he pointed to Lance, "a blonde-haired woman carrying a walking stick, and my, um," he paused, then continued, "a pretty, brown-haired younger woman. She's their niece." A blush filled Chris's checks as he hurried on. "Do you remember seeing them?"

"We are the cleaning crew," George explained, still clutching the mop in one hand, the trash bags at his feet. "We don't arrive until after everyone has gone for the night."

Neli stepped forward and spoke up. "We clean Castle completely; no one is here."

"So, you would have found someone if they'd slipped behind a chair or gotten locked in a restroom?" Lance asked, thinking back over the incidents of the past few days, including some of Stormy's previous escapades.

The woman looked up at her husband, unsure if Lance was joking with her, before carefully answering the question. "Yes, we would see someone if they were in Castle." She firmly nodded her head to emphasize her statement. "The only thing we find tonight is nice camera underneath chair near kitchen. The guests, they sometimes forget and leave things."

"What type of camera did you find?" Lance asked, anxious to discover anything linking to Stormy. "May I see it? My wife was carrying one, and I'm sure Ann would have had hers as well." Hope filled Lance at the possible findings, at the same time mixed with the dread of what it might mean.

"I know not cameras. I put in gift shop's lost and found box," the woman replied, adjusting the bucket of supplies from one hand to the other.

"Go and bring it, Neli," her husband directed her. "I wait here with these gentlemen." He handed her the keys. She set her bucket down, unlocked the door, and disappeared into the Castle.

Neli re-appeared after a couple of minutes, carrying a black camera case with the words "Nikon" spelled out on a small tag sewn to the front of it. She re-locked the Castle door and gave the keys back to her husband.

"I'm sure that's my wife's," Lance pronounced, looking over at the case she held in her hands. "May I see it, please?" He anxiety reached forth his hand toward the woman.

Neli looked questioningly toward George and he nodded in agreement. She handed the camera to Lance's waiting hand, then stepped back beside her husband.

Lance examined the case, then unzipped the top section. He withdrew the black and silver camera and turned it over. Holding it so the light from the wall's bulb shown on its surface, he carefully inspected the underside until he located what he was looking for, then excitedly held it out to Chris.

"This is Stormy's," Lance exclaimed. "Look right here." He pointed to the small set of carefully carved initials, *S. W.*, in the camera's silver edging. "She prefers to scratch her initials into things instead of putting labels on them," he explained. "As she says, 'it is easy to remove a label, not so easy to remove engravings'."

"Yep, it does read SW," Chris confirmed, nodding his head as he looked back at the couple.

"Let's see if there are any photos on here." Lance turned the camera back over and pressed the power-on button. With a small, musical chord, the digital camera came to life and was ready for viewing. He quickly pressed the menu button and brought up the photos. "Here we go. Here's one of Ann standing by a display of China dishes, and this one is of Stormy standing by a mannequin clothed in a long black and white dress. Presumably, these shots were taken inside the Castle?" He questioned, handing the camera back to the woman.

Neli looked at the photo of Stormy standing by the mannequin and nodded. "Yes, this is," she affirmed, a smile touching her lips. "Your wife, she is beautiful." Neli passed the camera back to Lance.

"Thank you. I think so, too." Lance briefly smiled back as he took the camera and thumbed through the rest of the pictures. "I hope you don't mind if I keep this. I'll make sure my wife gets it back."

"Yes, it is hers," George agreed. He flashed a smile of his own before his face became serious. "We are glad to help in its return and hope you find your wife and niece. We must go now. We have other places to clean."

"Thank you," Lance replied, "and for returning this." He held up the camera.

"In case you remember anything that might suggest where these women went after leaving the Castle," Chris said, reaching into his inside coat pocket, "here's my card. Call my cell, and if I don't answer, please leave a message and I'll call you right back."

George accepted the card and examined it. "Yes, we will do that. Goodbye." He and his wife picked up their bundles and hurried in the direction of the white van.

"Now what?" Chris asked, zipping up his coat as the two headed back down toward the SUV. Snow had ceased falling, a bitterly, cold wind taking its place.

"Let's warm up the car and take a closer look at these photos," Lance suggested, pulling his gloves over his reddened hands, the camera snug in its case over his shoulder. "I spotted something of interest in one or two of the shots."

"Look, right there." Lance pointed to the display on the back of Stormy's camera once they were in the vehicle. Chris studied the photo of a smiling Stormy posing alongside a mannequin in a full-length Victorian-style dress. "See the shadow back behind her, near the doorway?"

"Yes, I do," Chris acknowledged, examining it more closely. "It looks to be the effigy of a man most likely, though it's too dark to know for sure." He adjusted the camera in hopes of better discerning the image, leaning over in the warmed front passenger's seat of the Winters' vehicle.

"And check out this one," Lance said, thumbing the camera's button past several shots and coming to rest on one of Ann. Chris observed her standing between what looked to be the Castle's dining room and its kitchen. Behind her, protruding from a wall in the background, was what looked to be the blurred image of a man's head. "It appears as if someone might have been looking at the women from behind this wall, and when he realized that a photo was being taken, he tried to draw back to avoid being photographed."

"Now that's newsworthy!" Chris exclaimed, staring down at the shot. The warm air of the vehicle's heater had caused him to unzip his coat and remove his gloves.

"Newsworthy?"

"Yeah, that's news talk for 'I think we found something here'." Chris chuckled as Lance's eyebrow shot upward. Looking more closely at the shot, Chris exclaimed, "Hmm, I wonder. Didn't the cleaning woman say that she found this camera under a table in the kitchen area?"

"Yes, I believe she did. Why?" Lance asked, his own gloves removed in the warmth of the car.

"Read this sign, the one about the kitchen and how it was used." Chris handed the camera back to Lance.

After careful reading, Lance looked up at Chris. "So, this kitchen was mainly used at one time to just serve food, with no cooking involved. The tunnel that ran from the Sisters of Mercy's house to the kitchen here was a way for them to transport cooked foods to the Castle from their sanitarium, but it could also be used in reverse, I would assume."

"Like maybe to smuggle two women from the Castle, unseen and unknown by others here," Chris finished the thought.

"Yes. But is it still usable after all these years?" Lance conjectured.

"Did you notice if the Sisters' house is even there?"

"No, but let's go take a look. I think that road over there goes up to that back parking lot." Chris pointed out the window, then fastened his seatbelt.

As Lance pulled into the lot, the two men scanned the area surrounding the Castle. "I don't see any building that fits with the description of the Sisters' sanitarium," Chris remarked. "I'll look it up on the 'net." He withdrew an android cell from the depths of his coat, and, with a swipe of his finger, he was browsing the internet. "Here it is." He quickly scanned the page. "It says that an electrical fire destroyed the sanitarium in 1907. It seems it was located on this very spot, which is now a parking lot."

"Great. So that's a dead end," Lance grumbled, his face pinched in worry lines as he brought his hands down on the steering wheel in frustration. "That tunnel is long gone by now."

"Hey, what about that new cell phone Stormy just purchased," Chris exclaimed, barely contained excitement filling his voice. "A new android, right?"

"Yes, that's right," Lance affirmed, picking up the fervor. "Ah, I think I understand what you're getting at." He quickly withdrew his own android. "The latitude feature, right." He ran his finger sideways across the surface of his phone.

"Yes," Chris said, running a finger across his own phone. "And if she has it on, we may be able to track her location."

"Why didn't I think of that before?" Lance mumbled. "She didn't care about it at first, but after the saleswoman pointed out all of the ways it could be useful, she consented. Look, she's showing on here," he cried out, relief flooding his soul, before noticing the span. "But look at the time. It records her over two hours ago."

"At least it's a place to start from," Chris assured Lance, though concerned by the fact himself. "Scroll in closer and let's see where it's pointing to."

Lance did as requested and zoomed in on the location as close as the application would allow.

"I know that area," Chris shouted, looking up from the screen at Lance. "It's not too far from here. Let's go! I'll show you the quickest way to get there."

Nineteen

Stormy opened her eyes and tried to focus them on something-anything-in the pitch-black. She wondered if the snowstorm outside had knocked out the Castle's electricity, rendering the lights unusable. Certainly, someone from the staff would be along shortly to make sure any visitors still in the Castle were okay, and to assist them to an exit. Until then, she would attempt to make her way to a nearby chair to wait. Where her niece had disappeared was beyond her, but she would ask the staff to help search for Ann as soon as they came. Until then, she would sit there and try not to worry.

Sudden realization collided with her thoughts like a steam engine: she was already sitting down. As the fog in her mind began to clear, she became aware that she sat on a very cold dirt floor, up against what seemed to be a rock wall. *No rug, no wooden floor?* Stormy attempted to rise, but found both her arms and legs were too weak to respond.

What's going on? Why am I so weak, and where did this horrible headache come from? Her thoughts raced as she leaned back against the wall, her brain attempting to make sense of the disarray she found herself in.

As the dizziness subsided and feeling came back into Stormy's limbs, a sharp tingling sensation shot through her. She vaguely remembered a man catching her as she fell, then two people carrying her along a dimly lit passageway.

"Where am I?" she mumbled under her breath. She reached out for her walking stick, searching the floor around her. It wasn't there, but her efforts sent up a small cloud of dust. "Achoo." Her sneeze echoed off the surrounding walls.

"Bless you," a woman's voice softly murmured from somewhere close by.

Startled, Stormy hesitated a moment, then whispered back, "Is that you, Ann? Are you alright?"

No response came forth.

Stormy cautiously inched her way toward the direction of the voice. As she traversed through the dirt, her hand hit up against a soft object. She recoiled, then gingerly reached out once more. As her hand once again made contact, she realized that she was touching human hair. *This must be Ann,* she surmised, concern filling the pit of her stomach. She felt the face. Sure it was that of a woman's, she checked the neck for a pulse and was relieved to locate it beneath the skin, slow as it was.

"Ann, are you alright?" she inquired, shaking the shoulder tenderly. "Ann?"

"She'll probably be out for a while," a woman's voice declared from beyond them. "I heard them say that they had to leave the rag on her face twice as long in order to subdue her. I guess she put up quite a fight."

"Who are you? And where are we?" Stormy demanded. She hovered over Ann, instinctively ready to defend her from this unknown person.

"I'm a captive like you, locked in this cave, awaiting whatever fate they choose to hand out," the woman moaned. "That doesn't matter now anyway, after what they did to my husband." Stormy heard soft sobs coming from the direction of the voice.

"We're in a cave, did you say? Where? And who are 'they'?" Stormy continued to focus in the direction of the woman's voice, but it was hopeless trying to see anything in the darkness.

"Yes, a cave where no one will ever think to look for us. And it's all my fault that we're here to begin with." The woman continued to sob, the sound becoming desperate.

"The last thing I remember, I was in Miramont Castle looking for my niece and someone put a rag over my face," Stormy said, still holding onto her niece's shoulder. "How did we get in this cave?" She gently shook Ann's shoulder. "Ann, can you hear me, dear? Wake up, Ann."

"From what they said, they brought you and the young woman through some kind of tunnel from under the Castle, then by car from there to the Dwellings."

"Dwellings?" Stormy echoed, unsure of what she'd heard.

"Yes, we're at the Manitou Cliff Dwellings, a place made by the ancient Indians. Those men threw you in here with me, in this old burial cave under the cliffs," the woman explained, stopping to blow her nose. "I believe you were out for at least an hour after you arrived."

"How is this your . . ." Stormy began, pausing as she felt Ann's shoulder suddenly shift.

"Oh, my head." Ann moved as if to sit up, then fell back onto the ground.

"Just lie there for a few minutes and it'll pass," her aunt cautioned her, affectionately pushing back the hair from off Ann's face. "You'll be okay. It's just the effects from whatever they put on those rags they held against our nose."

"Rags? What happened to the lights? Where are we?" Ann asked, confused by her aunt's words and the engulfing darkness. "Wait, those two men. I remember now, they were trying to restrain me. Are you okay, Aunt Stormy? Did they hurt you?"

"No, I'm okay, just a headache. I'm just happy that you're here and okay, for the most part." Stormy continued to massage Ann's forehead, hoping to relieve some of her pain.

"I'm glad to see that you're alright, so far, that is," the woman uttered as she continued to moan. "I'm so sorry about the way they've treated you both."

"And who are you?" Ann answered, suddenly on guard as she tried once again to rise. "Are you with those two hoods?" she demanded, angrily. Her head continued to throb, but she sat up, assisted by her aunt. "Stay where you are."

"It's okay, Ann. It seems this woman is in the same boat as we are," Stormy explained, helping

Ann over to rest against a nearby wall. "Why do you say that this is all your fault?" she inquired of the other woman. "Who are you and who are these people that are holding us captive?" She sat down beside Ann, pulling her coat tightly about her against the chill of the cave's air.

"My name is Mrs. West. Sarah West. My husband, Peter, is the bank manager of the First Bank in the Springs," she began, her voice quivering as she tried to keep it under control. "I really thought I was trying to help these people with a good cause. I didn't realize that they were just using me to get to my husband and the bank's funds until it was too late. You have to believe me: I really didn't know."

"Mrs. West?" Stormy was surprised to learn this was the bank manager's wife. "What didn't you know? And who tricked you like this? Who are they?" Stormy prompted the woman. She realized that she was going to need some patience to obtain information out of this woman.

"Mrs. West? We met . . ." Ann began.

"Continue, Mrs. West," Stormy cut across, silencing her niece. She was not ready to reveal the fact that they knew her husband and several other things as well. *Why not wait and see where she goes with this?* Stormy thought.

"It's a branch of rebels who live here in the Springs. They've been in the U.S. for many years and have been aiding those in their country of Georgia who are working towards a better government." Mrs. West blew her nose once more before continuing. Stormy could hear the woman shift positions as she paused. Anger filled her voice as she resumed her story. "They told me of the conditions their families live in back home. Of the cruelty of their rulers, and that they are a poor and starving people. They said if I helped them, no one would be hurt. I felt like I was doing the right thing . . . helping the people of Georgia."

"It's sad how many governments and terrorist groups are affecting the poor people in their day-to-day struggles around the world," Ann commented from where she sat next to her aunt, leaning up against the smooth stone wall. "Where did you happen to meet these people?"

"The Country Club hired a new golf pro a few months ago," Mrs. West explained, slight embarrassment filling her voice "I'd been playing a few holes of golf with the ladies, but I'm not as good as most of them are. Just ask my husband." Her voice faltered as she choked back the tears. "When I heard about this new pro, I went to see about getting a few lessons. I wanted to look better in front of my friends, but when I saw how good-looking he was and how wonderfully he treated me, I guess all my good judgment went out the window. I began spending more and more time at the club just to be with him. Though I did improve my game." She sighed.

"Didn't your husband wonder at that?" Stormy asked, pondering whether she should tell the woman that she'd met her husband or not. "No, not really. He spends most of his waking hours working at that beloved bank of his," Mrs. West answered, bitterly. "I don't think he even missed me one bit."

"Some people can be real workaholics," Ann said, thinking of her own father. She shivered, wrapping her arms tightly around herself.

"After several lessons, the pro invited me to dinner, and he was ever so charming. I didn't even realize that all the time we spent together, he was pumping me for information about the bank. I was stupid enough to think he really liked me," Sarah declared, a note of sadness entered her voice. "I was even wondering if I shouldn't stay with my husband any longer. After all, he didn't seem to need me in his life, and without any children, he would forget about me quickly enough. Now I guess it doesn't matter since they shot him down like a dog. For all I know, he's probably dead now." This sent her into a wave of uncontrollable tears.

"Oh, Sarah, no, he's alive! I just saw your husband yesterday afternoon and he's already out of the hospital," Stormy assured the crying woman. "He looked a bit pale and worried, but I think he's going to be okay."

"Really? That's wonderful," the other woman cried out, brightening up as she softly sniffled. "Where did you see him?"

"I saw him at the bank. He said there was something he must do. He seemed quite determined."

"Oh, maybe he really does care about me after all." Hope was evident in the sound of Mrs. West's voice.

"Are the rebels after the bank's money, Sarah?" Stormy prompted again, certain this was the case. She stretched out one leg, then the other, in an effort to relieve the cramps she'd developed in them from the dampness filling the cave.

"Yes, they needed funds, a lot of them, transferred to their comrades in Georgia, and they wanted my husband to do this through his bank. They even . . ."

A loud scraping sound interrupted the conversation, followed by a strong beam of light, momentarily blinding the three women. The beam grew in intensity, then fell away to the floor as a man stepped inside the enclosure, juggling both flashlight and tray. Three bowls rested on top of the tray. A second man followed close behind, a scoped rifle under one arm and several blankets over the other.

"Here, I brought you some soup; I thought you might need it," the first man explained, his face shadowed from the light. "And some blankets as well. It'll get pretty cold before the night's over." He set down the tray as the man behind passed him the blankets. He tossed one to each of the women.

Stormy thought his voice sounded vaguely familiar but couldn't place a face to it. With the flashlight resting on the floor, she couldn't make out his features.

Ann, on the other hand, recognized the voice.

"Jeff?" Ann questioned as she leaned forward, trying to get a better view of the man's face.

"Look, Ann," the man began, still in a squatting position from setting down the tray. Before he could get another word out, Ann was upon him, springing like a ferocious mountain cat.

"You traitor," she yelled at the top of her lungs as she threw him backward to the floor sending hot soup flying across the cave. On her knees she straddled across his stomach and proceeded to pound on his chest with one hand as she pressed the other tightly against his throat.

The flashlight rolled on the floor beside them, and Stormy could see a look of alarm cross Jeff's face as he desperately fought for air.
Raising his arms in self-defense, he pressed hard against Ann's shoulders, fighting for his survival. A few more minutes without air and he would pass out, or worse.

She's going to kill him, Stormy thought. Momentarily frozen by Ann's movements, she now attempted to get to her feet and take hold of her niece.

However, before she could stand, the olive-skinned man behind Jeff lifted his rifle and slammed the butt of it into Ann's ribs. Ann winced with pain as she flew sideways into Stormy, sending them both tumbling back into the wall. The man with the rifle continued to point the weapon in Ann's direction while a gasping Jeff rose to his feet and stepped away.

"Are you alright, Ann?" Stormy queried, pulling herself up into a sitting position beside her prone niece. Movement caught her eye, and she was briefly aware of a very frightened Mrs. West inching her way back into one corner.

Ann lay there, clutching her side and attempting not to show the immense pain she felt as she glared at Jeff. She didn't answer her aunt, but Stormy had no trouble reading her thoughts.

"You don't understand, Ann. I'm sorry to disappoint you." Jeff shook his head.

Stormy caught a look of pain in Jeff's eyes before he turned and left the enclosure, pushing past the man holding the rifle. After a moment, the man retrieved the flashlight and carefully backed out of the cave, slamming the door shut behind him. Once again, the women heard a scraping noise as they were ensconced in darkness.

"Well, that went well," Mrs. West moaned from her corner. "Now you angered them even more. And on top of that, you spilled all of the hot soup they brought. I'm cold, and I'm hungry, and I want to go home." She began to weep even louder.

"We all do, Mrs. West," Stormy declared. She probed the ground about her, and finding a blanket, spread it over Ann. Searching further, she grabbed hold of the other two and tossed one in the direction of the sobbing Mrs. West. "Wrap this around you; it'll help warm you up. And get ahold of yourself. We'll think of something. How are you feeling, Ann? Does it hurt much?"

"A little," Ann responded as a moan escaped her lips. Stormy could hear further pain evident in her breathing. Ann started to sit up but quickly lay back down. "Guess I'm a bit dizzy."

"Just stay put and give yourself some time," Stormy advised her niece, trying to force a confidence into her voice that she didn't feel. "You probably just have a few bruised ribs, though he hit you pretty hard."

"I guess," Ann murmured, "but it was worth it." Ann mumbled several more words, too low for Stormy to hear.

Stormy was aware of the bitterness in what words she had heard as she helped to tighten the blanket around Ann's body.

She bundled herself into her own heavy blanket and leaned back against the wall to think things through. Resting a hand on her niece's shoulder to comfort her, she realized that it probably gave her as much comfort as it did Ann. As she sat there, she wondered how she'd let them get into this horrifying situation. But in truth, she couldn't think of how they could've avoided it.

After a time, Stormy heard a soft snoring coming from Ann and removed her hand from off her shoulder, trying not to disturb her. *She can use some sleep,* she thought.

As she set her hand on the floor of the cave, Stormy's fingertips brushed against what felt like soft leather.

"My purse?" Stormy mumbled under her breath. She reached out and grabbed hold of the object, pulling it to her. Relief filling her mind. "My phone!"

Why hadn't I thought of that before? she chided herself. *It must have been the drugs on the cloth they used on me,* she further reasoned. *It obviously fogs the mind, making one forget things.*

Stormy jerked on the purse's zipper and rummaged through it. After several attempts, she accepted the truth. The phone was gone.

"What happened to it? I'm sure I had it zipped in, so it couldn't have fallen out," she whispered. Images and sounds came flooding into her mind and she vaguely recalled her cell ringing and her attempt at answering it, only to have it ripped from her hand and shut off. With a heavy heart, she was sure that the call had been from Lance. He would've wondered why she'd not answered and been worried that she'd not yet returned to the hotel. How would he ever think to look for her here, let alone know of the kidnapping? Devastated, she pulled the blanket around her and leaned back against the cold stone wall.

Twenty

Stormy teetered on the edge of despair. As she attempted to work through her situation, her eye caught a small point of light shining from the opposite wall. Curiosity catching hold, she leaned forward and stared across the enclosure, trying to get a better look. This revealed nothing. She needed to move closer.

She continued to focus on the light as she inched her way across the otherwise pitch-black room, careful not to fall over her niece in the process.

Stormy arrived at the wall to find herself beside a moaning Mrs. West. A small hole of light shone low on the stone, almost at floor level. Further examination revealed it came from loose mortar between two adjacent stones forming a small portion of the wall.

"What are you doing now?" a distraught Mrs. West wined as she pulled her blanket over her nose in an effort to stave off the cold air.

"There's a space between these two stones," Stormy answered as she continued her probing. "If we can loosen more of the chinking

between these rocks, we may have a way out of here."

Lowering her blanket, Mrs. West asked, "A way . . . out?"

"It might be," Stormy said, "if I can just find something to loosen these." She dug at the stones with both hands, scraping her fingers in the process, only to find the rocks wouldn't budge. What could she use? She wondered where her walking stick had gotten to. It had no doubt been confiscated by the terrorists so that she couldn't use it as a weapon. And she would have tried; there was no question about that. It had proven to be of such use in the past.

"Do you think that's . . . wise?" Mrs. West stammered. "The terrorists . . . . are already upset, and who knows what they might do to us . . . . if they catch us trying to escape." Stormy could feel the fear of the woman trembling beside her. The very air reeked of it. Then she realized that it was not only Mrs. West who was afraid. She, too, was

Stormy sat in the dirt and took a few deep breaths in an attempt to quiet the fear and bring her torrent emotions under control. Would the terrorists hurt the women if they failed to escape? Maybe even shoot them and quietly dispose of their bodies? Or was she putting their lives in unnecessary jeopardy with her actions . . . . by trying to flee?

Probably not, she surmised. The women, especially Mrs. West, had seen the faces of several of the men, so they could no longer afford to release their prisoners after they got what they wanted out of all this. Stormy shivered at the thought. Was she never to see Lance in this life again? What about her children and the new grandbaby on its way? Would her family ever even know what had become of her and Ann?

Stormy prayed more fervently than she'd ever done in her life for both strength and guidance. As she waited, intently listening for the Spirit, both a reassurance and urgency flooded her mind.

You need to leave now. The thought came strongly to her mind, leaving no room for doubt, fresh determination flooding her mind.

"We must find a way to escape," she told the woman. "They won't be releasing us. They have no choice."

A low moan escaped Mrs. West's lips, followed by the sounds of sobbing.

Stormy thought back over the objects in her purse. She carefully crawled back to where she'd left it and began a search. "Here," she murmured, retrieving a metal nail file, "this might work." Turning around, she made her way back to the pinpoint of light. Inserting the file into the small hole, she began to file and chip away at the mortar. She was surprised at finding it so loose that it began to crumble and fall away.

The sounds awoke Ann. "What are you doing?" she inquired, failing to keep the pain she felt from her voice as she propped herself up on one elbow. "Aunt Stormy?"

"Stay put," Stormy ordered her niece. "I'm trying to get us out of here." Stormy continued to work at the stones with the file as she spoke. "If I can just get this loose, we might have a chance." No sooner had the words left her mouth when one of the stones moved, then rocked in place. She grabbed a firm hold on the rock and maneuvered it back and forth until it came free in her hands. Lowering it to the floor, she set it beside one knee. Moonlight beamed through the opening, filling the cave with several more rays of the precious substance.

"Great!" Stormy shouted, before realizing her error. Slapping a hand over her mouth, she listened, holding her breath all the while. Hearing no response from outside, she softly released the pent-up air. She must remember to withhold her excitement and confine it only to within her mind, she chided herself.

"Let me help you," Ann whispered, appearing at her aunt's side.

From the soft moonlight filling the cave, Stormy could see in Ann's face just how much it had cost her niece to move across the room. "You'd better rest. I'll keep at it."

"It'll go faster if we both work at it," Ann assured her. "I'm okay," she lied.

Against her better judgment, but realizing that her niece was right, Stormy gave in. "Okay, but be careful."

The two women worked at the wall, slowly loosening one stone after another, until there was an opening large enough for a single body to pass through.

Through the painstaking process, Mrs. West had eventually found the courage to lend them a hand, picking up the loosened stones and stacking them on the dirt floor of the cave, just beyond where they worked.

Stormy carefully poked her head through the opening in order to have a quick look around. Pulling it back into the cave, she quietly explained, "This wall comes out into a very small courtyard that appears to run but a short way before it turns a corner. I think it's safe for us to leave but wait here. I'll take a look around to make sure." As she started forward, Ann grabbed her shoulder, preventing her departure.

"Let me go," Ann told her aunt. "I have training in this type of thing and . . ."

"Maybe you do," Stormy interrupted, "but you're injured. I'll just be a minute." Before her niece could further object, Stormy was through the opening and crouching in the courtyard. She glanced around her for any signs of life before proceeding forward. Stealthily worming her way along the stone wall, she reached the corner and stopped. Slowly she peered around the corner, making sure to keep her head low. She was relieved, though a bit surprised, to find no one guarding the cave's wooden door. Evidently, the terrorists found the three women of no impending threat to them or their plans.

Stormy turned to make her way back to the opening and was momentarily startled to find Ann halfway out of the gap in the wall.

She hurried back.

"All's clear," Stormy told her niece, reaching down to take hold of Ann's arm. "Let's get out of here." She offered to help Ann up but was brushed away.

"I'm okay, but you might need to encourage that woman in there to follow us." Ann pointed behind her. "She refused my help."

"I'll get her," Stormy replied, an urgency filling her voice. Shoving her head back through the hole, she waited only a moment for her eyes to adjust to the darkened cave before speaking. "Mrs. West, we must hurry before they return." She reached out a hand toward the woman. "Our lives depend on it. Come on, I'll help you."

The woman hesitated, her fearful eyes studying Stormy's. Slowly she reached forth and grasped the proffered hand. "Okay, I'll come," she voiced, so soft Stormy had to strain to hear her.

The three of them crouched near the outside corner of the cave's stone wall, pausing to decide their next move.

"Mrs. West," Stormy whispered, "I don't know this area. Have you been here before?" She looked at the woman, awaiting a response.

"Yes," she said, a visible tremble shaking her body. "These are the cliff dwellings of the ancient Anasazi people. As I mentioned before, it is called the Manitou Cliff Dwellings and is nearly 700 years old. It's quite impressive, one of my favorite places to visit. You can explore and touch it all you want." The woman's face glazed over in thought.

"I wish we could've visited it under more favorable circumstances," Stormy breathed, "but we must hurry, Mrs. West." She took hold of the woman's elbow, guiding her to the front of their small group. "Now, where do we go from here to get to the exit of these dwellings?"

The woman focused on Stormy's face, then looked around as if coming back from some far-off place. "Please, call me Sarah."

"Okay, Sarah, it's very important that we get out of here before they discover we're missing." Stormy explained, looking firmly into Sarah's eyes. "Do you understand?"

"Yes," Sarah snapped in reply. "Come this way." She stepped out from the protection of the wall. Stormy and Ann had no choice but to follow. As Stormy did, she suddenly felt a little unsteady on her feet. Looking around her, she located a long stick and retrieved it. This would have to do until she could find her walking stick.

Sarah guided them along a moonlit path that led to a high cliff wall. "These are the caves the Anasazi built their homes in," Sarah pointed out. "We can slip through here." She indicated to a large crack in the cliff's wall with the wave of her hand. Stepping forward, she disappeared from sight. With a little insistence from Stormy, Ann went next, followed by her aunt.

The women found themselves in a semi-darkened cave. If not for the moonlight flooding throughout, they could've quickly become lost. Stormy spared a glance at the cave's high ceiling before her attention was drawn to the stone wall built to one side with an open doorway neatly carved into the rock.

Sarah continued to lead the women skillfully through the caves until they stepped out into the light of a pole lamp set near a set of descending cement steps, a metal railing running along its length.

"The exit is across there," Sarah murmured, pointing across a wide-open area. "It's past the parking lot and down the paved drive. I don't know how we'll get there without being seen." Tears ran down her face as she sank onto a nearby wooden bench.

Stormy glanced around the area as she and Ann stood in the shadow of the tall cliffs. Could they make it across the open space without being spotted? They would have to; they had no choice. But where were the men they'd seen earlier? Jeff and the guards had to be somewhere nearby.

As if in answer to her question, a roar of laughter exploded from the direction of a group of buildings up ahead and slightly to their left. The sudden noise forced all three women to the ground in fear of being discovered. After a few minutes, Stormy, along with Ann, ventured to raise their heads and survey the area.

While assuring themselves that no living being was in sight, Stormy noticed a sign bathed in the glow of a spotlight which read "Gift Shop and Museum" dangling from a chain a few yards in front of the buildings. She quickly pointed this out to her niece.

"I think if we were to skirt along the front of the buildings, keeping our heads low," Ann suggested, her hand pressing into her ribs, "we could make our way to those teepees beyond. I don't see a guard out, but we must keep our eyes open just in case."

"Okay, let's do it. It sounds like they're having a party, so this may be our best shot." Stormy grabbed Sarah's arm and pulled her to her feet. "We need to leave now. Come on." Looking over her shoulder at Ann, she asked, "How're the ribs? Can you make it okay?"

"I'll be fine," Ann whispered back, letting go of her side as if to reassure her aunt. "Let's get out of here. You two go first. I'll take up the rear and keep a watch for any movement on their part." She gestured to the buildings where another round of cheers filled the air.

Stormy led Sarah down the cement stairs and out across the graveled clearing before reaching the perimeter of the buildings. Ann shadowed close behind. They'd just passed the long sidewalk that led to the entrance of the gift shop when they heard what sounded like the flush of a toilet. Stormy pulled Sarah into a crouching position behind a thick scrub oak, with Ann joining them, just as two men exited a door set into the wall near the shop's front doors. A bright overhead light flooded the area around them.

As the women silently waited, the men came to a halt just outside the doors. The taller of the two withdrew a lighter from his pocket, and using it to light the cigarette he'd placed between his lips, he took a deep breath in. Withdrawing the cigarette, he puffed out a ring of smoke, before speaking. "You need to watch it with the vodka, my friend, at least until we are back home."

"Don't worry about me," the thinner man slurred his words, "I can drink with the best of 'em, but it has to come out some time." He laughed as he swayed to one side, then sadness filled his voice. "Home. It seems so very long ago since I saw my wife. And our baby, Fritz, he will be grown before I return."

"You worry too much," the tall man chided, stopping to take another drag on his cigarette before continuing. "This will all be over soon and then we can go home. I will be back with my sister, and you shall see your family again."

"Yes, yes, Hilda needs me," the thinner man brightened. "She needs a strong man around for Fritz. And he needs to know why his papa fights and what for. Hey, have I showed you his picture." He reached into an inside coat pocket, then another.

"Come, Comrade. You can show me inside where it is warmer." The man chuckled as he took hold of the thinner man's arm and assisted him to the door.

As the two men turned to enter, Stormy caught her breath. In the lamplight that illuminated the entrance, she focused on the taller man's profile: the crooked shape of his nose and his rather sharp facial features.

The man in the back seat? Stormy wondered.

Then to her further surprise, as the man held the door open for the other to enter, she noticed that one of the thinner man's pant legs was hiked up in the back, revealing his socks—bright orange socks.

"So, the gangs all here," Stormy mumbled under her breath as she fought the cramps building in her legs from squatting so long.

"Oh, no," Sarah whimpered, the color draining from her face.

"What?" Ann asked from behind her aunt. "Do you both know those men?"

Stormy turned to respond to her niece and noticed that Ann was tightly clutching her left side with one hand.

"I believe so," Stormy answered, glancing over at a ghostly-pale Sarah. "Let's get out of here before someone else shows up." She helped Sarah stand, then turned for Ann, but found her already moving. The three women continued in the direction of the teepee display. Although filled with concern for her niece, Stormy knew there wasn't much she could do to help her at this point.

Once near the front teepee, or wigwam, as the display's sign proclaimed, Stormy paused, noticing Ann's movements had slowed. "Let's stop behind here for a minute and catch our breath," she suggested.

"This is where my husband and I had our picture taken a few years ago." A smile flickered across Sarah's face before quickly disappearing, replaced by a deep frown.

Stormy felt a stab of pity for this woman she barely knew. As she stood there, knowing full well that there was little she could do to ease the woman's pain, but wishing somehow she might, a loud yell reached her ears, causing her to jerk back from her thoughts. She found herself turning in its direction.

"I think they've discovered we're missing," Ann exclaimed, peaking around side of the wigwam. "Let's get out of here." Holding her side, she took the lead, heading for the parking lot. Stormy once again urged Sarah to move, and they followed close behind.

They had gone no more than a few yards, when a shadowy figure darted from behind a second wigwam and headed in their direction. Ann immediately went into a defensive posture, stepping in front of her aunt. Stormy's heartbeat wildly in her chest as she held tight to a trembling Sarah and stared at the approaching form. As the object drew closer, a name formed in her mind.

"Jeff?" Stormy uttered as she tried to keep Sarah from falling to the ground. She steadied them both with the stick she still held.

"You," Ann growled, stepping forward, ready to strike.

"Wait," Jeff began, moving quickly, but cautiously forward. "Hold off," he told Ann, hands raised in front of him. "I'm not who you think I am."

"You don't say," Ann spat out. She took another step, then clutched at her side before pitching forward, crying out in pain.

Jeff leaped the few feet to her side, catching her in his arms before she could hit the ground. Before Stormy had a chance to react, a shot rang out, the bullet whizzing past her head, missing her by less than an inch.

"We need to move now," Jeff commanded the group, gathering up the limp Ann in his arms. "This way." He bolted for the empty pavement, the weight of Ann seeming not to hinder him in the least.

With heart racing, Stormy grabbed Sarah by the arm and the two fled in Jeff's footsteps as a second shot echoed off the cliffs.

Twenty-One

"The GPS last recorded Stormy's position as being somewhere in this proximity," Chris explained, looking down at the instrument in his hand, then back up at the moonlit landscape before them. "This is as close as I can pinpoint it."

Lance had brought the SUV to a stop along the side of Highway 24, not far from the city of Manitou Springs. The two men had exited the vehicle and begun a thorough search of the area for any signs of Stormy and Ann.

"They must be here," Lance insisted, his face full of worry as he quickly said another silent prayer, hoping for some kind of further guidance. He continued to scan the mountains to their left for any signs of activity.

"I think they would have taken the cell away from her and turned it off," Chris surmised. He looked across the highway and considered where he might have gone, given he'd just abducted two women. An eighteen-wheeler rumbled along the lane in front of him, splashing his pant-legs with cold, melted snow. "Hey, watch it." He jumped back as a chill ran up his legs, his pants wet to the knees. "Great."

"I think it's time to call in the police," Lance announced. He withdrew his cell phone from an inside coat pocket and dialed 911. A police dispatcher answered, and Lance quickly explained the situation, giving them the mile marker on Hwy. 24 where he was parked. He was told to remain where he was, and a unit would be dispatched to their location.

"Okay, they're on their way," he relayed to Chris as he ended the call. "Let's wait inside the car for them. It's a bit cold out here." Chris agreed and joined Lance in the SUV as Lance started up the motor and turned on the heat.

Fifteen minutes later, a black and white police cruiser, lights flashing, pulled in behind the SUV. The driver's door swung open and a sturdy, blond-haired officer stepped from his car and headed toward the parked vehicle. As he did so, Lance and Chris alighted from their own vehicle to join him.

"Hey, Officer Mulhound. How are you?" Chris offered his hand to the officer.

"Doing okay, Chris," the officer replied, shaking hands with him. "Out on a story?"

"No, but I think we're in the middle of one," Chris answered. "This is Lance Winters. We believe that his wife and niece may have been kidnapped from Miramont Castle. We tracked the last known GPS location for his wife, Stormy's, cell, but it ends here." He gestured with one hand around the area, the other resting on a hip.

"I see," Officer Mulhound said, addressing Lance. "So, it's your wife and niece involved in this?" He held a PDA in one hand as he took notes.

"Yes, that's correct," Lance affirmed, looking into the officer's eyes, then down at the device and back up again.

"What is it that makes you believe they've been kidnapped?" The officer tapped a screen on his PDA, then lowered it and studied Lance as he awaited a response.

Lance went back over what he'd related to the dispatcher, adding, "This just isn't like Stormy to be without her cell phone. She always has it on her. And she always lets me know where she is. She's now several hours overdue, both she and Ann." He shoved a hand into his coat pocket in a fit of anxiety. "I have to say, I'm very worried about them both."

"Ann had a date with me for dinner this evening," Chris interposed. "She just doesn't seem the type to be a no-show."

"Let me call and get us some back up out here," Officer Mulhound said. "Hang tight and we'll begin a search of the area as soon as they arrive." He headed back to his vehicle and reached for the radio. As the officer conversed with the dispatcher, the group heard the undeniable sound of a shot echoing off the mountains, followed shortly by a second one.

Lance stiffened at the sound, quickly looking around as a feeling of dread filled his soul. "Where did that come from?" he declared, as he heard the officer yell into his radio: "Shots fired. I repeat . . . shots fired! I'm going to check it out. Send back up."

"Sounded like a rifle to me," the officer yelled over to the men. "It seems to have come from the direction of the Cliff Dwellings. Wait here while I check it out." He jumped in his vehicle, lights flashing, and sped across two lanes of traffic, then on across the median. Executing a sharp turn, he headed down the highway at top speed.

"I'm not waiting here," Lance bellowed. He turned and ran to the driver's side of the SUV. "You coming?" he shouted to Chris as he flung the door wide and jumped in. Chris hustled to the other side and got in, barely closing the door before Lance put the car in gear and moved forward.

Wildly honking, with flashers on, Lance sped across the two lanes of traffic, barely missing being hit by a passing pickup truck. He sped across the snow-covered grass and followed the tracks of the police car. Quickly checking for vehicles, he slipped the SUV out onto the road and sped along, ignoring the speed limit.

"Where are these Cliff Dwellings?" Lance shouted to Chris as he raced to get around a delivery truck, then swerved back into the right-hand lane.

"The turnoff is coming up real soon, on the right," Chris directed, "but you'll need to slow down a bit to make it." He held tightly to the front passenger's sky hook with his right hand, glad he'd been able to fasten his seatbelt.

"Point it out when we get there, and I'll make it." Lance attempted to calm himself down. Chris was right; it would do no one any good if they crashed now. He took a few deep breaths as the SUV shot forward.

"Turn there," Chris pointed out with his left hand, before reaching out to steady himself against the dashboard. He still grasped the skyhook with his right hand.

Lance lightly applied pressure to the brakes as he guided his vehicle into the turn. The SUV momentarily skidded out of control before Lance got it back in check and they continued down the lane.

"Not bad," Chris complimented, though uncertain he would be able to pry his hand loose from the sky hook once the car was stopped.

Lance, upon approaching a huge pair of closed wrought-iron gates, slammed on the brakes, bringing the Santa Fe to a screeching halt, only inches from Officer Mulhound's cruiser. The officer, out of his car and peering through the closed gates, jerked his head back in concern as Lance and Chris jumped from their vehicle and rushed to his side.

"Are we locked out?" Lance demanded, grabbing hold of the iron bars and testing them.

"Yes, I'm afraid so," the officer replied. "I thought I told you two to stay put. We don't know who's doing the shooting." He looked back through the gates, making a snap decision as a third shot sounded from beyond them.

"My wife and niece may be in there," Lance pointed out, violently shaking the gates. "They could've been shot by those maniacs!" Chris was by his side, examining his options to climb over.

"Hold on, boys. I've got something in my trunk." The officer hurried to the back of his cruiser. He returned a moment later, a pair of impressive cutters in his hands. "Stand back and give me some room."

Stepping up to the gates, he clamped the large cutters onto the lock and squeezed down on the handles. As Lance and Chris watched, the tool sliced through the metal as if going through soft butter. Ripping off the lock, the officer tossed it aside and all three men pushed the gates wide open.

"Stand back and douse those headlights until we see what's what," Mulhound cautioned, heading for the cruiser, obviously knowing full well he alone couldn't make the two men remain behind. Better to let them tag along where he could keep an eye on them. He slid into the front seat and cautiously made his way through the open gates as Lance and Chris followed behind in the Santa Fe.

As they slowly made their way along the moonlit road, another vehicle swung in behind them. Lance cast a worried glance into his rearview mirror to get a better look at the light-colored SUV.

"That would be the El Paso Country Sheriff's Department," Chris affirmed, turning to look through the rear window. "They provide backup for the Manitou police when needed. They must have been nearby and heard the call."

As the convoy rounded a bend in the road, a shot rang out, striking the front windshield of the police cruiser, sending it careening into an embankment. Lance slammed on his brakes as Officer Mulhound threw open the cruiser's door and slid out of the front seat. Mulhound directed Lance to bring his SUV alongside the cruiser, then motioned for the two men to get down. As Lance did so, the sheriff's vehicle skidded to a halt beside Lance's, effectively blocking the roadway.

Both Lance and Chris quickly threw open their doors and cautiously slipped from their vehicle to make their way to the rear of the cars. The sheriff did the same, joining them as Officer Mulhound came from the other side.

"What do we have here, Mulhound?" the sheriff inquired, a rifle already in hand.

"We're not sure yet," Mulhound replied, toting a shotgun. "This is Lance Winters, and you probably already know Chris here, from News One Radio." He gestured to Chris before rising up to take a quick look around, then squatted again beside the reporter.

"Yes, we've worked on a few stories together before," the Sheriff acknowledged Chris. "Nice to meet you, Lance. Sorry it isn't under better circumstances."

A grim-faced Lance nodded in agreement. "Same here."

"Lance's wife is missing, along with his niece," Mulhound quickly explained. "They tracked his wife's cell latitude to a location near here. As I was looking into it, shots were fired from this direction." He looked over at his cruiser. "I think we've stumbled into something big here. As you can see, someone put a bullet through my windshield."

"I think you're right," the Sheriff agreed. "I believe we'd better get a few more guys out here ASAP." As he turned to leave, a deep blue, extended pickup with a shell-covered bed rolled in behind them. The four men tensed, then relaxed when the doors opened to reveal a shield with the words "Air Force Academy" emblazoned on it.

"How'd the Air Force get wind of this so quickly?" the sheriff questioned, a puzzled expression on his face. "And what're they doing here?"

Six men armed with M-16s, dressed in dark uniforms, Kevlar vests, and head gear exited the truck and advanced toward them. They came to a halt a few feet away. A man with a small Captain's patch on the front of his uniform stepped forward.

"Who's in charge here?" he demanded, looking at the group assembled behind the three vehicles.

"Better tell your men to stay down. Shots have been fired," the sheriff advised, remaining in a squatting position. "It's his call here," he continued, pointing to Officer Mulhound.

The captain signaled to his men, and they dropped down into position as he followed suit.

"Captain," Mulhound acknowledged the Air Force officer. "I'm Officer Mulhound and this is Lance Winters and news reporter, Chris Jacobs. You've probably met the sheriff before. What brings you out here?" He looked over the captain's shoulder to the five men crouched behind him.

"We received word from our man inside. It seems things are moving along on a much faster timetable than originally planned." Lance noticed a concerned look cross the captain's face, then disappear just as quickly. "We're going to need to move if shots are already being taken."

"Yes, Captain," Mulhound agreed, resting the shotgun across his knees. "And I'm glad you've joined us. You seem to know more about this situation than we do. Mind filling us in on it?"

"We have a cell of terrorists . . ." the captain began as another volley of shots rang out, followed by a cry of pain coming from several yards ahead along the right side of the road.

The captain sprung into action, signaling his men forward. They split into two groups of three and quickly took points on either side of the vehicles, keeping down as low as they could. Instructing Lance and Chris to stay put, Mulhound and the sheriff moved together in between the parked vehicles, resting their weapons on the doors, which they used as shields, as they peered into the moonlit landscape ahead of them.

"I can't just stay here with the possibility that Stormy may be out there lying injured somewhere," Lance exclaimed, starting to move. "This is about terrorists." His mouth formed a deep frown, his eyes filling with worry. He'd been in the Army, he knew how to handle himself.

"Wait," Chris commanded, grabbing ahold of Lance's shoulder in order to stop him. "I've seen these law enforcement guys in action and they're pretty good. If Stormy and Ann are out there, they'll find them." He rose up enough to get a glimpse through the SUV's back window, while pulling a small camera from an inside coat pocket. "Let them do their job." He snapped a picture. "However, I can't let a story this big go by without a few shots of my own." In rapid succession, Chris began taking photos of the vehicles and men around them, being careful not to expose himself or the others to the terrorists.

"You're probably right," Lance mumbled. "I take it you must have one of those special night shot lens, seeing as you're not using a flash on those photos," Lance stated as he intently peered around the Santa Fe, finding it difficult to stay put.

"Yes," Chris acknowledged. "Great invention." He snapped a quick couple of shots of Lance.

"Friendly. Hold your fire," a voice rang out into the night.

Lance, full of pent-up frustration, leapt into action and sprung around the side of the SUV, Chris close behind, in time to see a man step out onto the edge of the road, one hand raised high in the air holding a white handkerchief, the other hanging limp at his side.

"Halt!" the Air Force captain demanded, while all guns were brought to bear on the figure in the road. Lance could hear the clicks of the safeties being released on each weapon. "Identify yourself."

"Lieutenant Jeffery Davis, U S Air Force, sir," came the reply. "I have wounded with me."

"Hold your fire men," the captain declared, "he's one of us. Approach, Lieutenant."

Jeff slowly moved forward, being careful not to make any sudden movements. He knew that the men would keep their weapons trained on him until he was safely behind the barrier and they could see him more clearly.

"Captain," Jeff acknowledged the officer as he attempted to raise his right arm in salute. He groaned and grabbed at his shoulder with his left hand as he felt his head swoon.

"Hold on there." The captain grabbed hold of Jeff as he slid to the ground and leaned him back against the Sheriff's vehicle. "Sergeant, bring me the medical kit and a blanket."

"Yes, sir." The sergeant raced to the rear of the Air Force vehicle, making sure to keep low as he did so. As he returned with the requested supplies, Lance and Chris had made their way over to where Jeff rested.

"Can I be of some help, Captain?" Lance offered. "I've had some medical training when I was in the military."

The sergeant handed the supplies to his commanding officer, then returned to his forward position.

"Yes, I'd appreciate it." The captain withdrew a roll of gauze from the container. He opened Jeff's shirt and pressed the gauze against the wound. "It's not very deep, Lieutenant, but bleeding all the same. Here Mr. Winters, press this against his skin." Lance took over as the captain moved aside.

"Now what's this about having a wounded person with you?" the captain questioned Jeff. "Where did you leave them?"

Lance's heart skipped a beat. Was he talking about Stormy? Had she been hit by one of those shots they'd been hearing? Or could it be Ann? He pressed firmly against Jeff's shoulder as he awaited the answer.

"I left them in a . . ." Jeff moaned, then bit down on his bottom lip before continuing, "in a ditch a few yards ahead and to the right of the road."

"Them?" the captain questioned. "How many?"

"Three, all women," Jeff answered, shifting his body slightly to ease the pain. "One is Lieutenant Winters. She's been wounded from a rifle butt to the ribs. I was carrying her until one of the shots made me turn and it hit my chest."

Chris looked up, his face filled with anxiety. He'd been taking notes on his own PDA, as any good newsperson would with a hot news story playing out before them. Lance's head came up as well, but before he could ask the question, the captain was already moving away.

"Look after him, Mr. Winters. I'll see to the women." The captain hurried off toward his men.

Lance looked at Chris, then back at Jeff, while still pressing the gauze in place. "Jeff?" He hated to press the wounded man for information, but he could not help himself. "Is Ann going to be okay? And who were the other two women with you?"

Jeff looked up into Lance's anxious face. "Your wife, Stormy, and the bank manager's wife, Sarah West. We never meant it to get this far. It just sort of . . ."

"Is Stormy alright?" Lance cut across his words, fear clearly showing on his face.

"Last I saw of her she was," Jeff replied. Lance noticed the man was breathing a bit shallowly. "She's been a big help with Mrs. West," he added.

"How about Ann? Is she badly hurt?" Chris had stopped typing, concern filling his face.

"She will most likely have some bruised, maybe cracked ribs, but I can tell you this," Jeff's face split into a grin, "she fights like a wild cat. I wouldn't want to meet her in some dark alleyway, believe me."

Chris joined Lance in a chuckle. Both were relieved to hear that it wasn't any worse. Dealing with terrorists, anything could happen.

"I think I heard Stormy's voice," Lance announced as a soldier came around the end of the SUV and approached the group.

"I'll take over, sir," the young soldier said, crouching beside him. "The captain wants to see you."

Lance didn't need to be told twice. He jumped up and hurried around the vehicle, almost stumbling over the women who were resting up against it. His heart leapt as he spotted Stormy sitting alongside Ann. Mrs. West was resting up against the car beyond them.

"Stormy," he called out, relief flooding his soul. He noticed that her face was covered with smudges of dirt and there was a tear in one of her coat pockets. A stick lay on the ground beside her. But none of this mattered. His beautiful wife was alive and returned to him.

"Lance!" Stormy cried out upon seeing her husband as the held-back tears freely flowed down her face.

Lance sat down beside his wife and took her in his arms. He kissed her forehead as she snuggled in against him. They held tightly to each other, both aware that they might never have seen each other again in this lifetime. They knew they had witnessed a miracle and thanked God for it.

"Ann?" Lance said, finally releasing Stormy, but only enough to lean over his wife and place a hand on his niece's arm. "How are you doing?" As he spoke, he realized that Chris was already by her side, his hand clasped tightly in hers.

"I'll be okay," she said, turning her head from Chris to look at her uncle. "Just a few ribs. I'll be up and around in no time."

The sheriff approached as the captain and his men headed out into the dark and disappeared from sight. Officer Mulhound had vanished around the other side of the vehicles. "I called for an ambulance," the sheriff told them. "It should be arriving soon. I'll wait with you until you're out of here."

"Thanks, Sheriff," Chris replied, still holding onto Ann's hand. He looked up as Officer Mulhound and the young soldier came around the car, supporting Jeff between them. They settled him back against the vehicle.

"How are you feeling?" Stormy asked the lieutenant, worried by the paleness of his skin. "I want to thank you for helping to get us out of there." The group chimed in with their thanks.

"I'm okay, just a little blood loss. And you were already well on your way out of there when I caught up with you." Jeff looked down, then back up at Stormy. "I need to apologize to you though."

"To me? Why?" Stormy looked over at him, a puzzled look on her face. She watched as Jeff cautiously reached into an inside coat pocket and withdrew an object, holding it in his hand. She didn't recognize it from where she sat.

"When I heard that shot ring out," he explained, "I automatically turned to check on you two. In doing so, the bullet hit me just below my right shoulder. Thank the Lord that Ann was resting up against my other shoulder. It missed her by inches." He paused, looking over at Ann before continuing. "It was all I could do to get Ann down to the ground and motion for you two to drop."

"Yes," Stormy said, "I knew it must have hit you." She looked into his eyes, the moonlight shining on his face. "You assured us you were alright. If I'd known the extent of it . . ."

"That's why I didn't tell you," Jeff interrupted. "But that's not it." He reached out with his left hand and handed her the object he had been holding, the movement obviously causing him pain. "I'm afraid the bullet also hit and damaged it. I'm sorry, it's beyond repair."

Stormy looked at the object he'd placed in her palm. It was a moment before she realized it was hers. "Oh, no. How did you get this?" She held the cell phone up for Lance to view.

"On the way to these dwellings," Jeff began, "it started to ring. You came to and took it from your purse. As you attempted to answer the call, Aleksandre grabbed it from you and shut it down."

"Aleksandre?" Stormy asked, wondering if she'd heard him correctly. "You mean the golf pro from the country club?"

"Yes, the same," Jeff answered, then realized that he hadn't heard any more shots for a while, hoping the military would get the terrorist before they could flee the area. "Anyway," he continued, "I was able to get my hands on it apparently about the same time you were all escaping the cave. I made a quick call. That's how the Air Force knew where we were and what had happened."

"Wow, what a story," Chris exclaimed as he quickly tapped on his PDA.

"I didn't have time to put it back, so I shoved it into the top pocket of my coat," Jeff further explained. "I'm afraid that when the bullet hit, it struck your cell first, shattering it." He looked apologetic at Stormy.

"There's no need to apologize," she said, looking down at the broken cell, then back up at Jeff. "This saved your life. I believe it was supposed to be there."

"You're one lucky guy," the sheriff put in.

"I think so, too," Lance agreed, looking over the cell phone. "We can always get Storm a new one. You'd be impossible to replace, Jeff." "Only one problem," Stormy announced, grimacing. "How are we going to explain this one to the cell phone guys?" She looked up at

Lance. "Do you think the warranty covers terrorist attacks?" Lance looked up at the sky as a siren filled the air.

"If not, I'll buy you a new one," Jeff promised, holding his shoulder with one hand as the ambulance came to a stop behind them.

Twenty-Two

"This is a lot better than the room they put me in when I gave birth to my second son," Stormy commented as she studied the hospital room. "And when we were at that base in Germany, I had to change my own sheets."

A nurse breezed into the room and checked the IV bag hanging above Ann at the head of her bed. "It looks fine. I'll be back to check on you later." She flashed a smile at the group surrounding Ann and was out the door as quickly as she'd entered.

"They've been taking good care of me," Ann agreed. She took another sip from the long straw in the chocolate shake she held before sinking back into her pillows. "But they don't serve shakes like this one. Thanks, Uncle Lance, Aunt Stormy."

"You're welcome, honey," Stormy said, moving her purse to rest beside the recliner in which she sat. "What did the doctor say when you saw him this morning?"

"He said that I was lucky," Ann grimaced. "I only sustained hairline fractures on two of my ribs, along with several bruises. I should be out of here in a couple of days, and good as new in a few weeks or so."

"That's good news," Lance said, his eyes filled with relief. "It could've been much worse dealing with those terrorists."

"Yes, I know," she softly replied. "By the way, how did it go last night with that detective? Did he keep you late with all of his questions?" She took another sip from the straw.

Stormy sighed. "Yes, Detective Jarvis kept us for quite a while after they took you and Jeff away in the ambulance. He had a lot of questions for us both."

"And he bawled us out for not contacting him sooner with all that had been going on," Lance added, looking at Stormy.

"Yes, I know we should have," Stormy said, giving Lance an apologetic look, "but we told him our reasons. Though I think we should have kept it to ourselves about the list we started compiling on Lance's laptop. Jarvis gave us a further lecture about that. We never did finish it, did we? Oh, well." She shrugged before continuing on. "Finally, he said we could leave, but they might be getting in touch with us later if we need to testify."

Storm suddenly giggled.

"What's so funny?" Ann asked, reaching over to set her shake on a nearby stand.

"I just realized something. As Detective Jarvis walked away, he was wearing grey socks this time instead of bright ones."

"What's so funny about that?" Ann inquired, a puzzled expression on her face.

"When he interviewed me at the bank," Stormy replied, "he wore bright purple socks. I guess he decided to forgo fashion after all."

"Hi, everyone." Chris stepped into the room, a large smile on his face, both hands behind his back. He crossed over to stand beside Ann's bed and withdrew one hand. In it he held a large bouquet of brightly colored flowers. "For you, lovely lady."

Color rose up Ann's cheeks as tears moistened her eyes. "Oh, they're lovely, Chris. Thank you." She took the flowers from him and studied their various shades, apparently delighted with his choice.

Stormy sat forward in her chair to get a better view of the bouquet. She'd always loved flowers and the choices that Lance made when he occasionally surprised her with them.

"Thank you," Ann repeated as she clutched the flowers in both her hands. "But I don't have a vase to put these in."

"We can take care of that," Chris replied, "but first, I believe this is yours, Stormy." He grinned as he brought forth a dark-brown and black stick from behind him and handed it across the bed to a very surprised Stormy.

"My walking stick," she exclaimed, taking it from him. "Oh, thank you, Chris. I thought I'd never see this again. Where did you find it?"

Chris grinned. "It never hurts to know the local law enforcement." He laughed and the rest joined in. "They acquired it from one of the terrorists fleeing the gift shop when they approached. Sounds like it may have been the golf pro. He took a few swings at one of the soldiers with it before he was subdued."

"I guess it comes in handy as a weapon for others also," Lance proclaimed. "Not just for you, my dear." With raised eyebrows, his eyes sparkled with humor as he looked at his wife.

"I guess so," Stormy laughed. She leaned the stick against her leg, pleased to see that the charms were still firmly attached. "Thank you, Chris. I really would have missed it."

"No problem. Now, for a vase. I'll be right back." Chris hurried out the door.

No sooner had he left, than Jeff came strolling through the doorway, his right arm in an Air Force-blue sling, a heavy white strap holding it in place resting over the opposite shoulder. He held a book in his left hand.

"Hello," he greeted the group. They returned the greeting as he walked over to Ann's bed. "This is for you. I remembered how you like a good mystery novel and thought you might enjoy this one." Suddenly he became aware of the flowers she held. "Nice flowers," he mumbled. "Um, I'll just set this down here." He placed the book on the rolling tray next to Ann.

"That was very thoughtful, Jeff. Thank you." Ann blushed, then moved the flowers to one side. "I'm so sorry I attacked you the way I did." She spoke softly, her voice catching as her eyes filled with tears. "I should have known you wouldn't betray your country." She reached out her hand and took hold of his.

It was his turn to blush, a slight color creeping up his face. "No, I wouldn't, or you either," he replied, pausing, "but you had no way of knowing that the

Air Force had me go undercover at the time. They .
. ."

Chris returned, carrying a clear plastic container half full of water. "This is all they had, but I think it'll do."

Jeff released Ann's hand and stepped back, allowing Chris through. Stormy caught the look on Jeff's face. Did he, too, have feelings for Ann? she wondered.

"It's used for ice, so it's not very pretty, but it should hold the flowers nicely while you're in here." Chris took the flowers from Ann and placed them in the makeshift vase.

"Thanks, Chris," Ann said as the reporter set the flowers on a shelf across the room where she could enjoy looking at them.

"Jeff was just telling us what happened yesterday," Stormy told Chris. "Take a seat," she gestured to a hard-backed chair on the other side of Lance. "Please continue, Jeff."

"Well," Jeff began, looking over at Ann before turning back to the others. "Things snowballed pretty quickly. One minute we were to meet at their import store . . ."

"The one near Kim and Katie's design shop, the K & K, I'll bet," Stormy interrupted, leaning forward. "The one called 'Other Side of the Ocean Imports'? I thought something was familiar about that man stocking shelves."

"Yes, that's the one," Jeff answered, leaning back against the wall just as the nurse brought in another chair and offered it to him. "Thanks," he acknowledged her thoughtfulness as she turned to leave. Sitting down, he continued, "We were to meet the other terrorists there, but the man I was with got a call and everything changed. It seems you," he pointed at Stormy, "were making them nervous. They decided you had to be dealt with, and since you were with Ann, she'd be a bonus for them. They already had Mrs. West, and they knew it would only be a matter of time before you realized that you'd seen her in the car near the bank the day of the robbery. I'm sorry, but they didn't give me a chance to warn you, or even my commander at the Base."

"It's not your fault, Jeff. So, that really was her in the car window." Stormy thought back to the speeding sedan. "I thought so when we saw her photo on her husband's desk in his office, then met her in person in the cave."

"Who were these terrorists working for and how long have they been in this country?" Chris chimed in. He had his PDA in hand.

"All I can tell you for right now is that they were working with a splinter group in the country of Georgia. And it seems they have lived in the U. S. for several years." Jeff said. "Like most cells, it's about a perceived injustice, and to make changes, they need funds. That's where Mr. West and his bank came in. He admitted to being blackmailed by them."

"They needed him for the money he could provide," Lance suggested, "and I assume his wife was the perfect leverage." He looked over at Stormy and squeezed her hand.

"Yes," Ann put in. "Sarah told us when we were trapped in that old cave with her how the golf pro had been plying her for information about the bank. Most terrorists do their job well."

"I guess she and her husband have a lot of explaining to do," Stormy voiced, thinking of the frightened, remorseful woman.

"Yes," Jeff answered. "The police are holding the Wests downtown, and the Air Force wants a word them as well. They may possibly be facing some charges before all is said and done."

"What about the terrorist?" Stormy inquired, leaning a bit forward in her chair. "Did they capture them all?"

"Yes," Jeff said, grimacing, "though Ivan gave them a bit of trouble trying to avoid capture. The military has them on lock down."

"Good," Stormy said, letting out a sigh of relief as she sat back.

"But how did you get mixed up with these men, Jeff?" Ann asked.

Jeff looked over at Ann for a moment before speaking. "You know with all the classes and studying we do at the Academy, we need a break once in a while. I was out one night at that small cafe we all hang out at off Academy Blvd., but this night I was there by myself."

Ann nodded, knowing full well the pressure the Academy placed on its students.

"They were looking for someone on the inside who might be able to help, a sympathizer," Jeff said, shifting from one foot to the other. "They look for anyone who might look lonely. I guess that night I fit the bill." He chuckled. "I played it straight, and after our first discussion, I went back to the base and approached the captain with the situation. He talked it over with the commander and they asked me to go along with the terrorists and feed them certain info, so I did. I never thought anyone else, any of you, would get caught up in all this."

"Well, now we know why we were being followed all over," Stormy remarked, shifting in her chair, a large bruise smarting on one hip. "But I still don't know who tried to send me off of Pikes Peak."

"That was Aleksandre's younger brother, Ivan," Jeff told her, anger filling his face. "I thought we were there just to keep an eye on you and your group. It turns out Ivan had other ideas. It was after he gave me the slip at the doughnut shack, that I discovered he'd sent you down the slope. When his back was turned, I tied that rope to the tree and hung around long enough to make sure you were out of danger. I'm sorry, but I couldn't blow my cover and let you know who I was."

"I understand," Stormy assured him, shuttering at the thought of the entire experience. "Thank you for being there for me."

"Yes, thank you, I kind of like having her around." Lance smiled at Stormy, then looked over at Ann. "And I'm glad you're going to be alright, young lady. What is it with the women in this family?"

"We know how to handle ourselves, Uncle," Ann assured him, grinning. "We're just a bit passionate about it." She glanced over in Jeff's direction.

"I'll say so," Jeff agreed, feigning pain as he touched the scratches on his neck.

"Sorry," Ann muttered, before turning to Stormy. "Are you going to take Uncle Lance to see Miramont Castle? I think he'd like it."

"Not this trip," Lance chimed in. "I think we've had enough excitement this time. I think we'd better be heading back to Phoenix."

"Yes, but we'll come again," Stormy promised, then sighed. "There are still several places I wanted to see this time. I'm disappointed we didn't have a chance to try that geocaching."

"You can give it a try right there in Phoenix," Chris suggested. "I'll send you an e-mail with some areas near your neighborhood. But," he paused as he looked over at Lance, "I do have some free time in the morning in case you want to squeeze in a few before you leave."

"That sounds like fun," Stormy said, sitting up straighter and looking hopefully over at her husband. "Any chance we could spare the time? Maybe stay one more day?"

"I guess one more day would be alright," Lance agreed, smiling at his wife's enthusiasm over the idea. "But no more perils, just a nice, normal day."

Chris laughed, "I'll help you keep an eye on her."

"Hey, did they agree to replace your cell phone?" Jeff earnestly asked, looking from Stormy to Lance, and back again.

Stormy glanced over at Lance before answering. "We decided to wait until we're back home in Phoenix. Our cell phone person knows us better there, and frankly," she chuckled, "I think we'll need that for this story."

"Maybe so but have them call me if they need any convincing," Jeff advised, placing his left hand on his hip.

"Will do," Stormy agreed, re-adjusting positions in the chair. As she did so, her walking stick slipped from her knee. She managed to catch it before it hit the floor.

"Great catch, Stormy," Chris called over. "Criminals don't have a chance with you around."

"I'd just prefer that she stay away from them altogether." Lance groaned as he raised his eyebrows and shook his head.

Stormy shrugged and gestured with her hands as if to say 'It's not my fault'. The rest of the group burst out laughing

www.ingramcontent.com/pod-product-compliance
Lightning Source LLC
Chambersburg PA
CBHW021433240626
47153CB00001B/130